BETRAY

"We cannot go on like this," Uvallae said. The alien stood at one corner of the small lab, a vial in his hand. "You must cease your warfare against us."

"The vial? A bioweapon?" Walden stared at the small, stoppered tube.

"A derivative of the virus in you," said Egad. "Not much for them, but bad for you."

"*You* would have infected me purposefully?" Walden asked in astonishment. "You engaged in countermeasures even as I was trying to find a cure for the Infinity Plague, for you, for your people?"

Books by Robert E. Vardeman

The Weapons of Chaos Series

ECHOES OF CHAOS
EQUATIONS OF CHAOS
COLORS OF CHAOS

The Cenotaph Road Series

CENOTAPH ROAD
THE SORCERER'S SKULL
WORLD OF MAZES
PILLAR OF NIGHT
FIRE AND FOG
· IRON TONGUE

The War of Power Series (with Victor Milán)

THE SUNDERED REALM
THE CITY IN THE GLACIER
THE DESTINY STONE
THE FALLEN ONES
IN THE SHADOW OF OMIZANTRIM
DEMON OF THE DARK ONES

The Swords of Raemllyn Series (with Geo. W. Proctor)

TO DEMONS BOUND
A YOKE OF MAGIC
BLOOD FOUNTAIN
DEATH'S ACOLYTE
THE BEASTS OF THE MIST
FOR CROWN AND KINGDOM

The Biowarriors Series

THE INFINITY PLAGUE
CRISIS AT STARLIGHT
SPACE VECTORS

BIOWARRIORS
Book Three

SPACE VECTORS

Robert E. Vardeman

ACE BOOKS, NEW YORK

This book is an Ace original edition,
and has never been previously published.

SPACE VECTORS

An Ace Book/published by arrangement with
the author

PRINTING HISTORY
Ace edition/July 1990

ISBN: 0-441-06227-X

Ace Books are published by The Berkley Publishing Group,
200 Madison Avenue, New York, New York 10016.
The name ''ACE'' and the ''A'' logo
are trademarks belonging to Charter Communications, Inc.

PRINTED IN THE UNITED STATES OF AMERICA

10 9 8 7 6 5 4 3 2 1

For MacLean & TJ
8-8-88

SPACE VECTORS

CHAPTER

1

Jerome Walden ducked and swung to his left—too late. The wall behind him exploded in a shower of molten metal. Pain racked his body. He screamed and thrashed about. Robots came at him from all directions. And disease! It gnawed at his insides. He was rife with the Infinity Plague and the robots were going to kill him and . . .

He gasped as new waves of sharp pain coursed through his body. He stared at his hand. He had smashed into a bulkhead. He wiped sweat from his eyes and looked around, his heart racing wildly. He wasn't aboard the alien's huge space station. He was aboard the hospital ship *Hippocrates*. Walden put his back to the cool carbon composite wall and slid down until he sat on the floor in the corner of his sleeping quarters.

Slowly the hallucination faded, if he could even call it that. It had held images made all the more vivid because he had lived through the crises. Walden blinked hard and concentrated on things close to him. The deck. His own hands, including the left that he had swung at phantom robots and injured against the bulkhead. He tried to force away the insane urge to run, to flee, to get away. It wasn't possible. He and the others who had been aboard the Frinn space station— those who had *survived* Starlight—had been quarantined.

The Infinity Plague.

1

He shuddered. It might have been better if he had died in the fighting. Death by laser was quicker and cleaner than what humanity had unleashed on the aliens and, apparently, themselves. The Infinity Plague had been genetically engineered on the research world Schwann—Delta Cygnus 4—by North American Alliance scientists. How it had been released would remain unknown for all time.

The Soviet-Latino Pact scientists might have stolen it and gotten careless. Or the NAA might have deliberately vented it when the Frinn discovered Delta Cygnus 4. No one would ever know because the Infinity Plague worked more quickly on the piglike aliens. In self-defense they had destroyed the planet when they realized that they had become infected.

Those aliens had died, but others had lived and left Schwann before realizing they carried the seeds of infection. The plague spread across space, to the space station called Starlight and to the Frinn home world.

The graphic more-than-memory images of Schwann's destruction flashed in front of Walden. He threw up his hands to ward off rocky splinters from the exploding world. Only slowly did he realize that he saw ghostly images and not reality.

But the specters were so real. Too real.

He was going insane in the small space allotted him in quarantine aboard the *Hippocrates*.

Sweat poured down his face. He wiped at it halfheartedly. He had survived the fighting aboard Starlight and been exposed to the Infinity Plague. He had seen highly trained Extra-Planetary Combat Team members go berserk and slaughter their own men. He had been assured by their now-dead commander Edouard Zacharias this was impossible; EPCT training prevented such behavior. Even the civilian advisor Miko Nakamura seemed stunned at the notion of the EPCTs turning on their own.

Through combat suits, through solid walls, the Infinity Plague came after them. Walden cringed and tried to hold the apparitions at bay. Wetness ran up and down his hand. He flinched and again crashed into the bulkhead.

"Walden not well?" came a strangely pitched voice. Walden forced himself to look at the monstrosity speaking to him. The animal had its origins as a dog, but Walden's skill at genetic engineering had created Egad—an Enhanced intelligence, Genetically Altered Dog. A Saint Bernard head perched precariously on a whipcord-thin greyhound's body. A black ratlike tail wagged vigorously, and the dog's huge brown right eye peered at his master in concern. Egad turned his head and brought his smaller left blue eye around. The mismatched eyes stared.

"I'm all right," Walden lied.

"Smell like shit," Egad countered. His nose worked diligently. "Yes, like shit. You are frightened."

"I don't like being closed in. The quarantine is getting to me. It . . . it's making me uneasy."

Egad let out a noise combining the most derisive portions of a snort and a bark. He settled on his thin haunches and said nothing more. His eyes bored into Walden's very soul. Walden held himself in check. He almost reached over and turned off the computer-generated voice produced in the transducer at the dog's throat. He didn't want advice now, especially from an animal.

"All right," Walden said, relenting. "It's more than being in quarantine. I don't like the idea of going to the Frinn home world. The Infinity Plague must be devastating their populace by now."

"You are the reason," Egad said.

"I am not," snapped Walden. Sweat poured down his face again. He used his shirtsleeve to sop it up. "We can't tell who released it or how the Frinn were infected. They *did* and that's all we have to work on."

"How is cure work?"

Walden shivered with a sudden fever. "I haven't had time to work on it. Uvallae and the other Frinn scientists are still running tests. Without those results there's little I can do."

Egad sat and stared. Walden read disbelief in the gengineered dog's mismatched eyes.

"There's nothing I can do," he repeated, almost pleading with Egad to believe him. "The Infinity Plague virus changes constantly. It infects, then is transmitted in mutated form and might or might not cause the same symptoms in a second host. I'm not even sure if the mode of transmission is the same or if it changes, too."

"Computer works," Egad said.

"I've got simulation programs running," Walden felt more and more defensive speaking with the product of his own experiment. Only a few knew of Egad's intelligence or vocal abilities. This secret had allowed him to stay alive in an atmosphere of suspicion and double-dealing aboard the starship. One of his own staff had been a spy cosmetically altered by the Sov-Lats. She had been killed, but Nakamura had smoked out another spy already on the *Hippocrates*' staff.

"Leo Burch," he muttered. "He poisoned me with that damned cat."

"Cat!" Egad managed to snarl and speak simultaneously.

"He used the cat to poison me when he was supposed to be curing me. Some medical doctor he turned out to be."

Walden huddled down and wrapped his arms around his drawn-up knees. Putting his head down allowed him to shut out the world. He wanted nothing more than to be free of the pressures he felt now. Nakamura wanted results. She was only the Japanese Hegemony observer, a civilian observer for the NAA and nothing more—on paper. Her astute political maneuvering and willingness to assassinate had moved her into command of the expedition. The only military officer remaining aboard the *Hippocrates* was Vladimir Sorbatchin, the Sov-Lat liaison rescued from Delta Cygnus 4 hours before the Frinn destroyed that world. Sorbatchin had acquitted himself well in the battle on Starlight. Too well, for Walden's tastes. With the death of their commander, the EPCTs looked for leadership they could understand.

Sorbatchin spoke their language, even if they had been trained that the Sov-Lat Pact soldiers were their enemies.

Walden shook himself. It was hard to remember that old alliances crumbled everywhere around him. The EPCTs saw the Frinn as enemies. The aliens had destroyed a human-settled world, after all. And the robot armies facing them as they invaded Starlight had given unexpectedly fierce opposition.

"The Frinn aren't our enemy," he said to himself.

"Like Uvallae," said Egad. "He smells good. Wonder what pig-bitches are like."

"What?"

"No Frinn pig-bitches," said Egad. Walden had given up trying to keep the gengineered dog from referring to the aliens with the same obscenities used by the EPCT soldiers among themselves.

"There aren't any females?" He had not considered this. They had only limited knowledge of the aliens and their society. A captured ship and its isolated rooms had hinted at extreme introversion among the aliens. When they entered Starlight they had been met with instant resistance from robots revamped to be fighting machines. The Frinn were peaceful enough, but their abilities with robots allowed them to field deadly armies seemingly at an instant's notice.

Egad curled his short legs under him and lay flat on the deck. He still watched his master closely, as if waiting for the last shred of sanity to flee.

"Have you talked with Anita?"

Egad shook his huge head. Tongue lolling, the gengineered dog panted to cool himself. Walden shot to his feet, certain that the thermostat had been reset. That had to be the problem. The temperature had climbed too high in his quarters.

A quick check of ambient conditions on his computer vidscreen showed nothing wrong. Walden wiped more sweat from his face.

"She won't talk to me. She refuses. And I need her, Egad. I *need* her." Walden knew his shrill, strident voice irritated the dog. He couldn't control himself.

"She blames you for cat-shit major's death."

"You were there. You know Zacharias died accidentally, if dying in a combat zone can ever be described as an accident."

"Shouldn't have told her he died saving your life," said Egad.

Walden began pacing back and forth, as if unconsciously seeking the limits of his quarters. His gray eyes darted everywhere, seeking the smallest sign that he might escape this imprisonment. He didn't care if he infected the rest of the *Hippocrates*' crew. Getting out had become an obsession.

He wanted everything to return to the way it was, back on Earth, before he had been appointed director of research for the mission to Delta Cygnus 4. Anita Tarleton and he had a stable relationship then. There hadn't been any deaths—and he wasn't living in fear that he was infected with the Infinity

Plague and being driven insane by its insidious action upon the neurons of his brain.

Another memory became reality for Jerome Walden. He gasped and tried not to die in the imaginary grasp. It faded slowly, but it left him shaken. His worst fears sprang up in front of him forcing him to deal directly with them.

"No infection," Egad said. "You are like dog without place to piss. Pressure builds and you explode."

Walden barely listened to the dog. Soft chimes signaled the end of his computer program. He had been testing different combinations of drugs against the tricky virus using the computer. What slowed his progress was the difference in Frinn physiology. The aliens had twenty-five chromosome pairs compared to humanity's twenty-three. The plague worked to unravel the extra pairs and impaired their nervous system. But in humans?

Walden held his head. It mutated and transmitted differently from each host. How he needed Anita Tarleton's expertise! She had been sent to the research planet to work on the Infinity Plague and hadn't told him. He had been her lover, her superior, her friend and confidant, and she had not told him. The director of research back on Earth had decided Walden didn't have "a need to know."

"I need time. Everything's crushing in on me."

"Dr. Walden?" came a curiously inflected greeting. "Are you able to spare moments of your time for a question?"

Walden glanced up. He hadn't heard Uvallae enter.

"I thought you respected privacy," Walden snapped.

"Your door was open and Egad beckoned to me. If I intrude on your privacy, accept my apologies. I—"

"What is it?" Walden didn't want to be rude to the Frinn scientist. They had so much work to do, and Uvallae was a capable researcher. He could supply answers about the Frinn metabolism that would take months or years to learn. Walden remembered the vacuum freezers where they had stored Frinn corpses. Had he become infected while performing an autopsy on one of them?

"I have contacted Starlight," Uvallae said slowly, "and the situation is grim. Most have died. Order has returned to the station and robots once more perform peaceful tasks, but the plague runs rampant."

"How many are left?" Walden wasn't sure he wanted to hear.

"Fourteen remain." Uvallae hung his head and refused to meet Walden's horrified gaze. All Walden could see was the bald pate and rough, pebbly gray skin. He waited for Uvallae to lift his piglike yellow slitted eyes. Great emotion wracked the alien.

Egad howled and buried his head under a chair. Walden knew that the gengineered dog received more communication from the Frinn than he did. The aliens conversed more using their sense of smell than humans did with their mouths.

"I'm sorry. Thousands have died because of us."

"We never realized the biologic dangers as we explored," said Uvallae. "There was little need for it. We are a private people and communicable diseases are rare. Our medical science is so primitive compared to you because we—" Uvallae bit off the words, as if unwilling to discuss the shortcomings of his world's science.

"We must reach your home world and do what we can to prevent the spread. The Infinity Plague can kill billions."

"I fear for my world," Uvallae said. The tears vanished, but Walden saw the way Egad's nose trembled. The Frinn still emitted strong pheromones betraying emotional distress.

"I'll do what I can to stop the plague," said Walden. Even as the words left his mouth, another vision hammered at him. Ships exploded in front of his face. Battles raged. The NAA warships had fought well against the Frinn—until Walden realized the Frinn ships were not craft built for destruction. They were exploratory vessels.

"You are ill, Doctor?"

"I'm fine. Just an overactive imagination," Walden said. He went to his compact metal desk and fumbled open a locked compartment. He had hidden away two small capsules of pentagan, a drug that increased the resistance at nerve receptors making it difficult for the axon to fire. It worked well on migraine headaches. He swallowed the two capsules, hoping they would lessen the visions he barely survived.

"What manner of reception are we likely to get from your home world?" Walden asked. "Will they attack us on sight? You had pretty good defenses set up to protect Starlight."

"We are peaceable. What defenses are in place will be

recent. We used Starlight as a way station to protect our home. The residue left by the lift engines is hidden by Starlight's nearness to this system's primary.''

"How did you manage to mount such an offense in the Delta Cygnus system?'' he asked out of morbid curiosity. The weapons had been crude but effective. Zacharias had thought the Frinn had entered the system with the sole intent of invading. Nakamura's study of the alien weapons systems showed jury-rigging, as if constructed hastily out of available components.

"Our robots are efficient and more versatile than yours. Several of your warriors commented on using them on the battlefield. We know little of war, having never engaged in the all-out conflicts your species has endured.'' Uvallae made a face that twisted his pig's snout around. "I have read your history and do not understand much of the motivation for territorial conquest.''

"Your robots redesign themselves? We don't trust machines, even artificial intelligence computers, to that extent.''

"We program them with the details of their mission, then allow them to adapt. In many ways, we are advanced in technology and you have pursued biological sciences. It is a failing among us that we have not pursued this field more diligently. We will now pay for our ignorance. Our medical science is decades behind yours because we depend on—'' Uvallae clipped his sentence, letting it trail unfinished.

Walden didn't directly respond. The Frinn biogenetic knowledge was primitive by any standard. They hardly scratched the surface of what was known two hundred years earlier on Earth. Yet he would have traded such ignorance for the peace that had been the alien's legacy for so long. Earth had never destroyed itself with all-out nuclear war. The Soviet-Latino Pact countries and the NAA, with its ally, the Japanese Hegemony, preferred more discreet and less detectable ways of killing.

Walden specialized in creating gengineered diseases that destroyed the signal transmission in the human nervous system. Whether a nation or an individual, Walden could kill with the products of his research. But always there had been focus, direction, the need to contain and prevent rampant, unchecked spread. Deep down, he realized the combination of fear of his work and the feeling of power at designing such potent weapons had mixed inside him over the years. Now it all came back to haunt him.

Genocide. His species was responsible for a plague that might eradicate another. To men like Sorbatchin that meant nothing other than the power it afforded them. Walden was coming to see the danger of his work. He was infected with the Infinity Plague. He *must* be. What else would produce the visions he was enduring?

The pentagan deadened pain throughout his body and forced him to relax. His synapses stopped relaying complete information. The drug was dangerous to use. Too much permanently deadened delicate nerve fibers. And too little didn't serve his purpose.

"You are looking better. What is this substance that affords such relief?" asked Uvallae.

"It's nothing that will cure the plague in your people," said Walden. The pentagan allowed him to concentrate again on the immediate problem. "How are the fourteen alive on Starlight doing?"

"Robots tend them. Breathing becomes difficult for many.'

Walden nodded. The primary effect of this strain of Infinity Plague caused the Frinn autonomic system to cease functioning. Ordinarily bodily functions stopped as the plague interfered with the electron transfer that made respiration possible in protein molecules. What worried Walden as much as halting the progress of the disease in the Frinn was containing it. Epidemic seemed too moderate a term for its effect.

He dropped to the computer console and started working. His calculations hadn't netted him any new directions for research. In the back of his mind, Walden debated the morality of ignoring the Frinn plight and concentrating on his own. Spread of the Infinity Plague among humans was beginning and was potentially more devastating. The vector changed, as did the symptoms. Among the aliens, the symptoms were more uniform.

Or were they? He knew so little.

"Uvallae, how did the neurological autopsy results come out? Was death similar in each of the victims?"

"The robots work on this now. There is some evidence

that many died of suffocation, as we are witnessing on Starlight. Others, however, died from internal disorders.''

"What's that mean?" He couldn't keep the irritation from his voice. Uvallae was the most advanced of the Frinn scientists, and he lacked the basic knowledge that Walden relied on daily in his work. Communicating precisely was too difficult, especially with an alien more comfortable with communicating through scent.

"Blood oozed into the body cavities. Capillaries ruptured. There is some sign of other bodily juices leaving their traditional organ sites."

Walden worked at his console with the new information and decided that this was another manifestation of autonomic destruction and nothing unexpected. He might have to consult with another in his research team, Paul Preston, who was expert in angiogenesis factors and blood clotting. The Frinn gamete cells were damaged by the Infinity Plague but not the somatic cells. Reproduction of the cells became chancy and imprecise, leading to faulty organ performance.

"Dr. Walden, I need to know," Uvallae started.

"What?"

"Was I correct in giving your Miko Nakamura the coordinates of my home world? Will you destroy us completely?"

"We may already have," Walden said tiredly. He began working in earnest at his computer experimentation, hoping to stumble across something useful.

But he wasn't counting on it.

CHAPTER
2

Uvallae left Jerome Walden working on the computer program. The Frinn knew little about the Earthman's analytical procedures. Experimenting using a computer seemed strange to Uvallae, who had little experience with anything but empirical work. At the very least, Uvallae considered Walden's pursuit to be a substitution of mechanical logic for human instinct.

He went to his own laboratory, noting that his three associates had left their small labs to engage in meditation. Uvallae felt the need himself. He was crushed by the number of humans around him, even in quarantine. He needed time to recharge his energy, find new avenues of thought, make the effort to cope with his sorry position.

"Want company?" came a familiar voice.

Uvallae bobbed his head up and down in what he hoped was a successful mimicry of a human's agreement gesture. They depended so much on visual signs.

Egad sniffed and rubbed past Uvallae's legs and trotted on into the laboratory. The gengineered dog found a spot on the deck near a storage cabinet and circled about three times before settling down, this patch of floor now his.

"Are all humans like your Dr. Walden?" asked Uvallae. He went to his workbench and studied the progress made.

Little bubbles formed in the bottle of the gently boiling vacuum flask. Uvallae considered them, both in their context of invaders in a biological sense as well as thermal aberrations. They fit well into the matrix of the world he envisioned for them. No new information was gained. He turned his attention back to the patiently waiting dog.

Egad snuffled and scratched himself behind the ear before answering. Uvallae remained silent, as was fitting. He had asked a question; Egad had heard it. When the dog wished to respond, he would. This mutually understood ritual of silence between them lengthened. Uvallae continued to gather scent data from the dog that transcended mere words. The animal was more primitive than a Frinn but in curious ways was more advanced than the humans aboard the *Hippocrates*.

"Some are worse," Egad finally answered. "He tries to understand. In this he is different. But there is stress on him."

"Stress? To produce new work for Sorbatchin and the others?"

"Guilt. He feels guilty."

"I am not certain I understand guilt," admitted Uvallae. He used the computer console in the laboratory to get a definition of the word and dozens of examples. Ten minutes passed, and he was still not sure he appreciated the depths of this human emotion.

"Egad," the Frinn said, "he believes he could have acted in a way to reduce the death toll among my people. How extraordinary, since he was not in charge."

"His work," the dog said. "The burdens grow. He worries about how germs will be used."

"He did not develop the Infinity Plague. Others did. He is innocent."

"He feels guilt for the actions of others. Strange notion," Egad said. "Pretty bitch Anita knows more about it but has no guilt. She thinks it is right to work on it."

"I fail to understand the need for their species to conquer each other. Isn't the universe large enough to present challenges of *real* substance?"

Egad remained silent. He wasn't sure he knew what Walden—or Uvallae—meant when they talked of the universe. He had seen stars in the sky at night. He had watched vidscreen displays as the liftspace ships shook and moved. His concept of distance was limited to where he could run. The universe hardly extended beyond the range of his sensitive nose.

"Did I do right telling Nakamura where my planet is?" asked Uvallae. "I have insufficient information to decide."

"You did well," said Egad. The Frinn relaxed when he heard these words. He trusted Egad's opinion, limited as it was. "Walden is best hope you have of stopping sickness."

Uvallae settled into a chair and stared at a pattern he put on his vidscreen, his eyes unfocusing. He relived the past few months, examining his behavior and evaluating the decisions he had made for future use. Humans appeared to decide critical issues on spur-of-the-moment stimulus. The Frinn deeply considered important issues. That was the reason robots were so important. The metal devices freed organic brains for deep considerations.

For all the loss, for all the torment and terror he had endured, Uvallae saw that he had performed to the best of his ability. When data were missing, he could only extrapolate. He had done well. And still most aboard Starlight had died. The expedition into the human-settled space had resulted in massive destruction and death. And the Infinity Plague had been unleashed on the Frinn home world.

Uvallae had done all he could. Unlike Jerome Walden, he felt no guilt over his actions.

Egad watched the alien sink deeper into his trance. The odors coming from the Frinn changed subtly. The gengineered dog tried to make sense of them and failed. After another five minutes, the dog shook himself and rose to his bandy legs. Uvallae wasn't going to talk to him as long as he remained in this trance that wasn't sleep.

The dog left the alien scientist and returned to his master's quarters. The pentagan took the edge off Walden's hallucinations and allowed him to work. He ignored Egad. Ears badly in need of scratching, Egad left and prowled the tiny confines of the *Hippocrates'* quarantine section. He didn't understand the need to keep everyone who had been aboard the alien's space station penned up.

He not only saw no reason for it, he resented it. Nosing around kept Egad occupied for only a few minutes. He had explored the small suite of rooms before. Nothing smelled interesting to him. He had been raised in a laboratory cage, warned at every feeding about showing his true abilities. Egad wondered about the need to remain silent in front of most humans aboard the hospital ship. Nakamura knew—and he hated her.

Try as he might, Egad couldn't detect any odor. She masked her pheromones with chemicals to prevent sophisticated surface-acoustic-wave detectors from tracking her. The EPCTs used SAW-dets as part of their standard combat equipment, and so did most operatives in the spy business.

Sorbatchin might know that Egad spoke and thought as well as most humans. The Sov-Lat colonel smiled too much, and the smile hid his true intentions. Egad wondered if the man knew how obvious he was to someone with a nose.

Anita Tarleton knew, too. She had known and been a friend for as long as Walden. Egad missed her. He dropped into a corner, near the spot where a crude cage with a blanket in it had been set up for him. Egad didn't like the cage, and he hated the blanket's disinfectant odor. He was lonesome and wanted companionship.

Walden wouldn't do. He didn't like Nakamura. He hated Sorbatchin. Uvallae had lost himself in a daze. Egad decided to find Anita. She was such a pretty bitch and smelled nice.

Decided, Egad heaved himself to his feet.

He jumped to the top of his cage and got on his back legs. The shortness deterred him a little, but he kept at his task of snuffling around the filtration system mounted high on the wall. The solid state device attracted ionized dust particles and trapped them on its surface. As the day progressed, the surface of the filter slowly rotated. Devices scrubbed the face, disinfected, irradiated, and repeated the process to maintain the quarantined section's integrity even as it monitored the dust's content and composition.

Egad pushed and poked it and kept nosing until he loosened a bolt. His long tongue worked eagerly at the task. He seldom wished he were human. Now he did. It would make the work go so much faster if he had fingers. His intelligence and the need to find Anita kept him at the task.

A second bolt fell free. This gave the large dog the room he needed to get up into the opening. The filtration device had been installed for one purpose; no one thought of anything more than the hermetic plastic seal around it. The patients in quarantine were not supposed to be prisoners—and those occupying the quarters now were there voluntarily.

All except for Egad.

The tight fit around his head as he wiggled past the solid state filter eased suddenly. He fell into an analysis room. Small lights twinkled on panels showing the status of the quarantine, its air flow, oxygen use, particulate matter, virus and bacteria content, and dozens of other readings Egad didn't understand. But the gengineered dog knew the single red light flashing on the panel would draw unwanted attention if left untended.

He pushed the filter back into its slot. The blinking red light didn't stop. Egad used his tongue to press the panel immediately under the light. The detector reset.

Egad let out a short bark of triumph. Opening the door leading from the analysis room was simple; he knew how to open all but the most complicated cipher-lock doors aboard the *Hippocrates*.

He trotted into the corridor and got his bearings. He wasn't far from the EPCT barracks. Remembering how the soldiers had treated him before, Egad decided to make a short stop on his way to find Anita Tarleton. Some of the EPCTs even gave him candy and other treats. He felt he deserved something for the way the humans had been dealing with him.

Stopping just outside the door, Egad tentatively sniffed. He almost ran off when he smelled Colonel Sorbatchin. Then curiosity drew him into the long room set with dozens of beds. He saw more than half of them were empty. The EPCT had taken heavy losses, on Delta Cygnus 4 and later at Starlight.

Many of the personal equipment lockers had been opened and rifled. Egad jumped into an empty locker and settled down. The clothing at the bottom formed a nice bed and let him relax. He had been working hard and deserved a rest. He could get a treat from the soldiers later. The gengineered dog was drifting off to a well-deserved sleep when he heard Sorbatchin's deep baritone voice.

His blue eye opening, Egad peered down the long line of bunks. Eight EPCTs ringed the Sov-Lat officer at the far end of the barracks. Egad's keen hearing allowed him to listen without being seen.

"Your major's death was unfortunate, but he died like a soldier. He was a brave man."

One soldier chuckled at that. Another elbowed him in the ribs and silenced him.

"The major was a royal pain in the ass at times, but he knew his stuff," another soldier said.

"I have read the record," said Sorbatchin. "A hero, a true hero. You were lucky to have him in command for so long."

"Yeah, a hero. He whipped your butt at Persephone."

"Operation Pomegranate," said Sorbatchin, nodding solemnly. "Zacharias received your Starburst medal. It was deserved. We in the Sov-Lat bloc thought highly of him." Sorbatchin smiled broadly, throwing out his chest and squaring his broad shoulders. "I have been honored fighting alongside him."

"Why are you down here chewing the fat with us, Colonel?" asked Giovanni Hecht. "I know Nakamura told us we're all on the same side, us humans against the pigs, but you must have better things to do than hang out with us."

"Why should I, Sergeant?" Sorbatchin rested his hand on Hecht's shoulder. The EPCT sergeant started to flinch back and drop into a defensive stance. Egad saw that he restrained himself. "We are of a kind, you and I. Are we not both soldiers?"

"You're Sov-Lat."

"You are human—and so am I. *That* is what matters now."

Egad listened awhile longer, seeing how the Sov-Lat colonel worked on the soldiers and brought them around. He praised their military accomplishments, knew their fears, never spoke ill of Edouard Zacharias. If anything, this formed a stronger bond between the officer and the EPCTs. They all knew Zacharias had been a fool, lucky once in a critical battle and never again able to match that flash of genius.

Whatever else Sorbatchin was, he was no fool.

Egad crept out of the locker and went to the door. He disliked Sorbatchin and didn't want the man seeing him. The gengineered dog had no idea that the Sov-Lat colonel would have ordered him killed on sight for breaking quarantine.

In the corridor once more, Egad's loneliness mounted. He had meant to take a short nap and hadn't. He wanted to find Anita more than ever. He passed several crew members, but

they were too absorbed in their own work to notice him. Egad
decided not to bother them. He knew them by smell but not
to talk to. The old warnings Walden and Anita had hammered
into him made him wary of others.

More than this, Egad didn't want to be penned up again.
Let the humans play their silly games. He preferred his freedom. The wide-open corridors beckoned to him. He broke
down and yelped with joy, then ran as fast as he could. The
feel of freedom was almost more than he could stand.

Egad collided with a woman just as she came out of her
quarters. They tumbled to the deck together, arms and legs
and tail winding together. Egad recovered first, rolling onto
his paws, tail wagging and tongue flopping from his great
mouth. He licked the woman and tried to nuzzle her. She
pushed him away.

"Egad!" Anita Tarleton grabbed the dog around the neck
and wrestled him down to keep the tongue from drowning
her. "When did they let you out of quarantine?"

"Been out for an hour. Want to see you. Like Anita. You
smell good." He tried to lick her again.

The woman pushed her flame-red hair back into a sem-
blance of order. Cosmetic dyes swirled and flared brilliantly
under her skin, the organic luminescence powered by her
emotions. She looked up and down the corridor, then pulled
Egad into her cabin.

"Does anyone know you're out?" she asked. "If they'd let
you out, I'd've known right away."

"Scratch my ears? You do it nice." The dog presented his
shaggy head for her attention. She absently scratched his ears
with one hand as she reached to her computer console and
tapped in a request for the status of the quarantine. The lack
of information sent a chill up and down her spine.

"They haven't found the proper treatment for the Infinity
Plague yet, have they, Egad?"

"Don't understand. No one is sick, except Walden."

"What's wrong with him?"

"Crazy as cat-shit," the dog said, turning his head to let
her scratch a different portion of his skull.

"Is that caused by the plague?"

"He's always crazy, only more crazy now. Got tired of
being locked up. Nobody plays with me."

"So you got out and came here?" Egad bobbed his head up and down half as fast as his tail wagged. "Did you see anyone else before you found me?"

Egad considered the question. He had seen several people, including Sorbatchin and the EPCT soldiers. But that wasn't the way the woman meant it.

"No. You're the only one," he said.

Anita Tarleton heaved a deep sigh. She sank into a chair and held Egad's head between her palms. Green eyes bored into his mismatched ones.

"What you did was very dangerous. You might be carrying the Infinity Plague along with you."

"Is everyone going to turn crazy?"

"I don't know. I don't think so." She checked the biore-ports from quarantine and saw the high stress level reported for Walden. Other than this, he seemed to be in good con-dition. Anita dismissed the stress as insignificant since every-one aboard the *Hippocrates* felt the pressure. They had less than a day remaining in this system before the ship entered liftspace and hurled faster than light through imaginary frac-tal dimensions for the Frinn home world.

"You should have stayed inside with Jerome," she said sternly. "How did you get out? I don't see how you could reset the counters on any of the doors leading from the quar-antine chambers."

Egad said nothing. He liked Anita but she wasn't like Uvallae. She didn't understand that it sometimes took a con-siderable time to find the right words. She didn't wait but began a systems check of the quarantine section.

"There's trouble at one of the analysis rooms with its pres-sure," she said after five minutes of work. "We keep a lower air pressure inside so there is always a negative pressure gra-dient—air will always flow into the quarantined section rather than out."

Egad looked past her at the vidscreen and saw the small room where he had worked loose the filtration device. His path to freedom had been discovered quickly once the woman began looking. He'd have to find some other way out. He knew she wouldn't let him use the same route again.

"Do you want a nice bath?" she asked suddenly.

He tried to escape, but she already had him around the

body. He considered biting her, then relented. Being thrust into the small, efficient spray cabinet wasn't pleasant, but Anita wanted to do this. He kept his eyes tightly closed and only once did he shiver, sending droplets in all directions. Anita made angry noises but said nothing directly to him.

"We're going to use some ultraviolet on your skin, too. I'm afraid this might give you a bit of a sunburn. Consider it punishment for getting loose before you were told."

Egad endured the radiation lamps. He even endured the final antiseptic bath that made him cold all over, but he resisted when she started to drag him back to the quarantine rooms.

"Don't want to go. Not yet."

"I suppose it's all right," she said, staring at him warily. He didn't like her attitude. She acted as if he carried fleas and wanted to share them.

"Get lonely in there," he said, feeling sorry for himself. "Want to see you."

"You can have Jerome call me on the computer. Or you can work it yourself. You know how."

"Don't like to. Keys taste bad. Want to see you and Walden back together."

Anita Tarleton stiffened and moved away from the gengineered dog. "That's not likely," she said coldly.

"He misses you. I miss you."

"Thank you, Egad. That's the nicest thing that anyone's said to me in a long time, but Jerome and I aren't going to mend our differences."

"Cat-shit major smelled bad. Walden smells good. So do you."

"There's more to it than that among humans," she said, having been over this with the dog before. Trying to explain emotions the dog didn't share taxed her powers.

"You like cat-shit colonel?"

"What?" This took her by surprise.

"He is soldier. He leads the others."

"The EPCTs?" She shook her head. "Sorbatchin is an officer, but he's Sov-Lat. He doesn't command our soldiers."

"Who does?" asked Egad.

Anita started to answer, then fell silent. She didn't know.

Zacharias had been the last of the EPCT officers to die. There were two sergeants left but no one in the chain of command.

She stared at the dog and shook her head. For once Egad had seen something among the humans that she hadn't. And it frightened her. The EPCTs were combat-hardened veterans. What *would* Vladimir Sorbatchin do with them if he commanded their loyalty?

CHAPTER
3

Colonel Vladimir Sorbatchin stood stiffly at attention before Miko Nakamura. The small woman eyed him with some distaste, wondering how she could use him. Her grip over the EPCTs had weakened with Zacharias' death. The remaining soldiers resented her position with the Japanese Hegemony and had never accepted her as someone who could give them orders. She had controlled Edouard Zacharias perfectly. She now realized she had to control Sorbatchin.

"Please, Colonel, do not brace yourself in this fashion. It makes me weary looking at you."

"I always stand at attention in the presence of my superiors," he said stubbornly.

Nakamura's emotionless eyes studied him. Was the man serious? She did not think so. He was too experienced in the ways of manipulation. He sought only to confuse her, to delude her into believing what he wanted. The battle for control between them would be more difficult than she had anticipated.

A moment of blaming herself for being too involved following the research for a cure for the Infinity Plague passed. She concentrated on the Sov-Lat officer. He stood tall, strong, confident. If she had not been so self-assured of her own abilities, his height might have intimidated her. His crew-cut blond hair gave him a Nordic appearance, ruined only by his broken nose. She wondered why he had not had cosmetic surgery to re-form it. Not having it done properly was as much a vanity as overuse of the cosmetic surgeon's laser to redo every bump and blemish.

Where was Sorbatchin's vulnerable spot? Nakamura wondered if it might not be in his dead wife. She had been killed by the Frinn when they landed their robotic armor on Delta Cygnus 4. Did he hate the NAA for her death or was his drive for control aboard the *Hippocrates* derived only from personal ambition? She had to test, to probe, to discover what she could. Sorbatchin had consolidated his position quickly and well after the debacle on Starlight.

"Please, Colonel, my humble position with this expedition is one of advisement, not command. Sit, be comfortable."

He lowered his huge bulk into a chair carefully placed at the corner of the room. He lost his towering height advantage. Nakamura's cold black eyes were level with his pale blue ones. Every small advantage that aided her hindered Sorbatchin.

"We stand at a crossroads of momentous decisions," she said. "We have the coordinates of the Frinn home world. How do we use this knowledge?"

"Are you asking for my opinion?"

"Of course," she said easily. Nakamura poured tea from a self-heating pot. It lacked the deliberate, ritualistic movements of that of the *cha-no-ya* tea ceremony that soothed her so, but she had to forgo such pleasure. Her full attention must be on the Sov-Lat officer. Throughout the simply decorated cabin were spy devices of her own creation. No emotion, no physiologic response, went unnoticed by her guileful monitors.

"Why?"

"Ah, Colonel, you know the reason. You are the only surviving military expert aboard this ship. We should bury any differences in ideology, you and I. We are two humans against the aliens." She did not point out that her own grasp of strategy and tactics had been finely honed over twenty years advising the NAA. Both politics and military matters were her specialties.

"Let them die. The Frinn deserve no better. They destroyed a colonized world."

"There is some small evidence that the researchers on Delta Cygnus 4 brought on their own downfall," Nakamura said quietly. She sipped her bitter green tea with real appreciation. "We must pursue our own ends now."

"We can't return to Earth," said Sorbatchin. "The same argument applies now as applied before. The Frinn liftspace detectors are scattered throughout this system. If they return and read the residue left when we enter stardrive, they will know the direction of Earth. It is simple to follow that geodesic line and determine the stars capable of sustaining life."

"There is also at least one Frinn war vessel still roaming this system," said Nakamura. "I did not desire to return to Earth. I sought your opinion on the best way to approach the Frinn once we arrive in their system."

Sorbatchin sipped at his tea. From the way his upper lip trembled slightly, Nakamura guessed he did not like the tea. Yet he drank out of politeness. She could push him on small points to make the larger ones. This was important.

The Sov-Lat officer put down the half-empty teacup and said, "Why did you permit the EPCTs to return to their barracks rather than be put into quarantine?"

"You are the first to ask this question. Does it trouble you?"

"The soldiers showed signs of instability. One—or more—turned on his fellows. This flies in the face of their psychological training. Are you not worried about the spread of the Infinity Plague aboard the *Hippocrates*?"

"Not to any extent. All research shows the spread among humans to be almost impossible."

"That's not what Dr. Walden believes," Sorbatchin said.

"Jerome Walden is experiencing difficult times in his life. He is unable to cope properly."

"He is having a breakdown?" Sorbatchin sipped once more at the tea. Again Nakamura saw the tiny tremors of the upper lip. What else did Sorbatchin hide with this innocuous drinking of the ceremonial tea?

"That is possible. His is an unstable personality. Why Dr. Greene allowed him to be in command of the research team is unclear. Walden has some small skill at dealing with other scientists. This leads me to believe he might have been a marginally good choice."

"I would choose Dr. Tarleton," Sorbatchin said.

Nakamura hid her surge of interest in Sorbatchin's seemingly offhand comment. He must know of Anita Tarleton's involvement on Earth in the Infinity Plague project. There was no other reason for him to suggest her when any number of others in the research team were as capable. Nakamura's personal choice for leader would have been Paul Preston. The man's work with the angiogenesis factor was brilliant, and he dealt with his associates well. She had no reason to believe Sorbatchin would have chosen differently.

Hence, he knew of Dr. Tarleton's research.

"She is an able researcher," Nakamura admitted.

"She knows much of the plague and its effects. Has she told you it cannot pass between humans?"

"The only sure knowledge is what we obtained from autopsies on the Frinn," Nakamura said carefully. "Their autonomic system fails because of the unwinding of the extra chromosomes in their DNA. There are complex quantum effects occurring. Electron transport is denied in certain protein molecules. That is all we have gleaned from research to date. The Infinity Plague is a difficult virus to categorize."

"She is being allowed to work unhindered by Walden and the Frinn?" asked Sorbatchin. "Is this a wise course? She can learn more from the aliens and her lover."

"Her one-time lover," corrected Nakamura.

Sorbatchin nodded. "*Da*, it is wise to keep them apart. He will not distract her, and the Frinn are the only beings likely to be infected or transmit the plague. What has she found in her research?"

Nakamura poured more green tea, taking the time to order her thoughts. Sorbatchin, with his blunt Soviet manner, proved more direct in his questioning than was polite. She took it as an indication of how he perceived his position. Sorbatchin thought he was more in command of the situation than he was.

"There are interesting elements in her study of Frinn physiology. We have no need to see how best to propagate the Infinity Plague. It is doing a good job as it is gengineered. We have every reason to believe it begins the unraveling of the Frinn DNA, then transmits itself in myriad ways. There is no way to determine its modality of infection, its vector, or even *if* it will infect."

"In Frinn?" pressed Sorbatchin. "Not in humans."

"We have a gengineered disease that strikes only at aliens," Nakamura assured him. She had studied Walden's reports and found them hysterical and unscientific. He had lost whatever objectivity as a researcher he once had when he became so emotionally involved with the Frinn. Nakamura credited this with the loss of Anita Tarleton as a lover—to Major Zacharias. This unhinged Walden and caused him to transfer his emotional attachments to the aliens. In his mind, what befell them had to befall humans, QED.

"We can eradicate them!" crowed Sorbatchin.

"Perhaps," Nakamura said softly. In almost a whisper, she added, "Yes!"

"What is the peculiar odor?" Vladimir Sorbatchin sniffed tentatively at the air. "Is there a problem with your atmosphere-cleansing unit?"

"Not that I've noticed," said Anita Tarleton. She checked the computer vidscreen readout and saw that the content and purity was within the norms. She sniffed carefully and detected a slight amount of the antiseptic she had used on Egad. This must be what the Sov-Lat colonel smelled—and if so, he had a keen sense of smell. Or was he aware that the gengineered dog had been here and was tweaking her with the knowledge?

"I will have technicians double-check your system," he said. "We do not want your laboratory to become a death trap."

"It already is," she said dryly. "That's the intent of my research."

"I have spoken with Miko Nakamura about this," he said, settling down on the corner of a workbench. "We have agreed that the direction of your research should shift a small amount."

"Oh, you have?" Anita raised an eyebrow and stared at the man. Everything Egad had reported about Sorbatchin must be true, she realized. The Sov-Lat officer was unifying his position aboard the *Hippocrates*. She wasn't sure if this bothered her or diminished her own power. With Walden and many of the higher-ranking officers dead or out of action, she had assumed a position of preeminence. She was de facto head of the research team. Sorbatchin's obvious taste for power moved her down a notch.

"There is no need to continue research on the Infinity Plague," said Sorbatchin. "What we require are other bio-weapons."

"More? Why? The plague has devastated Starlight's crew. We can't begin to guess what it has done to the Frinn's home world."

"We *can* guess," he said with easy arrogance, "and the answers are disappointing. There will not be many casualties from the plague."

"That's not supported by other evidence," Anita said hotly. She had no qualms about developing bioweapons. It was her work, her life, and she thought that it gave needed stability to a dangerous world. In many ways the viruses she gengineered were cleaner and more predictable weapons than nuclear bombs. The Infinity Plague had been a deviation from her usual research direction. The notion of a disease that altered itself as it went from host to host—victim to victim—had appealed to Dr. William Greene and others in a policy-making position. She had failed; apparently those at the NAA station on Delta Cygnus 4 had succeeded, but only with the aliens.

"We believe the Frinn overstated their fatalities."

"As I said, evidence doesn't support that contention, Colonel. The unraveling of their DNA is always fatal. At least one ship carrying the contagion has gone to their home world."

"They are a solitary people. This will limit the spread of the Infinity Plague. You worry needlessly. Nakamura and I need other bioweapons, faster-acting ones. You will work on them for us since Dr. Walden is . . . incapacitated."

"He's been locked up," Anita said, bitterness in her voice. What feelings she had for Walden were past, but she resented the cavalier way Nakamura had quarantined him and the Frinn scientists. For the good of the ship had been the order. To keep them under close surveillance was more likely the reason. After all, Egad had reported that the EPCTs had not been quarantined. She wasn't certain but she thought that Sorbatchin had been aboard Starlight, also.

The brief examination she had given the gengineered dog had shown him to be free of any virus resembling the Infinity Plague. Although Anita had to admit her exam had been cursory and that the plague was insidious in the way it worked and propagated, Egad was healthy and so were the Frinn.

As to Walden, she couldn't say, but she doubted his problems stemmed from exposure to the gengineered virus.

"What kind of bioweapon do you want me to whip up?"

"Sarcasm is not called for, Dr. Tarleton," said Sorbatchin. "We must defend ourselves, if the need arises."

"There's a difference between offensive and defensive weapons. One kills, the other incapacitates."

"Tell me how your current research progresses," urged Sorbatchin. "You are close to knowing the function of the extra four chromosomes in the Frinn, are you not?"

Anita was startled, in spite of herself. Anything known to Nakamura must be known to the Sov-Lat officer. If those two worked closely now, she had no reason to hold back information. Yet she did.

"The function of those pairs is open to debate, but I believe they are almost vestigial. Their purpose seems to be to slow the Frinn metabolism."

"As if they hibernate? We have seen no evidence that they are seasonal creatures, like bears."

"They might have been at one time. This is only conjecture; you might verify it with the Frinn. I believe the need for hibernation diminished as their technology developed. Why hibernate when you can stay active all year, using artificial heating elements, insulation, clothing, shelter?"

"These extra chromosomes then serve no current use?"

"They're present. That means they can be activated again, under the proper conditions. I suspect that the Frinn can hibernate as they once did. My work shows certain chemical stimuli might trigger this response."

"The Frinn would simply . . . go to sleep?"

"They would awaken, Colonel," she said angrily. He twisted the purpose of her work. She sought ways to aid the Frinn in fighting the Infinity Plague. She believed, as did Walden, that the encounter between species had gotten off to a poor start. Destroying an entire world of sentient beings was not her intent or the purpose of her bioresearch. Weapons, yes, but weapons to be used intelligently. The Frinn had reacted to, not initiated, hostility.

"How long can they be kept in this state?"

"I've run computer analyses based on the body-fat ratios found during the autopsies." Anita shook her head. "I doubt they would last an entire year. Perhaps not even a month. The adipose tissue needed to support life, even in a slowed state, isn't present. The Frinn have evolved into slimmer, sleeker creatures than they were in their hibernation days."

"Put them to sleep, kill them by starvation," Sorbatchin said. "We might be able to use such a protective defense."

Anita stared at him, slowly realizing how Sorbatchin intended to use what she had discovered. "You want to blackmail them into submission," she said. "Put enough of them into hibernation that the rest must surrender or watch their fellows die slowly. That's no better than the Infinity Plague."

"No better," agreed the blond Sov-Lat officer, smiling wickedly, "but it is different. They might find a cure for the plague. If we keep them off-balance with several approaches, our ultimate victory is assured."

"You sound as if we're going into battle. Unless I'm mistaken, Nakamura has said our mission to the Frinn world is to rectify what has happened. We're going to aid, not to conquer."

"They destroyed our research station."

Anita Tarleton refused to go over the old arguments. "You have no position in our expedition. The *Hippocrates* is an NAA vessel. The *Winston* is, also. At best, you are an observer."

"As is Miko Nakamura," Sorbatchin said easily.

"She's an advisor. I don't like her assuming command, but there are too few left in the chain of command who know what they're doing."

Sorbatchin studied her intently until she felt like an insect under a microscope.

"We are alike, you and I," he said. "Power intrigues our kind. You fear a loss of your own dominion. Do not. We can work well together. Perform your assigned tasks and you will be rewarded with authority and respect."

Anita tapped in a question on her computer console. Nakamura's response was immediate. She was to cooperate with Sorbatchin. New bioweapons were required.

For the subjugation of the Frinn. All pretense of aiding them in their battle against the human-created Infinity Plague was gone.

"Very well," she said. "If you'll let me get back to work, we're more likely to have something by the time we drop back into normal space."

"We go into liftspace in a few hours," Sorbatchin said. "Prepare your experiments so they will not be destroyed by the entry into higher dimensional spaces." He rose and strutted out. Anita barely held her anger in check. For all the colonel's veiled promises at high positions for her, she knew he only led her on. He would use her, then cast her aside.

Anita sat in front of her computer console and idly tapped at the keys. She masked her work the best she could. Knowing that Nakamura—and now Sorbatchin—would access her every entry, she tried to bury what she had learned under gigabytes of electronic debris.

She was well on the way to determining how the Infinity Plague affected the Frinn. The site in the extra chromosomal pair where the virus began to cut and unwind the DNA determined the progress of the disease. One caused failure of the autonomic system. Another triggered the hibernation she had determined through her computer genome mapping. The former caused death within two months. The latter, chemically activated, took longer, slowing nutrient uptake, but was as deadly.

How long? Anita estimated this mode would kill within six months. But she had been given the authorization to pursue the mechanism triggering hibernation. She might work out a way of defeating the Infinity Plague as her work on the hibernation genes progressed. The two were related.

She rocked back and closed her eyes. Sometimes she missed Jerome Walden. He had always been able to block people like Sorbatchin and Nakamura and keep them at bay, allowing her to concentrate on her work. That had allowed her to do her research work more effectively. But dealing with them came along with the position she sought—and with the position came power.

Anita Tarleton, Head of Research Staff. She liked the sound to the title.

She left her console and returned to the half-dozen experiments she had begun to find the proper agent for triggering the Frinn hibernation. Several looked promising.

CHAPTER
4

Uvallae scratched his coarse-skinned, sloping forehead with both hands in a gesture of frustration. He tried to use the humans' equipment and it always turned on him. Their unsophisticated computer didn't speed his searching and computing as much as it wasted time through primitive keyboard input. Even the simplest of their robots refused to operate properly.

How he wished for his own lab aboard Starlight!

The Frinn scientist settled in the uncomfortable, poorly shaped chair and requested authorization to contact those remaining on the huge space station. From the delay, he knew his request was routed through Miko Nakamura. That bothered him less than wondering who else saw the request—and who listened in as he spoke.

This was but one penalty for being captured and belonging to a defeated species.

"Uvallae, it is good to see you once more," came the greeting from Starlight's controller. The man's appearance frightened Uvallae. He had lost weight and his hands shook when he made the traditional gesture of gathering together. Worse, his coloration was decidedly gray, a sure sign of infirmity. Uvallae wished they could communicate properly, as

31

they did aboard the space station. No scent transmission was possible between the *Hippocrates* and Starlight.

"Miggae, the pleasure rests with me," Uvallae said in response. "How is your research coming?"

Miggae's snout twitched, as if seeking the true question behind Uvallae's request. The space station's controller seemed to shrink and become even frailer.

"No work is conducted now. Maintaining the station takes all my time."

"My friend, you do not look well. What are you doing to counter this sorry situation?"

"No one remaining on Starlight is well," Miggae answered. "We try to maintain, not progress. Therein lies our slow death. The robots are once more working, but supervising their activity requires constant attention to all that goes wrong now. Starlight needs a full staff and repair technicians. The battle damaged more than we thought. It lies beyond the range of even a fully functioning robot."

"Is the space station in danger?"

"Not immediately," the other Frinn said. "However . . ." His words trailed off as he scrubbed vigorously at his sloping forehead in agitation.

"Are you eating properly? Take time to eat. You always enjoyed it so," suggested Uvallae. He tried to remember what Walden had said about the effects of the Infinity Plague. More than autonomic system failure might result. He had tried to convey his concern about the extra chromosomes sported by the Frinn. Uvallae was sorry he had not been able to concentrate more on the human's words. He would have to discuss this further with Egad before requesting clarification from Walden.

"There is no appetite," Miggae said. "I have no heart, either. Nothing is right. We are captives—and worse."

"How long has our exploratory ship been home?" asked Uvallae.

"Four months, plus an additional few days. I begin to hate myself for wishing that it had exploded when it left or is forever lost in liftspace."

"That is the lesser of the injuries possible to our species," said Uvallae, sharing his friend's disturbing emotion. He, too, had the thought that the Frinn would be better off if the ship never arrived home. Wishing ill of anyone did not come easily, even if it meant the greater good was served.

Such a liftship malfunction was almost impossible, though. Frinn ships were highly automated and performed redundancy checks constantly on even the least important systems. Unlike human vessels where many systems broke down at chaotic random intervals and needed supervised attention by organics, Frinn ships maintained zero defects. Again Uvallae wondered at the human philosophy of doing so much work personally. Some boring chores were better left to machines who could tirelessly pursue their mission.

"Do you make any progress in your work?" asked Miggae. "It is too late for those of us on the space station, but you might be able to save some of the more fortunate ones on our home world."

"Work is slow," said Uvallae. He wanted to boast and tell Miggae that a breakthrough on treating the Infinity Plague was imminent. To do so would put even more hurt on himself. The lie would magnify when Miggae and the others on Starlight died, beyond Uvallae's ability to save.

"I understand," Miggae let out a long, loud sigh that sounded like atmosphere rushing into a vacuum. "I appreciate the lack of guards on Starlight. The humans allow us to continue our lives the best we can without interference."

Uvallae started to warn his friend, then stopped. The comlink was being monitored. He had no doubt that Nakamura knew everything being said, and that Sorbatchin also eavesdropped. Again, he felt the sting of being a prisoner.

"All robots are functional?" he asked.

"As many as we need." Miggae rubbed his forehead even more vigorously, then stopped when he realized what Uvallae hinted at. A horrified look came over him. "I will do what is necessary, my friend. Can you do the same?"

"If I must, I will," said Uvallae. The thought of Miggae destroying Starlight to keep it out of human hands implied that they were at war. Walden had said repeatedly that he didn't blame the Frinn for destroying the human research world they called Schwann. Uvallae even believed this attitude was held by Miko Nakamura. However, the civilian advisor looked at the disaster as a way of advancing her career.

With Vladimir Sorbatchin also embarked on conquest to

further his own power, Starlight had become expendable. Somewhere in the system sailed a Frinn vessel hastily outfitted as a warship. Uvallae hoped that word could be sent to the ship about all that had happened. Wiser men might be able to find a course in the midst of momentous confusion.

Starlight would be destroyed when the *Hippocrates* lifted for the light-years' distant home world. Humans would never set up their own base here. Sadness filled Uvallae. Not for the first time he wondered if he had done the right thing giving Nakamura the coordinates of the world of his birth.

Egad said he had, but the gengineered dog was a second-class citizen in human society. The dog also had faith in his master, in spite of Walden's curious and deviant behavior.

"Is your quarantine effective?" asked Miggae. "We are so woefully ignorant of such things. I read of an *ugan* epidemic on the home world two hundred years ago. Everyone was instructed to remain at home. Less than one percent of the population perished as the disease ran its course."

"No other action was taken?" To Uvallae, this number seemed astounding. One percent of his entire race amounted to nearly one million deaths.

"New techniques for immunization were developed, but nothing more occurred." Miggae chuckled—or did he cough? "Our companionship with our world aided us greatly. The hospitals were seldom overworked, even with such widespread need for their comfort. And being a solitary culture has its advantages."

Uvallae felt uncomfortable discussing this with Miggae, even though he knew Walden and the other humans already knew of this facet of Frinn society. Even with almost fifty square meters of space exclusively for his own use, Uvallae felt penned in. He needed privacy and an area far exceeding that allotted in the quarantine.

"I begin to wonder about our need for quarantine on this ship," Uvallae said. "There is some evidence many of those humans who had extended stays on Starlight are permitted to roam freely."

"No verified case of the plague has been reported among the humans. It might not be necessary in their case," pointed out Miggae.

"Walden is penned with us, as is his canine companion."

"Humans have odd ideas, but they are more advanced in biological fields than we are. It is a pity we could not have met under more agreeable circumstances. They might be able to explain how our hospitals work."

Uvallae agreed, then broke the com-link with Starlight. The vidscreen turned pale and the illumination died. Uvallae felt as if a part of himself died with the picture. Miggae was a lifelong friend and highly valued. And he was going to destroy the space station when it became apparent he could no longer supervise the robots. Uvallae knew this was a controller's duty: Never endanger others. More poignant was the notion that Miggae did this to protect the home world from future human depredation.

"I did the right thing," Uvallae said to himself. He left the computer console and found a meditation niche. He settled in it and began reliving events from his immediate past, analyzing, pondering, deciding.

Only the humans could aid his planet against their Infinity Plague. He *had* done the right thing giving Nakamura the coordinates for the lift to his home. He *had*.

Vladimir Sorbatchin walked on cat's feet to the monitoring post Nakamura had set up outside the quarantine area. He pushed a small rice grain–sized camera into the room, then backed away and went to his own small room trailing fiber optic cable as he went. No one, not even Nakamura, could detect this passive-power bug. It used no energy and did not transmit a signal.

Once safely in his room, he attached the end of the foptic cable to an isolated receiver vidscreen. Sorbatchin crouched down and listened and watched as Nakamura's minion spied on the Frinn. The two scientists spoke in generalities, but certain phrases struck responsive chords in the Sov-Lat officer.

"They will destroy Starlight," he mused, understanding fully what Miggae had meant. He made small, crabbed notations in a notebook. One or two EPCT soldiers would secure the space station for human use—for Sov-Lat use.

Sorbatchin still needed to reach his contact back on Earth. Exactly how he was going to do this, he didn't know. But he would. Doris Yerrow had been exposed on the *Hippocrates*, as had Leo Burch. These Sov-Lat spies were known to Sorbatchin only through Nakamura's efforts at ferreting them out. A GRU officer on Delta Cygnus 4 had no need to know of intelligence operations aboard an NAA hospital ship, even one equipped for biological warfare research and escorting a scientific team. But, he thought, there might be others still undetected among the crew or staff who could be used.

He listened intently as the two Frinn talked. Sorbatchin worried at contacting Uvallae. How he could use the alien scientist was an unknown. The Frinn had lost all anyone could. That he had decided the space station must be sacrificed was obvious. It was also apparent to Sorbatchin that the Frinn were less than forthcoming.

They considered themselves, rightly, to be prisoners. He wondered if he could play on this to gain their support. If he made Nakamura the villain, he might gain sympathy and some allegiance. He had done well so far with the EPCT. Part of the *Hippocrates*' crew owed some small fealty to him. Among the NAA scientists he counted on minor support; from Anita Tarleton he saw no succor.

The conversation between Miggae and Uvallae ended. Sorbatchin reeled in his thin foptic cable and put the small camera into his pocket. He wished he had more places around the ship bugged. He needed better intelligence to form his plans.

His spying device safely tucked away, he strode out to find Miko Nakamura. As he had expected, she worked at the ship's console in the wardroom just off the bridge.

Her cool, dark eyes followed him as he crossed the narrow room and came up the length of the table away from her. She had seemed innocuous physically until he saw the edges of her hands. The fleshy pad had been surgically altered to support iron-bearing tissue. Nakamura's hands were deadly weapons, heavy bludgeons meant for killing. Even though Sorbatchin did not fear her physical attack, he kept the table between them—and felt the better for it.

"How may I help you?" she asked. If she was annoyed at his presence, she did not show it. He noticed, however, that she blanked the vidscreen so that he couldn't see what she worked at.

"We need to formulate an invasion plan once we reach our

destination," he said. Sorbatchin saw no reason to skirt the issue. They both wanted the same thing, with different players taking the important roles.

Nakamura wanted the Frinn to surrender to her; Sorbatchin wanted to rule their world. On Earth a commissar might control a few hundred thousand hectares under the Supreme Soviet. He would be the first Sov-Lat commissar to rule an entire world!

"We need to proceed slowly in this," Nakamura chided. "First, we enter liftspace. Then we consolidate our position." She eyed him, looking for a hint of disagreement. Sorbatchin kept a poker face, revealing nothing. When he moved to take control of the *Hippocrates*, he wanted it to come as a surprise. With the EPCTs behind him, he couldn't lose.

"What of the *Winston*?" he asked. "We need our sister ship to coordinate during the lift. It won't do to have either ship detected by the Frinn when we slip back into normal space. We must protect each other."

"This has been discussed with the appropriate flight personnel," Nakamura said. "Captain Belford is confident that we can come out of liftspace within a few light-seconds of each other, even with most of the crew on both ships inexperienced."

"Junior officers make mistakes."

"So true, Colonel."

Sorbatchin wasn't sure if she was chiding him for his impatience. He changed his tack slightly. "Is Captain Belford able to command this vessel?"

"I watch his performance closely. He and Dr. Walden share much in common. Both are unstable, yet have a usefulness that is not to be denied. I do not foresee any problems with the captain. He functions well enough in routine situations. I will command the *Hippocrates* when we enter combat."

"You are ready to fight when we enter the Frinn system, then?"

Nakamura sighed. She touched a button on the computer console and saved her project. Leaning back in the chair, she stared at Sorbatchin. "Yes, we will fight. Their exploratory ship that left the Delta Cygnus system has preceded us and knows nothing of subsequent events. However, the Infinity

Plague must have a toehold on their world and they will not greet us with open arms. They must believe we have only their extinction as our goal.''

Sorbatchin grinned. That was certainly *his* reason for pursuing the fleeing ship. Genocide would follow and he would claim an entire world for the Supreme Soviet.

''I have ordered Dr. Tarleton to change the direction of her work,'' he said.

''I am aware of this. I do not appreciate you intimating that this was also my idea. Your forgery of computer orders flies in the face of mutual trust and cooperation between us.''

Sorbatchin swallowed hard. She was good to have noticed the counterfeit orders he had placed in the computer for Dr. Tarleton's benefit. He worried at other particulars of his scheme to take over the ship that Nakamura might have spied on.

''I did not consider it important. We need other weapons for the invasion—we *are* agreed on this point?''

''That we enter the Frinn system as invaders?'' Nakamura nodded solemnly.

''Good. We need weapons, and Anita Tarleton is particularly capable with bioweapons. She should be given official command of the research group since Walden is incapacitated.''

''Your suggestion is duly noted,'' Nakamura said noncommittally.

''She believes she has learned something of an atrophied body function—''

''That they hibernate,'' cut in Nakamura. ''I am aware of this peculiar trait from other briefings. She can stimulate this in the Frinn at will?''

''By the time we reach the system, she will be able to do so chemically. Does she have your permission to experiment on the four Frinn scientists in quarantine?''

''An interesting idea, using them as experimental subjects,'' Nakamura said, as if she had never considered the matter before. ''Choose well which she uses. I want Uvallae left alive as long as possible. He is the most tractable of the aliens.''

''The key lies in the two extra pairs of chromosomes,''

said Sorbatchin. "Dr. Tarleton will unlock the secret, and we will use it to bring them to a quick surrender."

"Work out the details, Colonel. Delivery systems, timed action of the bioweapons, probable timetable until surrender, everything. You have experience for such a project?"

"The entire invasion plan will be submitted for your approval before we drop back into normal space," he promised.

"Sooner. I need to approve, to authorize, even to browbeat to insure we have everything in readiness. Time is of the essence. The *Hippocrates* will be the sole vessel to use these weapons. The *Winston* will only provide covering fire, if is proves necessary."

Sorbatchin wondered why she was in such a hurry to leave Starlight. A few weeks more in this system would not affect their arrival plans. If they got the bioweapons ready before the lift, both ships could carry the deadly cargo and emerge from liftspace, ready to attack the Frinn. If the *Hippocrates* launched, counting on weapons to be developed in transit, it reduced their chance for success.

It might even be suicidal. Sorbatchin knew the woman had something in mind. Whatever Nakamura might be, she was not self-destructive or stupid.

"Authorize complete file access, and I will begin my planning immediately," Sorbatchin said.

"Very well." Nakamura tapped a few keys on her console, waited, then entered the password that released the *Hippocrates'* complete data banks to him. It was everything Vladimir Sorbatchin could do to keep from laughing in glee. With this information, he would be undisputed commander of the attack force when they came nose to snout with the Frinn.

CHAPTER
5

Egad lay on top of his cage, eyeing the loosened filtration unit above his head. He had not told Anita directly how he had escaped before. She had sneaked him back in through a main door, resetting the door counter so no one would know he had ever left. For the dog, it was little more than a game. He understood what it meant to be sick; none of the humans looked sick. None of his new friends among the pig-aliens looked sick, either. Anita's concern confused him, as did Walden's, but he accepted it. There were so many things the humans counted as major that amounted to little more than cat-shit.

The gengineered dog heaved himself to his short legs and trotted from the room, wandering through the laboratories and checking the Frinn scientists. Uvallae sat with a glassy stare as he meditated. Egad wasn't sure what the Frinn did when he went away like this, but he always came back with more energy and often wanted to play. As he sat now, though, he was no more fun than a piece of furniture—and Egad couldn't even chew on his legs.

Finding Walden sitting and staring at a blank wall bothered Egad more than it did when he found the Frinn this way. Walden's hallucinations increased daily. He became paranoid and was sure everyone spied on him. The dog didn't know if

40

this was true. Why spy on someone locked up in a cage? He remembered his days as a laboratory animal back on Earth and how Walden and others had poked him, taking blood and making life miserable. No one took Walden's blood or shoved long glass sticks up his rear.

"Master?"

Walden jerked back from his reverie. A slow smile crossed his lips, giving Egad a moment's thrill. Perhaps everything was right once more with Walden.

"Good to see you, Egad. How's everything?"

"Boring. Play?"

"For a little bit," said Walden. "Are you ready to lift for another world?"

"Don't understand. We shake my guts again?"

"I'm afraid so. The entry into liftspace always does that, but it goes away fast."

Egad said nothing to this. He couldn't eat for a week after the *Hippocrates* started its stardrive engines.

"I've got so much to do. I feel the answer to breaking down the Infinity Plague virus is so close, but it keeps eluding me. The Frinn's extra chromosomes are the answer. But how?"

"Let's go find Anita. She's a pretty bitch. Nice."

A pained look crossed Walden's face. "I tried to contact her. She won't accept my call. And I need her help with my work. She still blames me for Zacharias' death, I suppose."

"What does the cat-shit Sov-Lat colonel plot?" the dog asked unexpectedly. "Overheard him with soldiers."

"Sorbatchin was talking with the EPCTs?"

Egad bobbed his head in agreement. Sometimes it hurt to talk too much. His throat muscles constricted and only ear-hurting shrill whines came out of the computer-driver transducer pressing into his throat. He had so much he wanted to say to Walden, but he didn't know the words—or rather, Walden didn't. It was easier talking with Uvallae since the alien knew the proper scent-words.

"How did you tap into the computer intercom?" Walden dropped down and scratched Egad's ears. The movement of human fingernails over his ears felt good. The dog barked in appreciation before answering.

"Sleeping in barracks when I heard him."

''Egad, you know that's not true. We're in quarantine. You couldn't have been in the EPCT barracks. And neither could Sorbatchin. The soldiers are all under quarantine, too.''

''They're not. He's not. We are. Gets boring here. Can't run and you won't play.''

Tiny clicks came from Walden's automated equipment. He stopped petting Egad to check the results from his experiment. Seeing that his master was again lost in the world of numbers and strange smells, Egad left. Walden never noticed.

Egad had enough of boredom. Sleeping was nice, but he preferred to do it where and when he pleased. He jumped onto the cage and began pushing the filtration unit back with his nose. Someone had halfheartedly replaced the bolts. Egad had learned how to use nose, tongue, and paws to wiggle the unit free again. Once more he slipped through the hole in the carbon composite wall, almost catching his head. When he got through on the other side in the analysis room, he knew exactly what to do. He reset the alarm he had triggered and then opened the door and ran into the corridor. His thin black tail wagged furiously. He was free again. What to do? Egad decided to check the EPCT barracks once more. The soldiers always petted him, and he hadn't gotten the treat he had counted on before.

The cat-shit colonel had prevented that.

To the gengineered dog's dismay, the barracks was empty. He sniffed around and found most of the equipment lockers empty. Wherever the EPCTs had gone, they had taken their weapons with them.

Disgruntled, Egad prowled the halls. He stuck his head into the infirmary and saw Leo Burch working at a desk, the pale glow from the computer's vidscreen giving the turncoat doctor a ghastly pallor. Of the fat cat that had been laden with spy equipment, Egad got no hint. He sniffed a few times. His nose wrinkled at the antiseptics on the air, but he didn't smell anything out of the ordinary. He left Burch working on the computer.

Frustrated, Egad turned toward the *Hippocrates'* control room. Captain Belford sat in the command chair but others did the real work. Egad had seen the crew preparing for a liftspace transition before. None of the frantic activity that preceded such a stomach-wrenching jump was evident.

"Don't like putting off the lift like this," one officer said.

Another replied, "We do what we're told." He cast a hot, angry look at Captain Belford and added, "By the *real* captain, we do what we're told. I liked it better when the *Hippocrates* was under his command."

"She's not so bad. She can make a decision," said the first.

Egad knew they referred to Miko Nakamura. Earlier, Captain Belford's command had been usurped by his first officer. Brittain had been murdered through Nakamura's machinations, and she had never relinquished the power back to the ship's rightful captain.

The dog left and went to Nakamura's cabin, listening hard. He knew trying to sniff her out wasn't going to work; she masked her scent too well. Faint sounds came to him. He knew he had found both Nakamura and Sorbatchin. Dropping prone on the cool deck, Egad pressed one sensitive ear against the bulkhead. As long as the liftspace engines didn't rumble and whine, he could hear well.

"We need to observe our troops in action," Sorbatchin said.

"There is little to test their mettle, Colonel," Nakamura replied. "Are you so sure your new tactics will work against the Frinn?"

"I am," the Sov-Lat officer said stiffly. "Major Zacharias had not learned what I have of their defenses, their robots' capabilities, their likely tactics and weak spots."

"We need to lift for their home world. Is this delay worthwhile?"

"It is. We cannot lift with their warship remaining undamaged behind us. They can follow and catch us between planetary defenses and a heavy cruiser."

Nakamura spoke for several minutes, and Egad failed to hear what she said. The dog's tongue lolled out, and he panted to keep cool. The air-conditioning in this corridor didn't circulate properly. Egad wiggled forward and found a nice current. By this time, Nakamura's voice had risen to a level he could hear.

"I see your projections are in order, Colonel. Apparently

we must give the EPCTs skill in dealing with the robotic forces the Frinn will field.''

"There is more. We must cut off communication between the *Hippocrates* and Starlight.''

"I understand," said Nakamura. "You don't want Uvallae speaking with those still aboard the space station.''

"Nor is it wise for those in the research area to find out we are practicing our techniques for fighting the Frinn. I detect an unfortunate bias among them to believe the aliens are nonhostile.''

"You will lead the EPCTs?" asked Nakamura. Egad's ear pricked up. The woman's voice quivered slightly. The gengineered dog wasn't sure what the tremor meant. In some humans, it meant a lie. But he didn't think so in this case. Nakamura was being crafty, as if telling him a full food bowl awaited him in the next room and he found only a vet ready to give a painful shot.

"With your permission," Egad heard a small quiver in the Sov-Lat officer's voice, too, but this he attributed to eagerness.

"I am only advisor to the expedition," Nakamura said. Smoothly, she added, "However, in the absence of NAA combat officers, I concur that you are the most logical choice for field command. Is there any problem with the EPCTs accepting your orders? You are, after all, a Soviet-Latino Pact officer.''

"Their training is to obey. They like me well enough, and we have developed what you call a rapport. The foray will go flawlessly. I am sure of it.''

"Very well, Colonel. Eradicate all the Frinn still aboard Starlight. Use whatever guile is required to lure their warship in, and see to its destruction, also.''

"I'll need the cooperation of the *Winston*.''

"I will transmit your commands directly to the destroyer.''

Vladimir Sorbatchin laughed, then agreed to this limitation on his power. "We work well together, Miko.''

"Yes, Colonel, we do. Let us concentrate on the details of your invasion before a small celebration.''

Egad got to his feet and dashed off, thinking to find Anita and tell her what was going to happen. The gengineered dog didn't understand everything he'd overheard, but he knew the

Frinn aboard Starlight had been promised immunity. Sorbatchin meant to kill them. Walden had worked on the concept of a lie until Egad thought he could detect it, even when it was couched in smiles and soothing voices and petting hands. If he had been able to sniff the Sov-Lat officer he would have known for sure. Humans emanated a curious odor when they lied.

Sorbatchin reeked most of the time.

Egad skidded to a halt when he realized Anita might punish him. She had been upset when he had come out of the quarantine room before. It didn't seem to matter to her that the EPCT soldiers hadn't been penned up. Egad remembered with no fondness the way she had treated him, too. She had scrubbed and dipped him in smelly chemicals. And the radiation bath still made his skin prickly. He stopped and scratched at a particularly itchy portion of skin just behind his floppy left ear. It made him feel a little better; at least the ear didn't bother him like it had.

The dilemma still tossed him back and forth. Anita wouldn't believe him, and he'd end up in a cage inside quarantine. Penned in a pen. Egad didn't want that. He trotted back to the analysis room and peered in. A technician finished going over the data gathered by the automatic equipment.

Egad slipped into the room after the woman left. It took him twice as long to push the filtration unit aside and force his ungainly head through the hole. He awkwardly tumbled into the room with his cage. He looked back at the filtration unit that had been his escape hatch twice now. It was askew. The dog wished he could somehow get it back into position, but he didn't know how.

Forgetting about it, he ran to Walden's lab. The door was locked and Egad couldn't reach the annunciator plate that would gain him entry. A growl formed in the dog's throat. This wasn't fair. He had information and Walden wasn't letting him in.

He turned and ran for Uvallae's lab. Egad lost his balance in his hurry and crashed into the side of the hatchway. But it didn't matter. The Frinn scientist wasn't inside. He wasn't even in his niche meditating.

Frustrated more than he had been in years, Egad went back

to Walden's door and lay down outside. He couldn't hear anyone inside, but he knew someone had to be there. Why lock the door if he was only going for a short stroll through the quarantine area?

Egad let out a long, loud howl that echoed along the corridor. It took Walden only a few seconds to slide open the hatch to see what produced such a protest.

"Egad! What's wrong?"

"Need to talk. Cat-shit colonel is invading space station."

"Please, Egad, not so fast. Your transducer is overloading. It turns everything you say into mush." Walden grabbed Egad and pulled him into the laboratory. Uvallae sat at the far side. He and Walden had been working on a problem using the computer.

"Uvallae, call Starlight," barked out Egad. The Frinn looked up, startled at the command from the dog.

"What is wrong? Has tragedy finally befallen my friends?"

"Call," said Egad. His speech unit malfunctioned. When he had crashed into the door of Uvallae's lab, he had struck the CPU and damaged part of it.

"Go on," said Walden. "I've seldom seen Egad this upset. It must be something important."

Uvallae turned the computer console around and tried to open a com-link with Starlight. Static greeted his efforts. He worked a few seconds longer, then rubbed his forehead with both hands in a sign of discouragement.

"Let me try," said Walden. "I've had more experience with it." He tried to establish a laser-link to the station and failed. Only static danced on the computer's vidscreen. Walden frowned, then called the *Hippocrates*' com officer.

"Yes, Dr. Walden?" came the immediate response. "What can I do for you?"

"I'm trying to reach Controller Miggae on Starlight. There doesn't seem to be a clear channel. I tried both standard com-link and a laser-link. Can you help?"

"Sorry, Doctor. All com is down right now. A tech blew the control circuits in the laser unit, and there's a hot proton storm boiling outside that chews up our usual circuits. We're looking at at least four hours before we can get in touch with Starlight again."

"Keep me posted. I want a circuit when one comes open."

"To Miggae," said the com officer. "Got it."

Walden signed off and just stared at the vidscreen. He shrugged and said to Uvallae, "They'll get back to us. There doesn't seem to be anything to worry about. Both the *Hippocrates* and *Starlight* are well shielded against proton events."

"The station is close to the primary," agreed Uvallae, "and is able to withstand heavy ionizing radiation."

They turned back to their work, leaving Egad in the center of the floor. He yelped and tried to get his voice back. Hisses and pops greeted him. He went and tugged at Walden's lab coat.

"Egad, we're busy. I'm finding out more about the Frinn physiology. Can't this wait?"

The dog backed off and stared. How did he tell them Sorbatchin was leading EPCT troops against the helpless survivors on *Starlight*? They refused to listen.

He raced from the room and hurried to a monitoring station loaded with equipment. The gengineered dog looked around frantically, trying to decipher the readouts. He had never been much interested in the humans' toys before, but he knew they told important things. What was it like outside the *Hippocrates* right now? He had to show Walden no storm was raging.

Which of the instruments showed the data he needed remained a mystery to Egad. He yowled in defeat. Nothing looked out of place. He trotted back to the laboratory and barked loud enough to get Walden's attention.

"Sorry, Egad. I'll fix your voder unit later. Uvallae and I are close to something. I feel it."

Egad refused to let his master slip away again. This time Walden's irritation reached the point where he said, "All right. If I fix your computer, will you leave us alone?"

Egad bobbed his head up and down, finally understanding the human concept of lying.

Walden worked for a few minutes, took out a circuit block, and tossed it away, replacing it from a box of the PLZT ceramic equivalents. He touched the self-test button and nodded to himself when he saw the small lights winking green.

"That fixes you up. Now scoot. Let Uvallae and me—"

"Cat-shit colonel goes to Starlight. To kill everyone!"

"That's not funny, Egad. You promised to let us work if I fixed your computer."

"A moment, Dr. Walden," Uvallae knelt and patted Egad's shaggy head. The Frinn's piglike snout worked actively to discern the truth. "Does Miggae know of this?"

"Secret," panted Egad. At last he'd found someone who believed him. "Colonel leads EPCTs and wants to practice killing."

"That's not very logical, Egad," said Walden. "We've already conquered Starlight. We've made our peace with the Frinn still aboard. We're trying to *cure* them, not kill them."

"Colonel goes there *now*!"

"Try to contact Starlight again," urged Uvallae. He stared at the dog, his catlike slitted eyes narrow above the bony ridges. The rough skin of his sloping forehead rippled and rolled, as if a hidden finger stroked it from underneath.

"No answer. The proton storm is still messing up com," reported Walden.

"Look at instruments. Check outside," yowled Egad. "No storm, no storm. I looked!"

Walden snorted and shook his head in disbelief. "You're just feeling neglected, Egad. You and I both know you can't read the instruments. You don't even know what monitors to track."

"Why—" began Uvallae.

"Egad is overwrought. The quarantine is working on all of us, including him." Walden knelt and held the big head firmly, looking into the dog's mismatched eyes, trying to convince himself as much as the dog. "Uvallae is going to contact his world after we lift into his home system. We're going to land as friends, not conquerors. There is no reason to harm the Frinn. We're friends, and we're trying to help them contain and defeat the Infinity Plague. Do you understand this, Egad?"

The dog bit him.

CHAPTER
6

"They tried to reach Starlight," said Nakamura. "The communications officer blocked them."

"What excuse did he give for the failure?" demanded Vladimir Sorbatchin. The Sov-Lat colonel settled the weapons around his body. He had found combat armor that fit him well enough, although most of the units were too small for him. Pirating from several sets of armor allowed him to move with relative ease. He extended his arm and pointed. A red aiming laser showed the spot where torrents of energy could be directed, or a single grenade, or any of half a dozen other directed weapons. If he wanted to take out an entire room, all he needed to do was switch to wide-beam weapons.

Sorbatchin felt invincible in the rig. He wished his own troops had such sophisticated devices. Their firepower would be increased tenfold. More!

Miko Nakamura tapped at the keys on her computer and read the information flashing across the vidscreen. "A proton storm is disrupting the com-link. A technician destroyed the laser-link. Com will be returned to normal soon. Those are the excuses."

"Not good," muttered Sorbatchin, fearing this. "Walden is increasingly paranoid. He has precision instrumentation in his lab to check such an excuse."

Nakamura smiled crookedly. "He has learned of our plans."

"What! How? That fool of a com officer! I'll flay him alive for this breach of security!"

"Do not worry so, Colonel. Walden has ignored his informant." Nakamura smiled even more as she considered the source. She knew Egad's abilities, even if Sorbatchin didn't. She intended to use the gengineered dog as long as possible before revealing his talents. How the canine had escaped quarantine was a matter to be investigated, but she overheard the dog's report and Walden's answer. Even Uvallae had been duped. The practice invasion of Starlight would proceed on schedule.

"If you are not concerned, I will ignore it, also," said Sorbatchin. The officer's sullen expression showed his anger at her. "I must muster my troops and be certain they are ready. Has the bogus message been sent?"

"We have every reason to believe the Frinn war craft has received the recall message and is on its way back to dock at Starlight's equatorial bay. All communication not originating on the *Hippocrates* is being blocked."

"Very well. Let us hope the Frinn robots provide an adequate defense for the space station. I want to test my theories of combat now, rather than when we invade the Frinn home world."

"All is ready, Colonel. Go."

Vladimir Sorbatchin saluted, spun, and left, his ill-fitting combat gear rattling as he went. Nakamura stared after him, her agile mind working over details of this mock invasion. Starlight had been subdued once. There was no threat left aboard, even if Miggae reprogrammed the myriad robots to attack once more. The true thrust of this engagement was capturing the Frinn war vessel. Nakamura agreed with Sorbatchin that it was bad tactics to allow it to remain behind in this system. Never put an enemy at your back.

Having a friend at your back was often as dangerous, she mused.

"Perhaps Colonel Sorbatchin will perish in this engagement. Perhaps the EPCTs will eliminate him for me." She had run computer projections and had decided a 50–50 chance

existed that one soldier would resent the Sov-Lat officer leading him and do something about it.

If Sorbatchin survived, so much the better. Nakamura
doubted he could succeed militarily on the Frinn home ter-
ritory. One way or another, Sorbatchin had to die to allow
her to gain undisputed control of this expedition.

Miko Nakamura began monitoring the progress of the human troops as they moved into battle formation. In many
ways Sorbatchin was more efficient than Edouard Zacharias.
But like the major, Vladimir Sorbatchin was expendable.

"Looking good, Colonel," said Sergeant Hecht. The non-
commissioned officer ran through a final checklist showing
the status of his men. The expedition had started with almost
two hundred EPCTs. Only forty were left, hardly enough for
a real battle. The Frinn robots had taken their toll, both on
Starlight and back on Delta Cygnus 4.

"We have some helpers," Sorbatchin said. "Three techs
will run them."

"Helpers?" Hecht looked across the *Hippocrates*' landing
bay and saw small robots scurrying toward him. Without
thinking, he flipped up his laserifle and started to vaporize
the leading mechanical device. Only Sorbatchin's hand on the
barrel of the weapon stopped him from spattering the ratlike
robot all over the ship.

"They're ours, Sergeant," the officer said. "The techs will
use them to support us, not cut us down."

"They look the world like the damned Frinn repair robots
that gave us fits," Hecht said.

"We modeled them after the pigs' robots. Repair rats, we
call them."

"Fitting," Hecht said. He stared at the dozens of ankle-
high mechanicals with undisguised distaste. When they had
faced the Frinn fighting machines on Schwann he had said he
wouldn't mind fighting alongside such powerful weapons.
Now he wasn't so sure. Too many of his friends had died at
their metallic hands for him to trust the robots as much as a
flesh-and-blood companion.

"You sure the damned things will work?" he asked Sorbatchin. "I've seen combat machines before. Even field tested
some. They fail when you need them most."

"These are patterned after the Frinn robots," Sorbatchin repeated forcefully. "Did they fail when you faced them?"

"Not many," Hecht admitted reluctantly. "But then, my life wasn't on the line because of some bit of twisted wire and block circuits. Did the captured Frinn help you build these?"

"No," said Sorbatchin.

"Good. I don't think I'd trust the damned things if the pig-faces had worked on them. They're plotting to get even with us. You can tell it by their eyes. Sneaky pig-bastards."

"It is we who will get even with them," Sorbatchin said softly. "We will destroy those on the space station—and their war craft. We can avenge the deaths of our comrades."

Hecht stiffened at this, but the EPCTs nearby didn't notice Sorbatchin's slip. Hecht had killed "comrades" in battle over insignificant real estate on other worlds. He wasn't a "comrade" any more than those in his squad were. Hecht ran his fingers along the firing toggle of his laserifle as he remembered that the Sov-Lats had been enemies not too long ago. The research stations on Schwann had been built to develop bioweapons *against* them. Being thrown together with Sorbatchin was pure chance—and it didn't change much, as far as Hecht was concerned.

The Frinn might be the primary enemy now. When they were whipped into submission, the Soviet-Latinos would again be the enemy. Hecht didn't much care who led them now if it was done with some intelligence and hope for winning. But later . . .

"Attention, troops," barked Sorbatchin over their command circuit. Hecht was glad to hear that the Sov-Lat didn't make the same mistake twice and call them comrades. Most of the men were pumped up for the battle, but even they would notice if Sorbatchin harped on using the offensive term.

"We are few in numbers. We are no longer able to take risks. This does not mean we will fight a defensive battle. The Frinn must be lured out of hiding. We have allies in robots built aboard the *Hippocrates*. Do not count on them exclusively. Your partner is your best defense in combat."

"What about the pig-faces' cruiser? How we gonna get it?" asked another sergeant. Hecht saw the irritation flash

across Sorbatchin's visored face. He wasn't used to under-
lings questioning him.

In some ways, this amused Hecht. EPCT officers held
nothing back from their men. The complete battle plan was
available to any man in the unit, from private up through the
ranks of officers, who cared to study it. Few did. Like Hecht,
they preferred to do as they were told by commanders who
ought to know every detail. Besides, plans changed drastically once the battle was joined. Hecht had never seen an
engagement go as scheduled. The only constants in combat
were screwups and death.

"The Frinn cruiser will be lured into a docking bay. We
must be ready to board and seize control. We believe there
are fewer than twenty of the pig-faces on the ship."

"Why do we believe that?" asked a private.

"Because that is the way their ships are designed. Most of
their controls are automated." Sorbatchin's temper burned to
a cinder now. Another flare up and he might use his laserifle
on anyone daring to interrogate him.

"Colonel, we're ready to go. Tell us what to expect with
these things." Hecht poked at a rat-sized robot with the toe
of his boot. The vicious little robot turned and buzzed at him.
Hecht checked power levels. If there had been the slightest
buildup in field charge around the robot, he'd have blasted it
into vapor.

"They were originally used as repair robots for small spots
aboard this ship," Sorbatchin said. "They have been modified in a way similar to the Frinn robots. We project an eighty
percent kill ratio for them. This frees the organic units for
more important duties."

"Organic units?" someone asked.

"He means us, sucker," Hecht said. A ripple passed
through the EPCTs that only the sergeant detected. Most of
the soldiers expressed their discomfort with this notion on the
non-com circuit rather than directly to Sorbatchin on a command channel.

"The Frinn cruiser will dock, we will board and secure.
Your individual assignments are programmed into your computers. Study them en route to the docking bay."

"Will we be going in at the same place as before?" asked

Hecht. "I can't make out the attack plan from what you've given me."

Again Sorbatchin stiffened at the implied criticism. "Where you enter the space station is of no concern. What you do once you arrive is. We regard this as a training maneuver, not real combat."

"Not your ass that'll die, is it?" grumbled one corporal. Hecht blanked the man's circuit for a few seconds to reprimand him for insubordination. They might not like Sorbatchin—and he might be an enemy officer—but he had been placed in command by their superiors. Hecht wondered at Nakamura's motives. He wished he had a few minutes to discuss this assignment with her. But he didn't. Sorbatchin urged them into the small shuttle craft.

Hecht herded his tiny squad into the belly of the craft. He had barely secured himself in the thick, unyielding webbing when the pilot accelerated violently. Hecht closed his eyes and rode out the abrupt vector changes stoically. He had been through this before—and it always bothered him.

Not knowing what to expect troubled him the most. Zacharias hadn't been the most concise officer Hecht had served under, but he had given his men as much information as possible. Sorbatchin gave them next to nothing.

"Sarge, do we have to put up with the little robot rats?" The soldier pointed toward the rear of the shuttle bay using his laserifle. Two techs worked with the nasty robots, making certain they were charged and ready for combat.

"Let them do your work for you, Hendrix," he said. "Just sit back, relax, and take a snooze. This is going to be a vacation."

"Sure, Sarge, a vacation in hell."

The shuttle vectored furiously and the ship crashed hard into the alien space station's docking bay. Before the shudders had died down, Hecht had his unit out of their webbing and into the airlock. He couldn't get used to the Frinn airlocks. He passed through . . . nothing. How they maintained a pressure gradient was beyond him. The atmosphere ought to rush out into space, but it didn't. Every step inward got harder until full friction worked against his suit and his external sensors measured full breathable atmosphere instead of hard vacuum. Hecht sent the code combinations to each man and dispatched them. The tiny colored display on his command computer showed deployment, status, and elapsed time.

"We got it, Colonel," he signaled Sorbatchin.

"The control center is ours. We met with only slight resistance," the Sov-Lat officer replied.

Hecht saw that the colonel has sustained only one casualty. He snorted in disgust. They had the easy part of the attack. The few Frinn remaining on Starlight were dying; the robots that had fought so fiercely before had been reprogrammed for their original maintenance duties. The real fight would be his.

"Where is their cruiser?" Hecht asked. His display failed to show anything outside Starlight's hull.

"The coded sequence has been sent. They'll be here in a few minutes."

"Minutes?" Hecht was startled. "They were closer than we thought."

"Less than five light-seconds away."

Hecht swore. That meant the alien cruiser had crept closer to the space station without anyone aboard the *Hippocrates* knowing. Or had Sorbatchin realized the alien vessel was that close? Hecht didn't like the idea that Sorbatchin and Nakamura were keeping such important information from them.

"Is the *Winston* ready to respond?"

Hecht fumed even more when Sorbatchin took a full minute to reply. "It will back us up, if needed."

Hecht switched to his local circuit, blocking Sorbatchin out. "Men, get ready to mix it up. We've got a tough one ahead."

"We're used to it, Sarge," said the unit leader carrying a set of war pipes. The meter-long tubes fired genius bombs capable of elaborate seek-and-destroy tactics, all computer-controlled.

"The cruiser is closing fast on us," Hecht said, not sure if it was or not. He settled down and studied the sketchy battle plan he had been given. Using the small robots as shock troops seemed a clever ploy, but total reliance on them taking the Frinn cruiser struck Hecht as ridiculous.

After the first few robots bored into the ship's hull, the Frinn commander should take steps to stop them. He had his own robots, after all, and they were programmed for repairing the damage caused by the intruders.

"Got radar contact, Sarge," came the advance man's report. "Sensors show this is bigger than a cruiser. We might be talking a battleship."

Hecht moaned softly. It was always like this. The best formulated plans fell apart when combat was joined. The enemy always did the unexpected. He couldn't change the attack plan now.

"We go for it. Ready with the pipes. Take out the airlock the instant it opens."

"Hell, if they used the same type as they do on the space station, we can fire directly into them," said the private manning the war pipes. The tubes flickered as electrostatic charge built up around them. The magnetically powered genius bombs would be mass-driven at minute fractions of the speed of light. Nothing could evade them, nothing short of Ultimate Strength Steel plate could withstand their impact.

"No sign they know what's in store for them," reported the scout in the space station's airlock. 'They're two klicks off, one, docking hard. Here they are. Let's do it, Sarge!"

Hecht moved the toggle that flashed orders on the vidscreens of his unit. The pipes flared as they discharged their loads of death. The genius bombs blasted through the side of the Frinn vessel, then sought out vital areas inside before exploding. Hecht watched a polarized picture of the alien war craft. From the ripples in the polarized field, he knew where the bombs had exploded inside.

"Their engines are gone. We took out everything aft of their control center. We missed the cockpit, though. Get the rats inside. Now, do it now!" he shouted at the technicians working the droves of mechanical vermin.

Hecht felt like a Piped Piper as the mechanical rats rushed forward, entering the battleship through the holes bored by the genius bombs. He cut into the techs' circuit and watched the progress of the robot shock troops. To his surprise, the attack went well. The Frinn were caught off-guard and failed to respond promptly.

"Follow up," he ordered. "Second flight, fire now!"

The pipes sang once more. A new launcher-load of genius bombs ripped into the stricken vessel. The stress indications in the hull convinced Hecht the ship was no longer space-worthy. Little more than a derelict connected to the space station.

"What now, Sarge? We go in?" asked Hendrix.

"Sure, why not," Hecht said, waiting for the proper instant to order the attack. A few sensors trailing foptic cables had been dropped by the genius bombs as they burrowed through the ship. The robot rats added a few more sensors. He scanned them all, isolating the areas where humans would be most effectively used.

"Go!"

He had only fifteen men with him. Hecht led the way inside, laserifle ready. He fired only twice on his way to the control room. The robot rats had used their minuscule lasers to cut through bulkheads—and aliens. The robots had sought the Frinn out, no matter where they hid. Many had been in their isolation niches doing whatever it was they did when they were alone. Hecht felt no sense of triumph at the slaughter. Even his own small part in the battle brought him no satisfaction.

Just as he thought they were going to take the powerful craft with no trouble, his defensive armor began glowing. He spun, following his instincts as much as the evasion advice given by his computer. He set his laserifle to continuous beam and slashed out in a half circle. The beam continued to heat him. He broke into a sweat as the outer portion of his armor sublimated. Hecht had only seconds left before he vanished in a greasy cloud.

Dropping to the deck, he tried to turn and roll to distribute the energy more evenly over his armor. The beam followed with unerring accuracy.

"Where's it coming from?" he demanded on his open circuit. "Somebody get it off my ass!"

The laser died as suddenly as it had begun. Hecht got to his knees, searching for the source. He still didn't see it.

"A robot," came another EPCT's report. "Don't know what it was used for, but it was high up in the corridor and it was deadly. One of our vermin got it."

Hecht advanced slowly, staying in a crouch. He found the module mounted on the bulkhead, hidden in a corner. A robot had burned through the protective shell and disabled the laser. Hecht had no time to mull over the effectiveness of the small robot. A new attack burned away a portion of his command circuitry.

He swung around, again using his laserifle beam as a scythe. A Frinn doubled over and then came apart when he cut the alien in half. Hecht wiggled forward, going past the dead Frinn and his sizzling entrails. He stood and entered the control room. Two others, possibly the pilot or captain and his first officer, lay dead inside. The vast control panels startled him. Only a dozen instruments were mounted amid the mostly blank areas. Even a nonwarship like the *Hippocrates* had thousands of readouts, instruments, and controls. The captain and a junior officer used laser wands and during critical maneuvers even helmet-mounted see-and-blink controls, in addition to touch toggles, to run the ship.

The Frinn let their machines do much more than humans did.

"Sarge, we got it. They're either dead or surrendered," came the scout's report. "Elapsed time is nine minutes from docking to complete domination."

"No casualties on our part?"

"I stubbed my toe. Does that count?"

"I'll put you in for a medal," Hecht grumbled. He shifted to the private circuit connecting him to Sorbatchin. The Sov-Lat colonel responded immediately.

"All is well?"

"We've got enough data to keep Nakamura busy analyzing it for years," Hecht bragged. "The ship is ours."

"Prisoners?"

"Nine. Another ten died. There were only nineteen crew members aboard."

"Excellent. Put them to death and return to Starlight immediately."

"Repeat that order, Colonel." Hecht rebelled at the idea of killing captives. These aliens hadn't fought as if they were military—they hadn't even fielded the robots that had been so deadly on Delta Cygnus 4 and on Starlight.

"You heard me. Do as you are ordered, Sergeant."

"I know my duty, Colonel." Hecht switched back to his private circuits and issued orders in clipped, terse tones. The Frinn vessel was completely secured in another three minutes.

CHAPTER
7

Jerome Walden stared at the vidscreen in disbelief. Sergeant Hecht was not joking, and this stunned Walden.

"You have nine *survivors*?" Walden asked.

"That's right, Doc. I thought you might be the best one to look after them. Colonel Sorbatchin wanted them tossed out the airlock. I'm an EPCT, not a murderer. You know our training regime."

Walden nodded numbly, his mind racing in circles. He tried to piece together the snippets Hecht had told him. The com blackout with Starlight hadn't been due to any proton event; Nakamura and Sorbatchin had engineered it to kill all the Frinn aboard the space station. Then they decoyed the Frinn cruiser in for the same treatment. They had butchered unsuspecting beings.

"We'll arrange for them to be brought into quarantine immediately," Walden said, thinking hard. The Frinn could be smuggled aboard with EPCT equipment. "They probably aren't exposed to the plague, but there's no way of telling for sure."

"Are you getting any better handle on it?" asked the soldier.

"We think so. The Frinn are especially susceptible because of their unusual chromosomal pairings."

"What about us? What about my men?" asked Hecht, worried.

"We haven't had time to do the intensive workups we need to find what caused some of the men to go crazy," Walden said. "It might be the Infinity Plague. I'm not so sure now."

"You staying in quarantine with them or are you coming out?"

"It might be a moot point. You and the others who were aboard Starlight weren't quarantined, as I'd thought. Sorbatchin has seen to that."

"With all due respect, Doc, it wasn't just the Sov-Lat's doing. He couldn't command anything aboard the *Hippocrates* unless Nakamura agreed to it."

Walden nodded. Miko Nakamura played a game that he didn't understand. Whatever her goal, Sorbatchin was a pawn in it. Everyone aboard the NAA vessel was a pawn.

"I just wanted to say one thing more, Doc." Hecht paused, his face serious. "It's been good knowing you. I saw the way you handled yourself back on Schwann. For someone without any training, you're damned brave."

"You make it sound final."

"It will be," the EPCT sergeant said. "I disobeyed Sorbatchin's direct order to kill the pig-faces."

Walden appreciated this, but he wanted to know more about the soldier's decision. He asked.

"Why did I disobey? Sorbatchin's a Sov-Lat. He's not my commander. Someone out of the unit should have been promoted up."

"You?"

Hecht laughed harshly. "Not me. I'm happy where I am. I don't need the extra headaches. But there are two or three eager young corporals and one sergeant who'd be damned good officers. They're even stupid enough to try."

"With the proper support?" asked Walden.

"They wouldn't find me disobeying them like I just did Sorbatchin. There are rules, Doc. Killing in cold blood isn't part of my training. I kill, but on command from those I rely on to know what's going on. Not even for Nakamura would I kill the Frinn."

"We'll see what can be done."

"You take care of yourself, Doc. You're looking drawn out. Pale."

The vidscreen blinked, replacing the sergeant's face with the readout of Walden's current experiment. He checked the results, sighed in exasperation, then leaned back to think through the problems brewing around him. He reached out and tapped in Nakamura's access code. Her sallow face appeared immediately on the screen.

"How may I aid you, Dr. Walden?"

"Tell me about the ambush and massacre aboard Starlight," he said without preamble. "And then you can explain why it was necessary to decoy the Frinn ship in and murder over half its crew."

"You are distraught. Perhaps your confinement is wearing on you?" the woman suggested.

"The quarantine is over, Nakamura," he snapped. "I'm having problems, but I'm sure it's not from the Infinity Plague. The Frinn might be infected but they are the only ones at risk."

"The EPCTs who went berserk," she protested. "Have you discounted the plague as a cause?"

"No," he said reluctantly, "but you lied to me about the EPCTs. They weren't quarantined. You put only me in this prison."

"The Frinn require our most expert researchers on hand to help them find ways of retarding or reversing the course of the plague. It seemed a simple solution to everyone's problem."

Walden spat out a curse. "Anita is the best qualified. You put me in here to keep me separate from my staff while you slaughtered the Frinn aboard Starlight and in their cruiser."

"You are reacting unduly to the circumstances. Colonel Sorbatchin and I agreed that we had to test the effectiveness of several tactics if we are to deal with the Frinn in the home system."

"Uvallae trusted you. You're planning an invasion of their home world."

"An invasion? Come, come, Dr. Walden. Can one hospital ship hope to accomplish much against an entire race on their home world? You know little of history if you think this is a plausible scenario for conquest."

"You're counting on the Infinity Plague having struck. The Frinn will be disorganized—and worse. And you conveniently forgot to mention the *Winston*. Its armament, with that aboard the Frinn cruiser you just captured, might be enough to get through liftspace to their home world."

"Their defenses, their fleet, their—"

"Their nothing!" raged Walden. "You know from Uvallae and the others on Starlight that the Frinn don't have a decent planetary defensive system. They aren't warlike."

"They—"

Again he cut off the worthless rationalization. "They had their robots build the weapons they used on us at Schwann. Those were repair robots turned into fighters that we faced on Starlight. They're experts at automation, not war."

"The difference escapes me, Doctor," Nakamura said coldly. "I have work to do. We lift from this system in one hour."

"After delaying it almost a day to put away the Frinn remaining in this system. You didn't want them warning their home world of your impending invasion. And what about Sorbatchin? He ordered nine Frinn murdered."

"He is a military officer. I needed someone to command the EPCTs."

"They're not dead," Walden said, savoring the flicker of dumbfounded amazement this caused. Nakamura struggled to regain her poise. "I'm putting them with Uvallae for the time being. We might be able to expand their quarantine area to make them more comfortable."

"They're aboard the *Hippocrates*?"

Walden took some small satisfaction in knowing that Nakamura wasn't as omniscient as she pretended.

"Why don't you ask Sorbatchin? The two of you know everything."

Walden savagely cut the connection. His vidscreen blinked and returned to the parade of data from his experiments. He had some small clues about the action of the Infinity Plague virus against the Frinn DNA. But was he right in thinking that it was completely harmless in humans? The plague changed its form when passed from one victim to another. The effects in the Frinn varied, making it hard to pin down a simple cure. How he needed Anita!

"They put ten men from the *Winston* aboard Starlight," Leo Burch told him. "They took the space station and the Frinn cruiser with only a couple casualties. A clean sweep for Sorbatchin."

Walden stared at the turncoat doctor. "You don't sound enthusiastic about it."

"I don't like this any more than you do, Jerome. Look, I was a spy, but I was doing what I thought was right. In some ways, I still believe I did the right thing in passing along information to them. The NAA is no better than the Soviet-Latino Pact countries. One triumphing over the other is no victory for mankind."

"I don't want to argue politics with you," Walden said tiredly. His anger at what Nakamura and Sorbatchin had done had faded. The *Hippocrates* shivered and shook and readied itself for the jump into liftspace that would take it to the Frinn's home planet. He looked down at Egad. The gengineered canine pressed his huge, floppy ear against a bulkhead.

The dog's brown eye looked up at Walden. He bounced his head twice to show that the *Hippocrates* truly launched this time. The telltale vibrations from the lift engines meant they finally entered the fractal-dimensioned space where faster-than-light travel was possible—or the ship simply vanished.

Either way, they were leaving Starlight behind and would probably never return. The conquerors, having triumphed, moved on to greater victories.

Walden flipped on the vidscreen and stared at the immense alien space station. It was a glory of engineering—and humans had slaughtered the race that had built it. When strength of arms wasn't enough, Nakamura had used subterfuge. Now they were going to carry the battle to the ultimate. Walden knew genocide was the only possible way of waging a war such as Nakamura planned.

"I want to help find the cure for them," Burch said softly. He laid his pudgy hand on his medical analysis robot's domed CPU. "It doesn't matter if you think you can trust me or not. What you're doing flies in the face of Nakamura's plans. Maybe that's enough for me."

"It also runs counter to Sorbatchin's."

Burch shrugged and smiled crookedly. "I don't see much difference between them right now, except that Sorbatchin is prettier."

Walden laughed at this unexpected comment. "Even with his broken nose?"

"Give me a chance. Albert and I could fix it up for him." He patted his medbot's chromed head again. "I'm not research grade, but I know medicine well enough to help you out."

Walden studied the corpulent doctor and decided his motives didn't matter. Walden had too few allies to hold a grudge against Burch. That the man had spied on him once meant he had the potential for doing it again. But who would he report to? Nakamura? Sorbatchin? Walden considered both of them his enemy, and both controlled him almost totally. They wanted nothing to run counter to their plans, whatever they might be.

"What are we going to do when we get into the Frinn's system?" he asked Burch.

The doctor shrugged. "Same as always. Blow the hell out of the poor bastards. Seems they adapt fast so we've got to do whatever we do fast. That was the whole point of the chickenshit ambush on their cruiser. Lightning strikes work, giving them time to retool their robots doesn't."

Walden shivered at the idea of landing on a world where every mechanism might turn against you. If the Frinn had been truly warlike, Starlight would have been an instant death trap for anyone setting foot aboard it. As it turned out, the Frinn were as much the victims of their robots as the humans.

"Let me run a complete med check on you, Jerome."

Walden tensed. The last time Burch had given him a checkup, he had been poisoned and almost died. He wasn't sure if the hallucinations he so vividly endured weren't the result of further poisoning. He could only guess at its source, but Burch wasn't out of the question as the instigator.

"I apologize for the poison, Jerome," Burch said in exasperation. "You are the most paranoid man I've run across in some time. It was Doris' cat that got to you. I didn't know she had it booby-trapped. Here, look at these. They're the gadgets that were stuffed into the poor beast."

Burch opened a cabinet and showed bank upon bank of

electronics surveillance gear. Most were microminiaturized cameras, smaller than a grain of sand. In spite of himself, Walden stared at the devices. He had a passing interest in spying on others. He had planted organically powered cameras and microphones on Sorbatchin and others. Some worked for a time but all died a natural death if they weren't discovered.

These were permanent bugs capable of spying for hours or even years. He had to admit the sheer number and variety of the equipment explained why the obese cat had slept all the time. It had been loaded down with the spy gear.

"I just use the countermeasures stuff," said Burch. "There's nothing going on in the ship that does me any good knowing." He heaved a deep sigh. "No one will have anything to do with a Judas. Not even Sorbatchin. But I do want to maintain my own privacy. Dignity is hard for someone like me to come by."

Walden looked around the infirmary and saw that the instrumentation wasn't adequate for research. The *Hippocrates* had been built for a war that had never occurred between the NAA and the Sov-Lats. As a result, refitting had been patchwork and slipshod for his purposes.

"Get me a few more computer consoles in here. I need at least a hundred more input lines for my equipment. I'll get Uvallae to start moving it out of the present quarantine."

"Consider it done, Jerome." Burch looked at him and smiled crookedly. "And thanks. It was getting damned lonesome around here. And I don't mean just being stuck in the infirmary at the *Hippocrates*' rim, either." Beyond the soft wall of the room lay the hard vacuum of space.

Walden glanced at Egad. The gengineered dog barked once, a sign that Burch told the truth. Whatever the doctor's motives, they didn't cross Walden's.

The ship shuddered and the lights dimmed. A siren sounded and the warning lights began flashing red and blue. The *Hippocrates*, the *Winston*, and the captured Frinn cruiser matched liftspace vectors and hurled themselves toward an imaginary point where the alien home world ought to be in a few hundred light-years.

● ● ●

"You're worn to a frazzle, Jerome. Take a break. Play with Egad. Go molest a nurse." Leo Burch hiked his feet to his desk and folded his hands behind his head.

"We're close. I feel it." Walden held back a surge of dizziness that threatened to make him wobble. Memories rushed back and became more substantial than reality. He relived every second of the time he'd spent aboard Starlight. The combat, the fear, the dying gasps of Frinn and human.

"Let me check you out," urged Burch. "There's some imbalance in your neurotransmitter system. I'll even let Egad stay and watch, if that makes you feel any better."

Walden looked sharply at Burch. Did the man know the dog's abilities? Or was he making a light joke?

"Is it obvious when this happens?"

"Obvious? Only if someone sees you turn pale, clench your fists, and look as if drills were rotating through your head. Other than that, there's no indication. What do you feel?"

Walden told Burch of the memory dumps of his recent past.

"Don't know what could cause it, but my guess about your brain oil being low might be 180 degrees out of synch. There might be a neurotransmission inhibitor at work."

"Like MAO?"

"More complicated. Let me do a complete enzyme and amino acid scan. It'll take a few hours, but it'll be worth it. The Frinn are like us, after all. You might have picked up something deadly from them—and something they look on as nothing more dangerous than a mild cold."

"I'm so close to solving the problem," moaned Walden. His head almost exploded as the hissing of laserifles made him duck. Robots rushed him—and the sight of the dead Sov-Lat scientists in their bunker on Delta Cygnus 4 turned his stomach and filled his mouth with bile. They had died horribly. If not from the Infinity Plague, then from what? Their own anthrax defenses? Something else? There were too many questions and not enough answers.

"I've been monitoring your tests. Uvallae agrees with you. The last batch came close to isolating the virus."

"I could have done it in hours if Anita had helped."

Burch said nothing to this. Anita Tarleton had refused to set foot in the infirmary since Walden had arrived. Burch wondered if she worked for Nakamura or if the thrill of power kept her away. Walden was the senior scientist of record. But Nakamura lent the other woman authority. If Walden ever got over his hallucinations, Burch knew most of the research staff would again look to him as their legitimate superior. Until then, Nakamura played on the division, kept the scientist working on her own projects and put Anita into the spot of returning to a former lover and losing her position.

It wasn't pretty, Burch decided. Power games never were.

"So close. I know it."

"The workup, Jerome. Let me do it. We've been in lift-space for almost a week now and you haven't slept more than an hour at a stretch."

"I don't need to rest."

"Egad," Burch said, changing tactics. "Tell him he needs me to check out his biosystems. He can't run like this for the rest of the trip. We're going to be in liftspace for another month."

"Do it," Egad said.

Burch blinked and stared at the dog, not sure that he had heard the animal speak. The mismatched brown and blue eyes fixed squarely on the doctor. Burch dropped his feet to the floor and wiped beads of sweat off his lip. He accused Walden of being unbalanced. He wasn't so sure about himself.

"I'll do it," Walden said. "Only if Egad can stay with me."

"Bring your teddy bear, too, for all I care. I just want you chipper when we drop back into normal space." Burch cleared his throat. "And it's likely to take the rest of the trip to do it. You're worn to a frazzle."

Burch put Walden into an analysis bed, started Albert on the basic tests, and returned to his office. A soft chiming indicated another of Walden's tests had finished.

Burch tapped in the request for a précis. He almost returned to the infirmary and stopped the tests on Walden when he saw the results. Walden had succeeded in isolating the Infinity Plague virus.

CHAPTER
8

Leo Burch sucked at his teeth, wondering what he should do. The computer analysis was complete. Walden had a complete crystallographic hologram of the Infinity Plague virus, had some idea how it interacted, and had even made a good start toward defining the chaotic nonlinear dynamic vibrations that turned it into a new killer as it passed from one infected victim to another.

"You're one hell of a researcher, Jerome." Burch stared at the screen, turning over his options in his mind. He checked Albert's progress with the physical work-over he had ordered. Walden would be on the analysis table for another hour.

Burch considered using the information to lever concessions from Miko Nakamura. All charges of espionage and treason against him might be dropped. Or he could sell out to Vladimir Sorbatchin. The Sov-Lat colonel would owe him protection if he delivered a detailed blueprint for the plague virus. With a simple cube of ceramic memory he could record every bit of Walden's work and preserve it—and erase both result and logic path from the computer's memory.

The physician heaved a deep sigh and settled down into his large, comfortable chair. There were other weighty factors to consider. With this discovery, they might stop a plague ravaging the Frinn. He could do nothing and let Walden become the savior of an entire race. Or he could do more.

More.

The ideas forming appealed to him. He hadn't distinguished himself on this expedition. His allegiance was too diffuse. He had thought the Sov-Lats were falling behind and by aiding them he helped maintain an equilibrium of power. No one wanted to see the world ripped apart by a war started because one side thought it held the edge. Balance of terror. Mutually assured destruction. The swinging sword of Damocles. He had heard the philosophy he followed called all this and more. Burch considered his actions patriotic, not necessarily for the NAA but for Earth.

He'd thought all that back on Earth. In space, away from the influences of his Sov-Lat control, he wasn't so sure. The Frinn had changed much in the way he looked at politics.

Burch saw the new elements in human history, even if Nakamura and Sorbatchin didn't. The balance of power shifted and the stakes in the game increased exponentially. One mistake caused billions of intelligent beings to die. And one intentional move might produce genocide unheard of on Earth.

He reached out and shifted Walden's results into a locked file. If anyone cared to hunt for it, they'd find it quickly enough. Burch wasn't enough of a computer virtuoso to protect his files from determined digging. A few more minutes started the computer program at work again, disregarding its previous logic path.

Then Burch began his own work in earnest.

"Let's see what Walden has really uncovered," he said, working slowly and carefully. "Is the Infinity Plague a danger to humans or is it only a Frinn problem?"

An hour passed as Burch was drawn increasingly into the problem. He had forgotten what rewards came from concentrated effort. When Albert beeped at him that Walden's bioanalysis was finished, he jumped in surprise. He wiped sweat from his forehead and blanked his computer vidscreen, replacing his careful work with the results of Walden's physical examination.

He muttered to himself, ordered a printout of the medical analysis, and then went into the infirmary. He looked down at an exhausted Jerome Walden.

"Whatever you've got, it's not the Infinity Plague. My guess isn't too good right now, but keeping you with the Frinn might not be our smartest move."

"What are you saying?" Walden pushed himself to one elbow. The room spun in wide elliptical orbits around him. He didn't resist when Burch pushed him flat.

"You might have picked up a bug from the Frinn."

For a moment, Walden simply stared at Burch. Then he laughed heartily. The laughter turned hysterical. Burch tapped out a command on Albert's small keypad. The medbot extended twin tentacles and clamped Walden's arm firmly. A third appendage administered five ccs of pentagan. Walden's hysteria faded as the drug worked on his axons, deadening sensation and slowing his reactions.

"Sorry, Burch. It struck me as ridiculous. *I* caught something from the *Frinn*?"

"I'm going to have Uvallae look you over later. He might be better able to decide if this is what's happened."

Walden reached over and patted Egad. The shaggy dog looked from his master to the doctor. He settled to the floor, his huge head resting on his tiny paws. This seemed to satisfy Walden.

"I'll rest for a while."

"I'll have Uvallae check you. Whatever it is you might've gotten from him, it's not going to get worse than it already is, not with Albert watching you constantly." Burch patted the medbot's shiny chrome dome affectionately. "There might be others from their ship who can help out with the medical guesswork, too. I haven't had time to talk to any of them."

"Sorbatchin wouldn't let you, even if you had the time. He wanted them all dead," said Walden. His eyelids drooped a little. The strain he had been under finally took its toll. Burch glanced at the readout vidscreen mounted on his medbot, then let out a gusty sigh. At last Walden slept peacefully, even if it took a considerable amount of drugging and exertion to do it.

"Look after him, Albert," Burch said. Egad growled when the robot rolled closer to obey. "You, too, Egad. Good dog. I think." He hurried back to his small office, the gengineered dog's off-color eyes on him all the way.

● ● ●

"I shouldn't allow this, but what the hell. We're all friends here." Leo Burch motioned for Anita Tarleton to enter the infirmary. Walden had been kept under close observation for over two weeks and hadn't shown any sign of worsening. His condition, whatever it was, remained stable. Uvallae and the scientists with him had been unable to shed any light on the malady.

"If you can't cure him, you're supposed to kill him," Anita said lightly.

"That was the old Leo Burch. This one just throws his hands up in resignation and retreats to his quiet office." He left Walden and Anita, Egad at their side.

"I've looked over Leo's reports. I think he's right. You've caught something from the Frinn." Anita Tarleton reached out tentatively and touched his forehead. It was cool, dry, and had the look of a man ten years younger. The treatment had done Walden a world of good.

"I've gone over his work, too, and didn't find any likely culprit. Did you see anything I'd missed?" Walden stared at the red-haired woman, drinking in her beauty. Just having her beside him again did more for his spirit than all the artificial boosting he had been receiving from the drugs.

"There are some lines of research that might pay off," said Anita. "My time has been . . . limited. We're almost ready to return to normal space. Captain Belford says we're not more than a week out from the Frinn home world."

"I know. I swear I can feel it when we're ready to drop out of liftspace," Walden said. His eyes narrowed. "What have you been working on?"

Her bright emerald eyes turned from him. Her avoidance cut him as badly as anything else she had done. Nothing had changed for the better between them, not really.

"You're working for Sorbatchin, aren't you? What does he want you to do? Find a new way of killing the Frinn?" Walden's anger pulsed through him, flushing his face and sending his heart racing. Albert flashed a single red light in warning at such unseemly arousal. Walden ignored it.

"What difference does it make?" she shot back. "They'll all be dead from the Infinity Plague by the time we arrive. So what if I find another way of killing them? They can only die once."

"That's the business we're in, isn't it? Why not see that it's bankrupt, that we have to change the way we're operating? We've got the technology to save, not kill. There's more to consider now than us versus them."

"We can't forget what they did," she said.

"Can we forget what we've done to them—what *you* have done to them? Aren't you the architect of the Infinity Plague?"

"I know something about it, damn you, Jerome. But I didn't gengineer it! Bill Greene put me in charge. I knew what they knew on Earth, nothing more!"

"You're saying you have no idea how to stop its spread? Would you know how if Zacharias had been dying of it?"

Anita Tarleton turned fierce eyes on him. She started to speak. Her varicolored cosmetic dyes swirled beneath her cheeks and turned her into something less than human. She clamped her lips tightly together into a thin red line. Without a word, she swung away and stalked off. Walden started to call out to stop her. A wave of weakness assailed him. As the room filled with frightening ghosts of his past, Albert moved closer, mechanically attentive to the wildly oscillating enzyme levels in Walden's bloodstream.

Egad looked from his master to the woman, let out a yelp, and raced after Anita. He skidded to a halt in front of her, his eyes imploring her for consideration.

"No," she said. "Leave me alone."

"He needs you. The sickness talks too much for him."

"He doesn't sound any different now than he did before. Vladimir is right." Anita pushed past the dog and stormed down the corridor toward her laboratory.

Egad hesitated, then followed her at a safe distance to avoid her wrath. He slowed his pace outside her laboratory, then cautiously peered around the opened door. Colonel Sorbatchin sat behind Anita's desk, as if waiting for her to return.

The dog dropped to the deck and watched and listened better than any electronic surveillance device.

"Was I not correct?" asked Sorbatchin.

"He tried to talk me out of working on the . . . project. I don't know what's happened to him. He used to be enthusiastic about the challenges in bioresearch."

"He has weakened. Only the strong participate," said Sorbatchin.

"Jerome's not like that," Anita said. "He's not a weak man. He's just confused now. Leo might be right about him incubating an alien virus."

"The pig-faces work against us even in this? Is that what you're saying?"

"They aren't sufficiently advanced for that. He might have caught something the equivalent of a Frinn cold." Anita took an involuntary step back at Sorbatchin's vehement response in vulgar Russian.

The Sov-Lat officer calmed and spoke in English. "He plays on your pity. This is the sign of a weak man. He cannot succeed on his own merit. Always he has ridden along on the wings of your brilliance. He does nothing without your pioneering efforts!"

Anita started to deny it, then stopped. She had often felt that Jerome took advantage of her work. He had been appointed the official project leader over her, yet their work was of equal importance. This had prompted her to accept the clandestine assignment to work on the Infinity Plague. At last she had an assignment worthy of her talents. The project in the NAA research center on Delta Cygnus had gone nowhere. She was going to turn it around.

Her! By herself, without Walden's help. No one could have denied her then.

"How is your work progressing, Dr. Tarleton?"

Egad heard the cunning in the Sov-Lat officer's voice. Anita didn't. She swelled with pride at his attention, at the obvious respect he held for her work—and for her as a person.

"Well enough. The hibernation mechanism in the Frinn's bodies can be triggered chemically. I'm not sure how long they can survive afterward since much of the fat required to live off has been lost through evolution."

"You can induce such hibernation, then they starve?" Egad wanted to bite Sorbatchin for his eagerness. The dog saw that this was precisely the type of weapon the officer sought.

"Eventually," Anita said. "There might be some utility to the hibernation triggering sequence if we can use it to fight the progress of the Infinity Plague."

"Why fight it?" Sorbatchin's voice was soft and menacing.

"You're right," she said, shaking her head. Red hair flew in wild disarray. She ran her fingers through the unruly locks and succeeded in tangling it even more. She didn't notice.

"Let the plague run its course," Anita said. "In a way, it's the Holy Grail we've sought for so long. It doesn't harm the user, is devastating to the enemy, and doesn't destroy the enemy's ecosystem. We can move in and take over without fear of plants or other animals being contaminated."

"You do good work, Doctor," complimented Sorbatchin. "I will see that you are rewarded." The colonel started for the door. Egad slunk back, then stopped when the officer did.

"Is anything wrong?" Anita asked.

"I worry for you," Sorbatchin said. "You are so gallant, so brave in the face of your loss."

"Edouard?"

"Who else?" Sorbatchin said smoothly. "He was a credit to his service. You must have loved him dearly."

Egad noticed the slight hesitation before Anita said, "Yes, of course." The dog wondered if the cat-shit major only provided a safe haven for her that wasn't Jerome Walden. She sounded as if she had no great love for Zacharias. Egad wished he could sniff more carefully to see if she lied.

He had no chance to do so. Sorbatchin strode from Anita's lab, his long legs swinging powerfully. Egad hunkered down against the bulkhead. Sorbatchin turned left and walked away from the dog, never seeing him cowering on the deck. The gengineered animal waited for the colonel to vanish before he moved.

When he did move, it wasn't to return to Jerome Walden's bedside. Egad sought out the Frinn in their quarantine that he now knew to be imprisonment. He wanted to speak with Uvallae and get the alien's opinion on how to proceed. If no one aboard the *Hippocrates* wanted to stop Sorbatchin, Egad would have to do it.

Cat-shit colonel!

CHAPTER
9

Walden stood at one side of the control room, watching as Captain Belford worked his way through the intricate procedures required for reentering normal space. The captain relied heavily on computers and the other officers. Walden watched as the strain mounted on the officer's face, and he knew why Nakamura had worked so diligently to replace the man in most command situations.

For reentry into normal-dimension space, however, the most experienced officers had to work. Captain Belford aimed his laser wand and sent the IR beam swinging across banks of controls, playing the instrumentation as if he sat at a huge electronic organ. He mumbled constantly into a throat microphone, but Walden knew these were mostly asides to the others on the bridge. The real work went on at the man's fingertips, using the control wand and the controls in the arm of his command chair.

"Does this amuse you, Doctor?" came Nakamura's cool question. Walden hadn't heard her enter. She stood less than a meter away.

"I want to see what happens when we drop back," he said. "I've been talking with Uvallae and the other Frinn about what to expect. It might not be pleasant."

"Your warning is noted," she said. Nakamura fixed her

cold eyes on Captain Belford. ''He does better controlling his nervousness now that Dr. Burch has him on medication.''

''I didn't know that,'' Walden said, startled. He wanted to appear as cool as the woman, but she always managed to slip past his guard. If Nakamura controlled the *Hippocrates*' captain with drugs, this explained why she trusted him more and more with the daily routine—and the always-touchy reentry. He wondered why Burch hadn't mentioned this to him. Walden bit his lower lip as he considered this. Burch might not be the repentant soul he professed to be.

Walden hadn't seen much of Burch after the doctor had diagnosed the strange malady afflicting him as caused by a Frinn virus. The chemicals pumping through Walden's veins kept the hallucinations from taking complete control of him, but they were getting worse. Walden disliked increasing the dosage to hold back the flood of visions, but he had to. The work on finding the cure for the Infinity Plague had not gone well, and he blamed himself.

Nakamura glanced at a small device in her hand. She smiled quixotically when Walden studied it and couldn't determine its purpose.

''You have never seen a remote monitor, Doctor? I watch Captain Belford's reactions closely. Every biological system in his body is summarized here.''

''If he starts to crack up, you'll know?'' He had never heard of such a device. What instruments had been implanted in the captain's body to make the sensor effective?

Walden shivered with dread. He didn't want to know. He was a scientist who had to deal with other scientists. He worked best when left alone in the laboratory, not in coping with the political aspirations of people such as Miko Nakamura. At one time he had thought she was sane. Now he wasn't sure.

The challenge of conquering an inhabited world seemed strong in her, even as she denied this was her goal. In Vladimir Sorbatchin, nothing but naked ambition shone in his polar blue eyes. Walden didn't even try to figure out the rest of those he dealt with.

''Captain Belford is performing adequately,'' Nakamura said. She slipped the monitor back into the folds of her watered silk kimono sleeve. "The others progress well, also. I am pleased."

Walden divided his attention between the approaching drop from liftspace and the woman. "What about the Frinn?" he asked. "They're complaining about being prisoners. And well they should. Sorbatchin tried to kill them aboard their own vessel. Uvallae wasn't happy with it."

"Uvallae misconstrues our motives," Nakamura said.

"I doubt that. Look." Walden pointed to a pair of officers working at a doppler radar unit. "That's been modified to guide in an EPCT drop force, hasn't it?"

Nakamura said nothing. Walden grabbed Egad's collar as the gengineered dog tried to push past. He wondered why he didn't let Egad rip out her throat.

He knew the answer to that even as the question popped into his mind. Nakamura must be a walking arsenal. She could hide away an enormous amount of firepower in the soft folds of her kimono. He wouldn't doubt it if someone told him she had a set of war pipes stashed there. Even more important, he could deal with Nakamura. Sorbatchin wouldn't speak to him—and Sorbatchin worked too closely with Anita. Egad had reported some of what the Sov-Lat officer had said to her. It saddened Walden to think that his former lover was no different from the military aboard the *Hippocrates*. Power—or the lust for power—drove her rather than scientific curiosity or desire to do a necessary job or even simple pride in a job well done.

"A wise choice, Dr. Walden," Nakamura said. "Egad is a special animal. I would speak at length with him when there are less pressing matters."

"You're invading this system, aren't you? You're going in with guns blazing. That was the whole point of murdering the Frinn aboard Starlight and decoying their ship. You wanted to see if a small strike force could prevail against them."

"Surprise has always been a potent element in warfare," she said. "We do not foresee any problem in our negotiations with the Frinn, but we must be prepared for any contingency."

"Coming out of starlift in one minute," called the first officer. Walden tried to place him and failed. The *Hippo-*

crates' original first officer had been killed by Nakamura during a clumsy mutiny attempt. He looked around the bridge and decided no further gambles would be made by this crew. Not with Nakamura watching them so intently.

He suddenly felt glad that she carried the weapons she did. From the gengineered iron in the side of her hand to the laser weapons she wore openly in her *obi*, Miko Nakamura was walking death.

"Any contact with our sister ships?" she asked. Nakamura stepped up to Captain Belford's side and began working the com-link that functioned as the nerve center for the *Hippocrates*.

"None. We have some evidence of liftspace ripples a few meters off. This is probably the *Winston*. We aren't sure how the pig-face's cruiser changes the geodesic," reported one officer working on the doppler radar. Walden knew then who reported to whom. Captain Belford was little more than a figurehead, in spite of his important work in preparing the ship for its drop.

"All systems ready. Prepare all EPCT crews," ordered Nakamura. She pulled a laser wand of her own from her kimono and began altering some of the settings Captain Belford had made on his control board. The officer started to complain, then fell silent.

The *Hippocrates* shuddered as the mighty engines began tearing through the fabric of space once more. The surface of the ship, once attuned to fractal dimensions, returned to integer space. Walden was thrown to one side and his stomach flipped end for end and came to rest at the back of his throat. Forcing back his rising gorge, he tried to focus.

The bridge was bathed in rainbow colors. Sounds tore at his ears. He screamed as robots attacked. Lightning from their lasers left glowing ionized shafts in the air. He was aware of Egad lying beside him, but the dog seemed oblivious to the danger. Walden tried the best he could to warn the others of the attack. Why couldn't they see and respond? From behind came a hard blow that knocked him to his knees. Egad growled and jumped, bowling him over. The gengineered dog stood over him like a sentinel, keeping the hordes at bay.

The impact shattered the illusion that the shift had brought about in him. Walden lay drained, panting, and weak. The hallucination faded swiftly once he recognized it for what it was.

"... under attack!"

Walden rubbed his eyes and tried to clear his head. He tried to correct the mistake he had made. He didn't want them believing they were being beset by robots. It had all been a delusion on his part. Only slowly did he realize that the *Hippocrates* really was under attack.

"The *Winston* got hit the instant it dropped from lift-space," came the report. "The Frinn cruiser is also damaged, but not as severely. They hesitated long enough in attacking one of their own ships. That gave us a small edge. The *Winston* took out two of the attacking vessels."

Walden forced himself to his feet. Egad growled again when Sorbatchin came close. The Sov-Lat officer held a short length of pipe—just the right size to be the weapon that had struck Walden on the back of the head.

"Don't," Walden warned. "He'll rip out your throat."

"Off the bridge," growled the colonel. "You have no business being here."

Walden ignored him. If Sorbatchin pressed the attack, he'd find out how strong Egad's jaws were.

"What happened?" he demanded of Nakamura. The sallow advisor had pushed Captain Belford from the command seat and worked furiously at the *Hippocrates*' controls.

"We entered the Frinn system. They were waiting for us."

"Spies!" cried Sorbatchin. "Uvallae betrayed us. He let them know we were coming!"

"Don't be absurd, Colonel" snapped Walden. "There's no way to communicate when you're in liftspace. We triggered their system-wide defensive system."

"Not so, Doctor," corrected Nakamura. "Those were robot ships programmed to patrol and destroy. They did not lie in ambush. They simply responded to the starlift residue formed by our engines when we came back into normal space. It was our misfortune to reenter near their orbit."

Sorbatchin began barking orders. Several of the bridge crew started to obey. Nakamura used her laser wand to override those who tried. Walden saw that she brooked no interference with her control of the *Hippocrates*.

"Colonel, compose yourself. We are engaged in delaying tactics for the moment while we assess our position. It might not be as bad as it seems."

"Not as bad!" roared Sorbatchin. "We had intended to drop the EPCTs onto their home world in a first strike. How can we surprise them when they know we're here?"

"We find other courses to our goal," Nakamura said calmly. She worked at the command chair's arm, tuning, adjusting, sending orders. The IR laser wand flashed across the large control board that directed every important system on the hospital ship.

Walden backed off as Sorbatchin started to argue. He didn't want to get between them as they fought over control of the *Hippocrates*. If he had to bet on the outcome, he'd go with Nakamura. She controlled more than her own emotions.

The Sov-Lat officer realized his precarious position and subsided. More calmly, he asked, "What do we do now? They are swarming toward us like flies to shit."

"How apt," Nakamura said dryly. "We send messages proclaiming our peaceful intentions. Dr. Walden, transmit the full details of your research toward a cure for the Infinity Plague. Do it on whatever frequency Uvallae gives you. We must convince them to break off their mindless attack."

"Those are only computer-guided ships," reported an officer on the far side of the bridge. "No readings to indicate organic life. Hell, they didn't even bother pressurizing the cabins."

Walden watched the huge vidscreen at the far end of the bridge. Useless most of the time, it now showed a magnified real-time picture of the swarming Frinn war craft. Everywhere he looked on the screen he saw tiny glistening pinpoints of death.

"They're locked on. Transmitting our intent isn't going to stop them," said Captain Belford. "They're machines. They can't be programmed to save us."

"Get Uvallae on the com," urged Walden. "Let him see if he can stop them."

"No good. We fight." Sorbatchin pushed an officer out of the way and began working on his board. Walden wasn't sure what the officer's position was, but the *Hippocrates* lurched as the guidance rocket engines ignited.

"We do not go into battle," Nakamura said. "They outgun us. We cannot reach their planet's surface with the EPCTs before they blow us out of space."

"We can!" cried Sorbatchin. "All we need is nerve!"

The battle between Nakamura and Sorbatchin for control ended abruptly when Egad launched himself across the bridge. The gengineered dog's teeth closed on the Sov-Lat officer's leg. Egad twisted and turned, putting his powerful jaw muscles to good use. Sorbatchin screeched in pain and tried to draw a small pistol.

"Stop!" Nakamura's command froze both Egad and Sorbatchin. "Do nothing more to disturb me. This is crucial."

The woman began working with the *Hippocrates*' guidance computer. Tentative tracings appeared on the vidscreen, showing possible escape orbits. Walden frowned. Nothing looked plausible to him. The robot ships put into space by the Frinn had blocked them effectively from reaching the solitary planet circling the distant sun.

"We go now," she said quietly. The *Hippocrates* bucked again, this time finding a different acceleration vector. Nakamura worked at a com-link that bound both the *Winston* and the captured Frinn ship to her command.

"They committed themselves too early," she said, sitting back in the command chair. "They cannot alter course quickly enough to stop us from slipping past their cordon."

"But the Frinn vessel. The one—" Walden's words died abruptly as the star pattern blossomed on the screen. Nakamura had sacrificed the captured alien ship and a dozen human crewmen to get past the Frinn picket ships.

"The *Winston* is engaged with two of the robot ships about three light-seconds away," came the report. "They request immediate aid."

"Prepare the EPCT troops," Nakamura ordered. "And let the *Winston* know they are on their own. If we do not penetrate and occupy quickly, all is lost."

"Negotiate!" cried Walden. "Talk to them. Get them to call off their robots. Let Uvallae speak to them."

"I have done so already," said Nakamura. "I hoped the transmission to his home world would give them pause. It did not. Since that ploy failed, we have no choice but to push on boldly. Better a thousand arrows in the forehead than one in the back.''

Walden looked around frantically, trying to think. Too many items bored into his head. He couldn't concentrate. Worst of all, the fringes of his sight began blurring as the hallucinations returned. He forced himself to settle down and not to panic. This drove away some of the garishly colored phantasms working their way into his field of vision. Egad helped, pressing warmly against his leg and giving a steadying influence.

Of all things in the control room, only Egad seemed natural, normal, understandable.

"Take me to Uvallae," he ordered the dog. Egad looked up at him quizzically. The bridge—and Nakamura—formed the center of command. To leave here was to abandon the chance to influence the course of battle over the next few minutes.

The gengineered dog shivered slightly and obeyed. Walden held on to Egad's collar, almost strangling the dog as they left the bridge. Captain Belford sat nervously at one side, his face gray and his hands shaking. Whatever drug Nakamura had pacified him with seemed to be wearing off.

The farther he got from the control room, the more Walden regained his senses. Stress brought out the worst in him, he realized. Whether the alien virus in his bloodstream accentuated already existing problems or produced new ones had to remain unanswered for the moment. He had a more important mission than solving his own predicament.

He came to the quarantine sign on the door just inward of the infirmary. He looked around for Leo Burch and didn't see the doctor. Walden heaved a deep breath, then began working on the cipher lock. In less than a minute he had breached the quarantine and opened the door. The entire *Hippocrates* would have to serve as a ward now, if it was even necessary.

The more Walden saw of the Infinity Plague and its effects, the more he thought it worked only on the Frinn. Whatever bubbled within his own veins was not spawned by the ever-mutating virus created in a human bioweapons laboratory.

"Uvallae!" he called. "Where are you?"

Egad trotted down the corridor and stopped in front of the alien's laboratory door. He edged the door open with his nose but did not enter. Walden pushed past the dog and stopped to stare.

"We cannot go on like this," Uvallae said. The alien stood at one corner of the small lab, a vial in his hand. "You must cease your warfare against us."

"What are you doing? We've got to contact your leaders and put a stop to—"

"No!" The Frinn's emphatic reply caused Walden's heart to miss a beat.

Egad barked and flopped onto his belly in the middle of the floor. He put his huge head on his paws and looked up at the alien. Frinn and gengineered dog stared at each other for what stretched to an eternity for Walden. He wasn't sure what went on, but Uvallae began to relax. He placed the vial down on a counter and rubbed his rugose forehead hard with both hands.

"I no longer know what to do. The overcrowding aboard the *Hippocrates* wears on me—on all Frinn. I go crazy from the imprisonment. And for what? Do we carry the seeds of your plague within us? What difference does it make since it does not affect you?" Uvallae dropped to his knees and fell forward, banging his piglike snout against the floor.

Walden didn't know what to say or do.

Egad looked up. "Odors are heavy. Can you smell them?"

Walden's nose wrinkled. He detected a musky, unpleasant scent that made him slightly sick to his stomach.

"Frinn fear. Frinn uncertainty," the dog said. "I convinced Uvallae not to kill you all."

"The vial? A bioweapon?" Walden stared at the small, stoppered tube.

"A derivative of the virus in you," said Egad. "Not much for them, but cat-shit bad for you."

"*You* would have infected me purposefully?" Walden asked in astonishment. "You engaged in countermeasures even as I was trying to find a cure for the Infinity Plague, for you, for your people?" Walden's surprise turned to feelings of betrayal and outrage.

"You humans live this way. We do not. How can we adjust to you? Is this not the way you fight? We are prisoners and helpless, except for what we do to save our own."

"I was trying to help. You know that."

"Egad assures me this is so. I am shamed."

Human stared at alien. The gulf between them wavered, becoming wider—and lessening as understanding grew in Walden. The Frinn scientists could not hope to cure or slow a complex virus like the Infinity Plague. Uvallae had tried to find a weapon of his own to force all the humans into stopping the plague. Baring that, the humans would perish along with the Frinn.

"We must work together. The Infinity Plague wasn't an accident; your exposure to it was. We've got to stop its spread across your home world. Look, Uvallae. Look at this and tell me if it is going to help any of us."

Walden adjusted the vidscreen on Uvallae's computer to reflect what showed on the master screen on the bridge. Nakamura tracked the Frinn robotic warships. The *Winston* fought well but lost the battle by slow millimeters. Of the captured Frinn cruiser he saw no trace. Nakamura had sacrificed it.

And the woman had cleverly evaded the Frinn's automated outer defenses and bored straight for the home world, a brown and green and blue glowing ball of gauzy clouds and life. The *Hippocrates* would soon disgorge its load of EPCTs and bring death even faster to an innocent world.

It took Uvallae several seconds to understand what Walden showed him. The alien moved with astounding speed when he saw how Nakamura intended to establish contact with his home world. Not even Egad's reflexes were quick enough to stop the Frinn from dumping the vial of his gengineered bioweapon into a small funnel.

"It is done," Uvallae said, resignation apparent in his stance. "The liquid has been introduced into your air system. All humans aboard the *Hippocrates* are infected. Fatally infected, even as you are, Dr. Walden."

CHAPTER
10

Jerome Walden stood and stared in helpless fascination. Uvallae had poured the vial of his bioweapon liquid into the ship's air filtration system. His feet turned to lead. Walden went to stand beside the shaking alien.

"Was it worth it?" he asked. "You might have killed us all."

"My world is dead. If the Infinity Plague has not devastated it, then your soldiers will. I saw how effectively they worked on Starlight. Miggae told me of their power and determination to overcome, no matter what the odds."

"There are only a handful of the EPCTs left," Walden said. "Do you really believe they can conquer an entire world?"

"Mine, yes," Uvallae said. He tossed the empty vial into a closed sink unit. "We are not warriors. The robot ships you now face are makeshift. The explorers must have returned and told the controllers of the meeting on Delta Cygnus 4. Then the Infinity Plague must have begun its deadly course among my unsuspecting people. This is our only possible response. We want to keep you at bay. They do not know of your vicious attacks at Starlight, but they do know you for the plague-carriers you are."

Walden kept silent about Nakamura and Sorbatchin. Their

plan to take over the Frinn home world might succeed, if what Uvallae said was true about the lack of military preparation. He wondered what it would be like living on a world where there was no armed strife on a national or interplanetary scale. He tried to imagine and failed. All his life he had lived with war, the threat of war, and his deadly biological research.

"What did you put into the air system?" he asked.

"You cannot stop it. I may not have your expertise at bioweapons, but I know you cannot stop this, not in time to prevent death."

Walden put his hand on the Frinn's sloping shoulder and said, "Can you cure it?"

"Not in humans. In Frinn, it is a minor discomfort."

"That's another good reason to choose it," Walden said. "The Infinity Plague affects only your race, what you just introduced into the air system only mine."

The two stared into each other's eyes, Walden's gray eyes fixed on Uvallae's cat-slitted green and gold ones. Uvallae broke off the contest of wills first.

"I have failed. You will be able to isolate the virus and cure yourself. You will concentrate on this to the exclusion of work on the Infinity Plague." Uvallae shuddered and rubbed his forehead. "Not that you would have succeeded. Too much rests on the Infinity Plague's destruction of my home."

"I *am* working on a cure," Walden said earnestly. "You Frinn seem to be of one mind on many things. This might be why you don't have wars. It's not that way among humans. We . . . contest everything."

"You would still work to undo what you have done?"

"I can only try," Walden said. "The course of your virus has been checked. Leo Burch found drugs that reduce its effect. And if I don't get upset, the hallucinations don't take control. Is there any other side effect I should know?"

"In Frinn, this is a minor disease, one hardly mentioned. We have few diseases. The *menla* fever affects only children, who recover quickly. Our medicine has not progressed as has yours; we Frinn seldom come in contact to worry about contagions."

"This might have saved your world. The plague might not

have spread. We don't know, Uvallae. We've got to contact your controllers to find out.''

''The *Hippocrates* cannot reach my world. The soldiers are prepared to kill. We have no defenses.''

Walden took a deep breath. ''Counter the *menla* fever solution you introduced into the air system. I'll try to stop the EPCTs from landing—I'll try to stop Nakamura and Sorbatchin.''

The *Hippocrates* shook, throwing Walden hard against a bulkhead. For the ship to experience such a quake meant a powerful impact against its hull. For all Uvallae's talk of the Frinn's inability to defend themselves, Walden wondered if they hadn't whipped up a surprise for their unwanted human visitors.

A second tremor wracked the ship. Egad let out a howl of hurt, then put his paws over his ears. Walden swallowed to clear his own ears. He barely heard the high-pitched whine. For the gengineered dog, it had to be a painful sound.

''I'm going back to the bridge. Look after Egad, will you?'' Walden didn't wait for Uvallae to agree. He hurried out, not bothering to shut the quarantine door after him. The entire ship had become a thriving pesthole. Infinity Plague and *menla* fever abounded, leaving no one untouched.

Walden considered there might be one intelligent being aboard the ship who would be left untouched. Egad was neither Frinn nor human. He vowed that the dog wouldn't be left the only living being aboard the *Hippocrates*.

Walden slowed as he went past Anita Tarleton's laboratory. Did she still work inside? And if she did, what was she working on? She might be the deciding factor in a race to find a cure for the Infinity Plague in the Frinn, but she wasn't likely to be working toward such an end. She and Sorbatchin had chosen the course of finding different bioweapons to use against the aliens. Walden forced back tears thinking how needless this slaughter was. He believed Uvallae. The Frinn were inherently a peaceful race.

Although he slowed, he did not stop to beg her for help. Anita made her own decisions. He raced onto the bridge where Nakamura sat stolidly in the command chair, using the laser wand and a heads-up visor that allowed instant access to any readout on the ship.

"Dr. Walden, you have returned. We need your skill. The Frinn laid a trap for us."

"Trap? How?"

"We slipped past their automated cordon and into a passive mine field."

"We started triggering the damned things the instant we neared their planet," cut in Sorbatchin. "There is no way to land the soldiers. The mines are not detectable. This is a pathetic excuse for a war vessel!"

"It's a *hospital* ship, Colonel," snapped Walden. "It's not supposed to have battle sensors aboard."

"It is equipped with EPCT delivery systems," Sorbatchin said, his anger matching Walden's.

"Gentlemen, arguing solves nothing," said Miko Nakamura. "We cannot penetrate to deliver the EPCTs using only the *Hippocrates*. We must call in the *Winston* for minesweeping work."

"What kind of mines are out there you can't see on the sensors?" He stared at the huge vidscreen at the front of the bridge.

"There are many possibilities," said Nakamura. "Plastic casing and triggers with only a minimal amount of metal, nonnuclear explosives differing from those we expect—"

"You can detect only those you think the Soviet-Latino Pact uses," accused Sorbatchin.

"A minor point when we are in danger of being nibbled to death by Frinn explosives, Colonel," Nakamura said. "We must work as one in this endeavor."

"Pull back and let Uvallae try to contact the planetary controllers again," urged Walden.

"This did not produce results before. There is no reason to believe it will now. We need your advice in other matters, Doctor."

"What?" Walden wasn't sure he liked the woman's tone. Nakamura was usually deceptively docile, even humble. No longer. Arrogance billowed from her like hot, fetid gusts of wind.

"The *Winston* has eluded its attackers. We have a chance of being reinforced by it and its more sensitive detection equipment. However, we need to know about delivery systems. Can we reach the planetary surface with an aerosol release at this distance?''

Walden looked past Nakamura's arm to a small readout showing the distance from the Frinn's home world. In spite of himself, he thought in terms of delivery systems and vulnerability. It was his training and the job he had worked hard at for years.

"You might get one in a hundred through at this range. The problem with aerosol bombs lies in their containment."

"You still think about human contamination. We have no need to worry about this. If the device leaks, it leaks into space, not into our own troops."

"True. There's not much time to eat into a plastic container, if we use Impervo casing."

"It will melt on atmospheric entry. I have considered this." Sorbatchin stood with his arms crossed belligerently over his chest. His square jaw jutted and his eyes burned with insane light. Walden was suddenly afraid for his own life.

"We must use a metal cylinder, even if the inner containment vessel is of plastic," said Nakamura. "Who on your staff could design such a system and build it?"

"Burnowski might be able to. Or Chin. We do more with designing what goes into the bombs rather than how to deliver them." Walden stared at the vidscreen and saw the slow progress made by the blinking dot he assumed was the *Winston*. "How did the *Winston* get away from the Frinn robot ships?"

"He does not need to know. This only wastes our time," said Sorbatchin.

"He is correct. We need your aid, Doctor. Will you do this for us? For humanity?" Nakamura eyed him coldly. He wondered if she had ever felt a touch of the humanity she bandied about so easily as an argument to sway him?

Walden backed away from the pair and started to speak. No words came to his lips. He hadn't told them of Uvallae's actions. The *menla* fever might already be working its insidious way through Nakamura's and Sorbatchin's mouth and nose and lungs, finding a home on brain receptor sites. He tried to decide how telling them of this subversion from within their own fortress would affect their actions.

Killing Uvallae and the other Frinn would be their first act.

From there, they might decide that leaving the alien's home world intact was not worth the effort. Even though the *Hippocrates* and *Winston* didn't have the heavy weapons of NAA or Sov-Lat battleships, they could devastate a world.

Especially if that world was already ripped apart by the Infinity Plague.

Walden wasn't sure if it might not be better to let the hallucinations caused by the alien fever start in the two. He smiled bitterly when the thought came to him that he might not be able to tell the difference. Both Nakamura and Sorbatchin had delusions of grandeur. Never before had anyone been given the chance to conquer an entire world.

He spun and went to Captain Belford. The gray-haired man had grown increasingly restive. He paced back and forth until scuff marks showed on the deck from his boot soles.

"Captain, may I have a word with you?"

"What? Eh, certainly, Dr. Walden. What is it?" The officer's eyes darted around the bridge, more like a trapped animal's than a ship's master.

Walden took him by the sleeve and led him from the bridge. He didn't doubt that Miko Nakamura had every likely spot aboard the *Hippocrates* bugged, but she was busy at the moment fending off Frinn attacks and avoiding their deadly plastic space mines. By the time she listened in to the conversation, Walden hoped he would have accomplished his ends.

He closed the door to the wardroom off the bridge and said, "Do you approve?" He pointed to the smaller version of the bridge's vidscreen showing the battle in progress. The *Winston* still fired its laser cannon to defend the *Hippocrates*. The Frinn robot ships had been reduced in number but not in the ferocity of their attack.

"I don't want to fight. I never did. I am a hospital ship's captain, not a battle master." Captain Belford almost broke into tears of rage. "She took my ship away. And the damned Sov-Lat bastard helped her!"

"It's your ship," Walden said with quiet confidence. "You're still the commander of the *Hippocrates*. You know more about the vessel than they do."

"No, I don't. She knows everything. It's uncanny. I don't know how she does it. I've tried to wrest control away and

. . . and I failed. I don't know why." The man's eyes clouded over. Walden saw that the drugs Nakamura used on him still dimmed his self-confidence and made him a pawn in her power game. He hated himself for doing it but he used this hesitation for his own ends. He had to, if he wanted to see significant progress made toward stopping the spread of the human-spawned Infinity Plague.

"They claim they'd let Uvallae contact his world. Is this true? Or did they jam the transmission?"

"I don't know. I was there, but Nakamura is so clever. She might have done any number of things to block the signal."

"Did any of the Frinn give you the proper hailing frequencies? Or did Nakamura supply them?"

"She did."

Walden sighed. Nakamura hadn't wanted to contact the aliens. She had wanted them kept in ignorance until the EPCTs landed and took over their centers of power.

The *Hippocrates* rocked again as another mine detonated against its hull. Walden knew the vessel wasn't built to take such punishment. When they had engaged the Frinn exploratory ships they had sustained considerable damage—and little of it had been fixed. The battle at Starlight had left the *Hippocrates* untouched, but this only gave Nakamura a false sense of security in the ship. It wasn't a war vessel to be whipped about at will.

Captain Belford touched the vidscreen control and got a new picture of the battle raging in the vacuum beyond the ship's hull. His fingers tapped restlessly until Walden wanted to scream in frustration. He held back, knowing the captain's nervousness came as much from the drugs Nakamura gave him as the pent-up desire to act.

"There is the *Winston*," he said, pointing to a small dot moving at crazy angles from the *Hippocrates*. "Its captain is good, I'll give him that. I can't believe we've lost so many men, though. It hurts. I have never lost more than one or two during a mission. I don't want to file the reports when we return to Earth."

"We won't be going home," Walden said rancorously. "Nakamura is going to destroy us." He didn't add that he would let the *menla* fever run its course aboard the ship before he joined in the genocide pursued by Nakamura and Sorbatchin.

"Not if they keep doing this," Captain Belford said, not hearing Walden's resentment. "The space mines are diabolical. They might even have rudimentary AI circuits in them. If we had a decent minesweeper in front of us, they wouldn't bother us one whit. But we don't—and the *Winston* has its hands full keeping their robot killers at bay."

"We can contact the Frinn. Let Uvallae speak with them. We have to stop the plague. We caused it, we must stop it."

"It is very hard to get a free circuit with Nakamura watching, unless I . . ." Captain Belford's words trailed off as he began following a thread of thought. Walden didn't pester him. He let the officer work out his own plan. He spun the vidscreen around and ran it in split mode, the battle still playing out on the top half and Uvallae appearing on the bottom.

"Come to the wardroom off the bridge," he said. "Do it, Uvallae. We can get through to the controllers. You can tell them whatever you want."

"Why are you doing this? Are they not monitoring everything that leaves the ship?" asked the alien. His rough-skinned forehead rippled with dismay.

"Believe what you will of us. I'm trying to stop the plague. I don't want to die of your plague, either, but it's much slower acting. Your problems are more pressing."

"This is so confusing," whined Uvallae. "You humans are not of a single mind." The alien turned and spoke rapidly to someone off-screen. When Walden heard a sharp bark, he knew the Frinn consulted Egad. Whatever the dog said, it satisfied Uvallae. "I will be there quickly. You have opened the way."

"Hurry, there may not be much time."

To Captain Belford he said, "He's coming. You can open a com-link to the planet?"

"For a few minutes we can connect. Nakamura will see it. She monitors everything all the time. I don't know how she does it. I never could. I only watched summary displays, but her—" The officer shook his head.

Walden wasn't interested in Nakamura's strengths or the captain's failings as a commander. He wanted Uvallae in touch

with the Frinn controllers. Stop the robot attacks, get through
the mine fields, and guarantee that the EPCT troops wouldn't
be sent down, and they might get on with their real work.

He glanced over his shoulder when Uvallae entered. Walden motioned for the alien to sit beside Captain Belford.

"I've got a small laser com-link patched into this vidscreen," the Captain told Uvallae. "The center for your
world's communication is rotating around just past the horizon. We've got half of your world's day to reach them."

"We've got until Nakamura stops us," corrected Walden.
He saw that Uvallae understood the dissension in the human
ranks. Egad entered and flopped onto the deck at the doorway. The gengineered dog had told the alien as much as he
could. Walden hoped that Egad understood the situation
aboard the *Hippocrates*.

"Go. Transmit. Do it now. I've got the power on the small
lasercom unit." Captain Belford went pale and sat down
abruptly in a chair, at the end of his strength. The drugs and
tension had finally broken him.

Uvallae began a slow, systematic speech. He continued for
several minutes, then leaned back.

"I am not getting through," he said. "There is too much
interference."

"Not with a laser beam! That's closed to interference! Keep
trying!" Walden refused to be thwarted.

"It is no use, Dr. Walden," said the alien. "The use of so
many energy weapons in nearby space affects the beam's integrity. And there is a further problem."

"Keep trying," urged Walden. "You can—"

"The major obstacle to establishing contact," said Uvallae, "is the destruction of our communications site. The
Winston scored a direct hit with a missile."

Walden started to tell him to keep trying, to find another
com unit able to receive when he saw the vidscreen go dark.
Even if Uvallae could reach a planetary station, it now meant
nothing. Nakamura had discovered their feeble attempt to
communicate and had cut the power to their lasercom.

The battle raged, silent and increasingly deadly. And Walden was powerless to stop it.

CHAPTER
11

"Gentleman, you should not do such things. I do not like having anyone sneaking around behind my back." Miko Nakamura stood in the doorway of the wardroom, the long silk of her kimono sleeves hiding her hands. Egad snarled and rose to his spindly legs. The woman moved slightly, shifting her weight to fend off an attack. The silk sleeves rustled, as if she reached for weapons.

"No, Egad. Down." Walden didn't want the dog going for the woman's throat. He was afraid Egad would lose. Even if she wasn't armed, Nakamura had gengineered hands, the edges implanted with iron-hardened cells. He had no idea what other modifications she had accepted in her body.

"That is the first smart thing you've done all day, Dr. Walden," she said in her quiet, coolly menacing voice. "Allowing Uvallae and the other Frinn to leave the quarantine is a mistake, however. The plague might spread among our kind."

"You know it can't," he snapped. "The Infinity Plague affects only the Frinn. As far as Anita's research goes, the plague is a failure against humans. I've guessed this much. You've seen her reports; you must know that for a fact."

"That conclusion seems true." Nakamura studied Uvallae rather than Captain Belford or Walden. She ignored Egad

94

completely. "You are not showing symptoms of the plague. Do you feel well?"

"I sorrow for the loss of my home world," Uvallae said. He rubbed his hands across his forehead and backed away. Walden wondered what psychic pressures were placed on him being surrounded by so many people. He had seen Uvallae cope with public appearances by stoically accepting. What emotional price did he pay later? Did he have to rush off and be alone for hours? Longer? There was so much to learn about the Frinn and so little time.

"Your world is not lost," Nakamura said in her low voice. "We can save it. Let Dr. Walden help us. We need to get through the mines and the robot ships. If we—"

"That's bullshit," Walden said. He lacked the energy to feel moral indignation at her easy lie. "You want to destroy his world, not save it. You didn't put Anita to working on a cure for the Infinity Plague. You and Sorbatchin have her working on different bioweapons to use against the Frinn."

"Your source of information is wrong," Nakamura said. She glanced at Egad when he growled. "I see. You've used a four-legged spy." She settled herself and turned to Uvallae. "They have misinterpreted Dr. Tarleton's mission. Her research is directed at slowing the course of the plague."

"Quit lying, Nakamura." Walden sat on the wardroom table and stared at the vidscreen. The *Winston* worked well against the robot ships. Nakamura had penetrated the enemy's computer battle plan and exploited it now. For all their adaptability, the aliens' robots proved no match for human intuition and genius.

"Rudeness is no answer, Doctor," the woman said. "I come from a polite society. If you had said this to Colonel Sorbatchin, he would have reacted badly."

Walden knew he had made an implacable enemy of the woman. He shrugged it off. He hadn't rated high on her list of favorites before this.

"Let me contact the Frinn. Let me try to stop the plague. They are providing their own vector for its spread."

"No one is preventing you from doing your own work, Doctor," Nakamura said. "Why don't you allow us to conduct this mission without your interference? Your laboratory is a more appropriate place for you to do your best."

"You want to eradicate them," accused Walden. "Genocide. It's not a pretty term, is it, Nakamura?"

"Wars are fought to be won at any cost."

"This isn't a war!"

Walden wanted to shake the woman in frustration, to rattle her teeth and make her see that she couldn't have it both ways. One instant she told Uvallae she wanted only to preserve his culture. In the same breath, she spoke of war and total destruction of an enemy. The Frinn were innocent victims, as much as those humans they killed back on Delta Cygnus.

More. If the humans hadn't worked on bioweapons, the Frinn would never have contracted the plague.

Walden swallowed hard and tried to imagine describing anyone engaged in biological warfare research as innocent. Such sophistry was becoming harder for him, if not for Nakamura and the others intent on invading an alien planet. Yet if he hadn't spent years gathering the expertise in killing, he wouldn't have the knowledge now to counter the plague's effects. If only he could work on the Infinity Plague unhindered, if only they would let him get to the classified data.

If only they would break off their attack on Uvallae's home world.

"The *Winston* is prevailing against the defenders," said Nakamura, seeing his interest in the vidscreen display. "We will attain orbit soon enough."

Uvallae bowed his head. "I have already surrendered to you. Is there more you desire?"

"No," said Nakamura. She looked from human to Frinn to the gengineered dog still growling deep in his throat. Without another word, she turned and left.

"We tried and failed, Uvallae. I'm sorry." Walden's mind raced. They couldn't reach the controllers on the planet's surface. What else could they do?

Nothing came to him. Nakamura had ordered him back to the lab to work on staying the spread of the Infinity Plague. Walden saw little else for him to do.

"Let's go," he said, putting his arm around Uvallae's shoulders. The alien shied away. Walden cursed himself for forgetting that they were aliens, that they respected privacy, *needed* it in ways even the most introverted human did not.

"We've got work to do. If we can retard the plague's spread, that will be a major accomplishment."

"For what? You heard her. She seeks only my planet's domination. You speak of genocide. This is a word unknown to me, but it sounds as if you mean total eradication of a native population. This is what Nakamura seeks, is it not?"

"It might be. She's working too closely with Sorbatchin for my liking. The Sov-Lats have a long history of genocide dating back centuries. Afghanistan, Angola, Iran, Lithuania, Germany, and France. I'm surprised Nakamura accepts it so quickly."

"She takes easy way out. *Hippocrates* is wounded," said Egad. "*Winston* is, too."

"You may be right. We can't wage a real war, so she's doing everything possible to eliminate possible opposition. She wants to be remembered as the woman who conquered the first intelligent aliens we ever discovered."

"They found us," pointed out Egad.

Walden looked at Uvallae's bowed shoulders as he walked dejectedly in front of them. It was a black day in Frinn history when their explorers found the humans in the Delta Cygnus system. It brought them plague and conquest.

The *Hippocrates* rocked as a new wave of attacking ships fired kinetic weapons at them. A round hole appeared centimeters from Walden's head. He spun to see where it came from, only to see a matching hole in the far bulkhead. A steel pellet had penetrated both exterior hull and interior walls. With any luck they wouldn't lose much atmosphere before repair crews glued the hole.

"With any luck," Walden said, repeating it over and over. Luck for the Frinn was different from that of his own species. If he destroyed the *Hippocrates*, it might save the Frinn. But could he turn traitor to his own kind?

He couldn't. No matter how viciously Nakamura and Sorbatchin pressed their war, he could not act as a betrayer of faith and humanity. But that didn't mean he had to tell them about the *menla* fever.

Leo Burch shivered with fever. He barely succeeded in programming his medbot to take the blood samples and run analyses on them.

"You are anemic," warned Albert. "Too many specimens have been taken in a short span."

"Pretend I'm an old-time doctor using leeches to bleed my patients," Burch said.

"I do not understand."

"It's not necessary, Albert. Just do your work." Burch lay back on his bed and stared at the gray composite ceiling. The *Hippocrates* vibrated so hard it threatened to bounce him onto the deck. He hadn't followed the course of the battle, but he knew it had turned bitter. Burch tried to concentrate and couldn't. The plague racing through his veins was taking its toll. He had used Walden's work, carried it a bit further, and had succeeded.

Too well he had succeeded. He had infected himself with a mutated version of the Infinity Plague.

Nausea rose. Burch tapped an order into Albert's keypad to inject a broad spectrum of drugs. They seemed to do little to impede the course of the plague, but they worked against his churning gut and the insufferable headache threatening to split his head like a plutonium atom in a bomb.

"Computing resources are nearing their limit," Albert reported.

Burch was too sick to curse. "Keep everyone away from me. Don't think quarantine's the answer. Damned plague is too sneaky. Can get out and infect everyone." He tried to follow his line of thought and failed. Too much jumbled in his head. He felt as if he had turned to dust internally. "But keep the computer working. We need a full workup on it. Everything. Pathology, crystallography, projections, everything. Do you understand, Albert?"

The medbot beeped once.

"You're better than any human. You're even better than that damned cat Doris left me. Keep working, Albert. No matter what." Leo Burch closed his eyes and let the tide of drugs wash him into a land less wracked with pain. The medical robot would work tirelessly to delineate the Infinity Plague and find its cure.

Leo Burch would erase the shame of turning against the NAA and spying for the Sov-Lats by giving the answers they sought. Jerome Walden wasn't the only brilliant research scientist aboard the *Hippocrates*.

"Not the only genius . . . " Burch crooned as he fell into fitful, drugged slumber.

"They do not array against us quickly enough," gloated Vladimir Sorbatchin. "See how they hesitate? We can drive through and destroy their world!"

"No," said Nakamura, musing over the course pointed out by the Sov-Lat officer. "They respond slowly because their ships are entirely automated. This is one reason I do not approve of using only computer-driven forces. If we follow your plan exactly, they will have time to recompute and we will prove vulnerable. We must always do the unexpected."

"Attack! Now!" Sorbatchin slammed his fist down on the arm of Nakamura's command chair. She silently reset the controls he had disturbed with his outburst.

Eyes colder than space turned on the colonel. "You forget your place, sir. We are not a full armada. We have only the *Winston* and our own vessel. To lose either ends the battle."

"Boldness. We must attack. They do not expect it from us."

"They are not reinforcing their ships," Nakamura said obliquely. "What we have met, those we see in space around us now, constitute their entire force."

"That is defeatist thinking. From this position comes a synthesis we can exploit for our own benefit," said Sorbatchin. "I did not expect cowardice from you."

"You see no weakness," she said in a tone with a chilled steel edge. "I seek ways of winning without dying." Nakamura studied the vidscreen showing the relative positions of the Frinn ships and the *Hippocrates* and *Winston*. "We have no information about their planet-based weapons. If we rush forward, we might find ourselves caught between heavy ground lasers and surface-to-space missiles and their robot ships."

"This is all they have. Look! Is this a world that can do more? They teeter on the brink of defeat. The plague has reduced them to using machines!"

"Those machines destroyed a human-colonized planet," Nakamura said. "We proceed slowly." She touched a toggle on the chair arm. Captain Belford dutifully came to stand beside her.

"Do I take over again?" he asked.

"For a time. I must use the ship's computer to project our chances of victory. There are several possible ways of attaining *sustainable* and *safe* orbit around their world." Nakamura swung from the chair and walked off on silent feet, never looking back at either Captain Belford or Sorbatchin.

The Sov-Lat colonel snorted and left the bridge. Less than a minute after he had gone, Nakamura returned.

Captain Belford looked up, startled. "You want to—"

"Remain where you are. I merely wanted our Sov-Lat friend to leave for the moment." She worked at a control board, following Sorbatchin's path through the *Hippocrates*. When she was sure he was safely out of the way, she turned her attention fully to the tactical problem.

"*Winston*," she called, using a lasercom to link with the NAA destroyer. "Do you have any sneak missiles left? I want a complete scan of the planet's surface."

"None left," came the immediate reply. "We stripped out the camera gear and installed conventional explosives. We've needed everything that has an engine in it to defend ourselves. When are they going to pull back? Our laser cannon are overheating. We need time to repair the damage."

"Soon," Nakamura promised. "I will use equipment from my own stores." She looked over a computerized inventory of all that remained aboard the *Hippocrates* and chose carefully. Swift fingers tapped out orders. The EPCTs were better suited to combat than maintenance, but she trusted them implicitly. They began work converting a small shuttle into a spy craft for her.

As they worked, so did Nakamura. The computer gave her projection after projection on the likely outcomes of her plans. None suited her. She needed more data on the Frinn's on-planet capabilities. The *Hippocrates* and *Winston* maneuvered to avoid conflict now, only occasionally exchanging fire with a robot ship rapidly crossing their attack vector.

More than anything else, the random path through space gave the ships time to repair and her time to plot. In two hours the EPCTs had converted the small shuttle into the type of vessel she needed most. Surveillance equipment, of necessity, was makeshift, but the CCD cameras and radiation detectors were easily scavenged from existing parts from all over the *Hippocrates*.

"Launch," she ordered. On the bridge's vidscreen she watched the tiny dot marking the shuttle leap away from the *Hippocrates*. In twenty minutes it had penetrated the ring of protecting Frinn ships. In fifty, she was certain it had crossed the orbits of the deadly space mines swarming around the planet like killer gnats. And in three hours it skimmed the planet's atmosphere.

The intelligence it lasercommed back was sketchy; the equipment placed aboard the shuttle wasn't as sophisticated as she would have liked. But the information relayed after one complete orbit of the Frinn's Earthlike home world convinced her that victory was within her eager grasp.

The vidscreen showed only desolation. The few cities appeared deserted, abandoned, in ruins. The bucolic country-side seemed untouched by the ravages humanity had inadvertently inflicted, but occasional close-ups showed cemeteries with more new graves than old.

The Infinity Plague had done everything she had hoped it might. The Frinn's planet was hers for the taking.

CHAPTER
12

"You've doomed us!" cried Vladimir Sorbatchin. "You have us trapped between ground forces and their damned robot ships!"

Miko Nakamura scowled. How could she have miscalculated so badly? She dared not show any hint of indecision in front of the Sov-Lat officer. He worked assiduously to undermine her position among the crew of the *Hippocrates*. She had to maintain an aura of invulnerability and control over them. Otherwise, they would all perish quickly. The Frinn defenses had proved more obdurate than she had anticipated from her first look at the planet.

"They hid their capabilities well," she said. "You have seen the shuttle's reconnaissance material. Did you detect any laser cannon on the surface?"

"You did not show the photos to me. You hid the entire mission from me. I would have gone personally to be sure we saw only the parts of the world that would give us the most intelligence."

Nakamura snorted. She knew Sorbatchin would never do such a thing. He would have sent some of those loyal to him. She frowned. Could her failure to find the Frinn's true defensive capacity be traced back to the EPCTs? Had they betrayed her at Sorbatchin's command? They followed him naturally, a military leader among a shipload of scientists. She had to check their alliance with the Sov-Lat officer.

"We are caught in orbit, passing over their laser cannon every ninety minutes. The last pass ruined our external sensors. We are blind on most frequencies."

"Give me command of the *Winston*. I will show you how to deal with those swine!"

"Captain?" she asked. Nakamura did not budge from the command chair. Sorbatchin could rant and rave all he wanted, but she was still firmly in control of the ship—and the expedition. Even Captain Belford agreed to that.

"What is it?" the drugged officer asked in a dull, listless voice.

"Colonel Sorbatchin wishes to head an expedition against the Frinn. Prepare the landing craft and tell the EPCT unit that he will lead them into combat."

"I . . . never said that," Sorbatchin muttered.

"What? Did I hear you wrong, Colonel? You want someone else to lead the soldiers? Very well, I can get—" Nakamura held back a thin smile when she saw how neatly she had trapped the Sov-Lat officer. He dared not lose face in front of Captain Belford and the other crew on the *Hippocrates*' bridge. They would quickly tell the EPCT soldiers how Sorbatchin had backed down and any position he had among them would vanish quickly. As it was, Nakamura hoped that the loutish colonel led them directly to hell and died there. It would solve many of her problems.

She wasn't strong enough to kill him outright. He had done well in cementing his position among the crew and soldiers, in spite of being their "enemy." Nakamura had to remind herself constantly that she had no position in the chain of command, that she was only a civilian advisor and not even a member of the ship's crew. If Sorbatchin's position was tenuous, hers was like vacuum.

Sorbatchin's normally cold pale blue eyes burned with a fever that amused her. He knew what she had done. The only way he could redeem himself was to win against the enemy.

From what she now saw in the photographs of the planet's surface, Sorbatchin had little or no chance of surviving longer than a few minutes, even with the highly trained EPCT company backing him. She hated to sacrifice such devoted warriors for the simple purpose of ridding herself of an unwanted, if temporary, ally but such were the ways of war.

Von Clausewitz had said that war is nothing more than the continuation of politics by other means. She would combine the steppingstones to her power. Rid of Sorbatchin, she would be left as ruler of an entire world!

"I will return with their written surrender," Sorbatchin told her.

"Do so. I am entrusting this vital mission to you, Colonel. Take with you all the photographs you require for planning your mission. I suggest you land near the largest city."

"Their capital," he said, glaring at her. Sorbatchin swayed slightly, sweat beading his forehead. He started to speak but his tongue expanded until it filled his mouth and he choked.

"Colonel, are you ill?" She looked at him curiously. The officer swayed and turned pale. Nakamura did not want him easing out of this suicide mission with a claim of sickness. He *had* to descend and die on the planet's surface. She could use a martyr, a new hero, someone for the survivors to focus on and forget their own misery.

"Everything turned red for a moment," he said, wiping away the sweat. He glared at her again, then saluted smartly and left without another word.

Nakamura put a constant monitor on Sorbatchin. She didn't want him escaping her carefully baited trap. No matter what he did, if he dropped planetside with the EPCTs, he aided her cause.

But she preferred that he die. Nakamura touched the com button on the command chair's arm and asked, "Dr. Walden, could you spare a moment?"

His haggard face appeared at the corner of the bridge's vidscreen. Beside him stood Uvallae. She smiled. She had all the actors assembled for her play.

"What is it?" Walden asked. "I'm busy in the lab."

"Would you like to pursue your research at a more basic level?" she asked. "I need volunteers to assist Colonel Sorbatchin when he lands on the planet."

"You want me to go with him and the EPCTs?"

"Only if you can aid the populace. I am sincere in desiring an end to the Infinity Plague ravaging their world. I have evidence that it has decimated the population." She ran some of the CCD pictures assembled from orbit.

"I know that place. It is less than a hundred kilometers from my dwelling," said Uvallae. "The cemeteries! They overflow with the dead from the plague. My world *was* infected!" Until this moment, hope had burned in Uvallae that the returning exploratory ship might have been spared the horror.

Nakamura silently urged the Frinn to continue. Walden's resolve melted instant by instant.

"I'll go down. I can work better with more patients to study. I need to know how the plague runs its course and how it mutates. Without more comprehensive data, it might take years for my computer work to return decent results."

"I will arrange for Sorbatchin to accommodate you on the landing. Your equipment cannot take up more than five cubic meters of space, however. This is an EPCT landing, and they need weapons."

"Against a sick world? I doubt one in ten of the population is functional," Walden said, studying his vidscreen.

"It is as bad as we feared," Nakamura said. "Uvallae, do you wish to return to your world? You and the others?"

"Yes, we will return. We have tried to aid Dr. Walden aboard ship, but we can do more on-planet. We have full facilities there. I would check the hospitals."

Nakamura watched Walden's reaction. He turned to Uvallae, then toward the vidscreen. He started to speak, as if to confess. She puzzled over this response. What could he have to confess?

"Yes, Doctor?" she prompted.

"Nothing," he said, lying. He covered himself by asking, "Will Anita come with us?"

"I have not asked Dr. Tarleton." Nakamura cut the audio on the vidscreen for a few minutes as she pretended to speak with Anita Tarleton. She wanted the red-haired scientist to remain aboard the *Hippocrates*. After Sorbatchin and Walden were removed, Tarleton would be the perfect figurehead to keep the scientists in line. Nakamura had seen how the lure of power had enticed her into doing Sorbatchin's bidding. Even more important, the scientist worked on new bioweapons useful against the Frinn. Nakamura wasn't persuaded that Sorbatchin and his small force could conquer an entire world, even one brought down by the Infinity Plague. Further warfare would be required, and Anita Tarleton was the perfect one to show the way with new bioweaponry.

"She wishes to remain aboard the *Hippocrates*," Nakamura said to Walden after restoring the audio linkage. "Hurry and get what equipment you will need down to the cargo bay. Colonel Sorbatchin intends to leave within the hour."

The *Hippocrates* shivered as it absorbed a new round of missile fire from the attacking robotic fighters. Nakamura glanced at the pattern of incoming ships and saw that the *Winston* would be able to interdict most of the missiles and deflect all the laser fire. In space, they were secure for the moment. From the planet, however, came the real menace after orbital insertion. She had identified no fewer than six sites capable of blasting them out of the sky while they were in orbit.

"Will we be able to maintain contact with the ship?" asked Walden. "I'll need the use of the ship's computer."

"Doubtful. Take a portable machine, if you feel it will help you." Nakamura's generosity was fed by the need for haste. The sooner she got Walden and the others planetside, the sooner they would be removed as pawns in her power game.

"Very well," said Walden. "We'll get everything ready. It's not much time, but we have no choice."

"No, Doctor," she said softly after she turned off the audio on the vidscreen, "you have no choice at all." She diverted her attention back to the attack patterns and how she would take over the planet. Once that lay behind her, she could get on with the business of setting up a provisional government. A few Frinn would remain, she knew. Lifeforms tended to be persistent.

"No, Egad, you have to stay here. Go to Anita. She'll look after you," Walden said to the gengineered dog. Egad didn't budge.

"Go with you. Not stay on this cat-shit ship."

"Please, Dr. Walden, allow him to come with us. He . . . it is difficult for me to say these things."

"You can communicate better with him than you can with humans, is that it?" Walden had seen the way Egad and the

Frinn worked together well. He hated to put the dog into danger, though. On-planet was a hellhole. Nakamura's pictures had shown the widespread devastation brought about by the Infinity Plague.

"Everyone getting sick here," said Egad. "Don't want to stay."

"The *menla* fever," he said softly. He had seen many of the crew members wobbling, looking pale and frightened as hallucinations seized them. He felt guilty about not warning them, yet he couldn't come out and tell all he knew. It was a small hold he had over them, a very small one. He wasn't even sure how he would use it. The disease slowly worked on the humans and didn't seem to be a truly serious one. The drugs Leo Burch gave him held the disease at bay as much as his self-control. If he didn't get too upset, the phantoms didn't return to bedevil him.

"You should tell your Dr. Tarleton what I have done," suggested Uvallae.

"If I do, it won't take her long to find a cure for it."

"I made a mistake loosing the disease," said the Frinn. "Tell her, tell the others. Do not make them suffer."

"We'll tell them after we've whipped the virus on your world," said Walden. "We shouldn't diffuse our time and talents and resources." He grinned wickedly. "Besides, we might have to use it as a bargaining lever to get what we really need."

"You would blackmail your own kind?" asked Uvallae, startled. "For us?"

"Yes." The answer bothered Walden, but he didn't stop to analyze it. He had too much to do to get his equipment ready. He had several promising starts on a cure for the Infinity Plague. A few breaks and he could stop the spread.

"I will help you with these crates." Uvallae and two of the other Frinn helped Walden wrestle his equipment down to the cargo bay where the EPCTs prepared a shuttle craft.

"Hey, Doc, you going with us?" called Sgt. Hecht. "This is going to be like old times. Almost." He eyed the Frinn suspiciously. "They going down with us, too?"

"They are. We're all going down to help the Frinn."

"That's not what the buzz is telling us, Doc," said Hecht. "We're going down to kick pig butt. If they want to help, fine. Otherwise, I'd advise them to stay clear. The colonel isn't likely to put up with them this side of a barbecue pit.'' Hecht gestured with his chin in the direction of Vladimir Sorbatchin.

"You're actually letting a Sov-Lat lead you," Walden said sadly. "I didn't think you'd ever do it."

"He's a military man. He's got odd ideas, but we can track him better than the others."

"A Sov-Lat," Walden said, sowing all the seeds of discontent he could. Hecht didn't seem pleased with the idea of a Sov-Lat officer leading them, but the EPCTs had been devastated in combat. All the NAA field officers were dead. The sparse table of organization in the Extra-Planetary Combat Teams didn't provide much depth in leadership. There had been only four officers for more than a hundred men. Zacharias hadn't been any loss, as far as Walden was concerned, but the deaths of the other three officers left the combat team without leadership.

"We'll make do, Doc. Don't worry. We're EPCT," Hecht said. The sergeant wheeled and bellowed orders at the small squad of a dozen soldiers struggling to get their equipment into the shuttle. From the amount of weaponry Walden saw, he knew they meant to make a direct landing on the planet.

Before, they had power-chuted in. Not this time. This would be a full-scale invasion—or as full-scale as fewer than forty men could make it with jury-rigged equipment.

"Inside, Doctor. We launch immediately," said Sorbatchin. The Sov-Lat officer's pale face betrayed the strain he felt.

"Are you feeling dizzy, Colonel? You don't look too good."

"Silence! Nakamura said the same thing. I am a Soviet-Latino! I do not share your bourgeois weaknesses!"

"Sorry I said anything." Walden herded the Frinn inside the cramped shuttle. Uvallae tugged at his arm. When they weren't likely to be overheard, Walden asked what he wanted.

"The *menla* fever seizes him harder than the others. See his eyes? They burn."

"We'll watch him carefully. I don't want him crashing any more than you do," said Walden. He knew the descent would be automatic. The fight-or-flight circuits in the shuttle would stand them in good stead. Once on the ground, it didn't matter what Sorbatchin's condition was. They could slip off and do the work he had to do. The Frinn had to be saved.

He might do better to try to save them from Sorbatchin's mission of conquest.

"All in, everyone down. We're going to do this one right. No more pig-faces kicking us around," Hecht said as he herded his squad into the shuttle. He cast a look in Walden's direction, as if apologizing for what he had to say. He smiled weakly at Uvallae as he pushed past and buckled down beyond the Frinn.

The shuttle exploded from the cargo bay. Walden closed his eyes and let the acceleration knead his rigid muscles. The new pressures only increased his tenseness. Twice on the way through the Frinn mine fields and robot ships and savage fire from ground batteries, he had to use pentagan to keep the *menla* fever hallucinations from possessing him totally.

"We're almost down," came the pilot's warning. "We're landing near their capital. Heavy fire. Two laser batteries. Something spitting energy donuts at us I don't recognize. But we're going to make it."

"Compact toroid cannon," murmured Hecht. "We saw the pig-faces use it back at Schwann."

The small torus of energy spat from the end of its launching tube at ten billion gravities of acceleration. Walden had wondered about them before and Zacharias had satisfied his curiosity. These were not permanent weapons but makeshift ones rushed into use out of necessity. The donut of energy might move at significant fractions of the speed of light and explode like a dozen nukes, but in an atmosphere they fell apart quickly. The Frinn had to use them solely to keep away atmospheric invasion.

"They're getting desperate," Hecht said. "The compact toroid gun is a better space weapon. Attenuation length must be less than a kilometer." He studied his small panel of instruments. "Their lasers aren't too good, either. Beam attenuation is extreme in the atmosphere."

"They defend themselves and little more," said Uvallae. "We have no planet-based weapons."

"For no weapons, pig boy, you sure gave us hell getting down," spoke up another EPCT.

"That's enough, Lloyd," Hecht said in a tired voice. "He's right. This is nothing compared to a real ground battery. All we need to do is dodge around just outside the ionization cloud and we're safe."

"No EPCT is ever safe. We're goin' in, Sarge. We're goin' in!"

The shuttle hit the ground with a bone-jarring impact. Walden fought down the new bout of phantoms creeping into his field of vision. Increasing the dosage of his nerve-numbing drugs would cause him to pass out. He concentrated on remaining calm, in spite of his hammering heart rate.

"Out. We got to get into the tanks before they get their heavy armor after us," ordered Hecht. He stopped beside Walden and stared at him. The sergeant touched the readout on Walden's wrist and asked, "You all right, Doc? Your readings are off scale."

"Go on, Sergeant. I'll be fine." Walden forced himself to his feet, ignoring the return of memories he had no desire to relive. He had to keep telling himself it was the effect of the Frinn's fever, not cowardice on his part. Egad bounced against one leg and steadied him; Uvallae put an arm around his shoulders and helped him out of the shuttle.

Walden thought the hallucinations had seized him again. He stepped out into a newborn hell of destruction. The ground smoldered from the shuttle's landing jets' back-blast. Everywhere he looked he saw impact craters.

"We're being bombarded. Robot armor less than five klicks off and getting closer by the minute," he heard the report over a command circuit. He didn't bother asking Hecht for confirmation. The EPCT sergeant had his hands full getting the small tanks out of the shuttle's cargo bay.

The automated skirmish tanks each carried ten men inside and provided armor shielding for an additional twenty clinging to the outside. Sorbatchin had crowded five of the tanks into the shuttle; no one needed to ride outside. Walden heard the hiss and crackle of commands. The EPCT company worked smoothly to get their tanks on-line and into action.

Even as he watched, two tanks began a slow, methodical firing of their two-hundred-millimeter turret guns. He had no idea what their target might be, other than the Frinn robots rushing toward them. The cannon fired projectiles that vanished over the low hills surrounding the bowl of a valley where the shuttle had landed. Once aloft, artificial intelligence circuits took over inside the projectiles to guide them independently to their targets.

"How do we move our equipment?" asked Uvallae, indicating the pile of crates. "If we stay here, we will be killed by our own robotic devices."

"There's a cargo carrier," he said, pointing to a lightweight, sturdy electric motor device left behind by the EPCTs. "Load what we can on it." Walden helped the Frinn get the boxed equipment onto the small flatbed truck. "We might be able to keep up with Sorbatchin's tanks, though I doubt it. Top speed for the carrier is less than ten kilometers an hour."

"So slow?" asked another of the Frinn scientists from Starlight.

"It moves heavy equipment and isn't a racehorse."

The Frinn started to ask what a racehorse was. His question died on his lips as a screaming came across the sky. Walden instinctively dropped flat on the ground. Egad knocked over Uvallae and another Frinn. The others stood and stared as the rocket drove directly for the vulnerable shuttle.

The air filled with molten steel, sizzling nuts and bolts, and carbon vapor as the missile scored a direct hit. However the EPCTs left this world, it wasn't going to be in that shuttle. Only smoking ruin remained.

"Any injuries?" asked Walden, struggling to his feet. He saw the answer to the question was going to depress him. Only three Frinn, other than Uvallae, had survived. They had been killed by their own defensive fire.

"We've got to hurry," Walden said. "The tanks are already at the rim of the valley. I don't know what Sorbatchin's battle plan was, but he's the kind to prefer a blitzkrieg attack."

Uvallae looked at him curiously.

"Sorbatchin will drive directly for the heart of the capital. He will destroy what he can to prevent retaliation, but he is depending on speed more than firepower." Walden still wondered at any soldier willing to take on an entire world with only five tanks and fewer than forty men, even if they were EPCTs. Nakamura and Sorbatchin had refined their attack techniques using Starlight as a testing ground, but this was more than a space station. This was the Frinn's home world.

"What are those?" asked Uvallae.

For a few seconds, Walden didn't know what he meant. Then he saw tiny explosions all around. The ground had become pockmarked not from pieces of the shuttle but by aerial bombardment. Small pellets fell like a deadly rain. Each sphere exploded and blew a meter-wide crater. They didn't seem dangerous at distances more than a few meters, but Walden realized enough fell to make it increasingly unlikely anyone would escape. They were on the receiving end of a huge shotgun firing explosive buckshot.

Egad let out a squeak like a mouse when one pellet exploded only centimeters from him. Walden shouted, "Uvallae, look at Egad. I've got to drive this damned thing."

Walden fought to keep the cargo carrier on an even course. Slow, ponderous, it had a mind of its own. Worse, the ground shuddered under them, causing the cargo handler's guidance computer to overcompensate and threaten to send them wheeling in wide circles. He wondered if they shouldn't have crowded into one of the skirmish tanks and let the Frinn robots blow up the equipment. What experimental implements he had in the truck bed wasn't likely to turn the deadly tide caused by the Infinity Plague.

Dirt flew into the air in tiny fountains all around. The explosions almost deafened him. He checked his suit and made sure the air filtration system worked well; he sweat more than usual and overloaded the capacity of the circulation system. When perspiration poured into his eyes, Walden ripped open the face plate and let the warm, dry planetary air erase some of the dampness.

After what seemed an eternity dodging craters and avoiding the falling pellets of death, he wrestled the cargo carrier to a halt along the ridge overlooking the valley. He glanced back and shivered. The deadly rain of kinetic particles had turned the once-green valley into a churning sea of death. No spot showed more than ten square centimeters of untouched grass. Chipped rock looked like broken white and gray bone as it poked through the surface. In spots, notably around the destroyed shuttle, cavities meters deep were common. Walden wondered how they had survived such a fearsome rain.

"They leave us behind," moaned Egad. "Cat-shit colonel is leaving us!"

"That's no loss," said Walden, watching as the five EPCT skirmish tanks weaved their way across a plain toward the distant Frinn capital.

"They leave us to die!"

It took Walden several seconds to see what the gengineered dog meant. The robotic defenders had not pursued the skirmish tanks toward the city. A dozen or more of the automated death dealers circled and came directly for them.

CHAPTER
13

Leo Burch screamed as pain tore at his guts. He rolled onto his side and tried to reach his medbot. Albert hummed and purred mechanically just beyond his reach. Mouth too dry to form words clearly, Burch fought for the medication he needed to dull the suffering that killed him slowly.

"Albert," he whispered huskily. "Help me."

"You are infected with the Infinity Plague," the medbot told him. "Analyses of your blood are being performed to determine how it propagates in your body."

"I'm burning up." Burch wasn't sure Albert heard him. "Thirsty. My nerves are all telling me I'm dying. Can't breathe, either. Check the air supply. Something wrong with it. Whole damned ship is hot and stuffy."

Albert rolled closer, then adjusted the oxygen tube running up Burch's nose. The robot determined the flow had not changed, but Burch's uptake had. His lungs stopped functioning of their own accord. His autonomic system was slowly rebelling, refusing to work at ordinary tasks.

Burch tried to scream when iron bands contracted around his chest. His eyes opened and he saw a blurry image of his medical robot beside him. The medbot had wrapped a metallic tentacle around his chest and contracted. When the pressure from the oxygen hose up his nose had mounted enough to inflate the lungs, the robot relaxed its grip. In this crude way the medbot kept Burch breathing.

"Drugs. Convulsants," croaked Burch. "That will make me jerk and twitch but it ought to get me breathing." He found Albert's keypad and tapped out the prescription. Obediently, the medbot injected the proper amount of the drug.

Burch gasped and lay back on his bed. "I've done it now, Albert. I took Walden's work and isolated the Infinity Plague. I went him one better. I got it to take in humans. In me."

His annunciator sounded, signaling that someone out in the infirmary wanted to see him.

"Doctor's not in," he said weakly.

"Leo, are you all right? You sound like warmed-over death," Anita Tarleton said. "Let me in."

"Can't do it," he said. "Got a bad case of the bads."

"What's wrong?" Anita's voice turned shrill. "You don't have the fever that is spreading through the ship, do you?"

Fear clutched at Burch's throat. How had he spread the Infinity Plague? He had tried to be careful, not leaving this room during his experiments. Albert worked through electronic connections. All the blood work had been done in the medbot's small but powerful workup kit. He tried to check Albert's progress and failed. His eyes refused to focus on the readouts that would tell whether he had found the appropriate IGG factor in his blood required to generate either an inoculation against the plague or an outright cure.

"You sound awful, Leo."

"That's what is great about me, notable sex appeal. The women all line up for hours to tell me how rotten I sound." Burch collapsed to his bed, this small banter tiring him. He began gasping again. Albert helped with the constricting metallic tentacle until Burch was able to continue breathing without assistance.

"I'm coming in, Leo. You need a doctor. Where's Albert?"

"Albert's not a doctor—and don't come in!"

"Why did you weld the door shut?"

"Anita, leave me be. I'm going to be fine." Even as he spoke, he knew she heard the lie in his tone.

Anita Tarleton left. Burch closed his eyes but sleep refused to come. He wondered if Albert still worked on the chore of isolating the Infinity Plague virus and working up a counter-agent. He couldn't stir himself enough to see.

"Leo?" He heard his name called, as if from light-years off. "I've got the way to break in, if I have to. Are you going to make me use the laser torch to cut through?"

"Go away, Anita. Go away. You don't understand."

"Make me understand." She hesitated, then said in a low voice, "It's the plague. What have you done, Leo? Tell me!"

"It's all Jerome's fault," he said. "He started his work in computer simulation. I came across a good result while he was down and out, some fever he'd picked up from the Frinn by the look of it. I stole his results. He never knew. He thought that line of inquiry was discarded by the computer. I started the computer on another program, a bogus one."

"The plague, Leo. What about it?"

"I've got it."

"You can't. It didn't work in humans. I have the reports."

"I did some gengineering on it. You're not the only whiz in the lab, Anita. I accomplished what you had tried and failed." Burch coughed. He noted almost clinically how difficult it was for his body to perform autonomic responses. Coughing, sneezing, breathing, they all grew increasingly difficult to do.

"You have the plague?" Anita's disbelief rang in her words. "This isn't some disease we picked up from the Frinn?"

"I'm sure. I isolated the virus, did a crystallography workup on it, did some splicing using the gamma-ray cutter according to Walden's computer guesswork, and voilà! I have a full-blown case of the plague."

"We need to tend you, Leo. You'll die. You saw what it did to the Frinn."

"It's doing the same thing to me. Albert's doing all he can, but I don't want to spread it. That's why I sealed the room. Don't unseal it." Burch slipped into unconsciousness. The strain of speaking with Anita had drained him.

"Albert, are you there?" called Anita. She tapped her fingers impatiently against the intercom beside the doctor's door. She wished Leo had installed a standard vidscreen link as everyone else had done aboard the *Hippocrates*. She knew the reason he hadn't, though.

He had spied for the Sov-Lats and needed privacy beyond that of others.

"Working," came the medbot's calm mechanical voice.

"Give me a full status report."

"Still working. There is no progress to report until the blood sample analysis is finished."

"What is the purpose of your testing?" She worried that Burch had lost control of the medbot. Her fear was realized.

"Cure of the Infinity Plague using Dr. Burch's blood as an active immuno-agent. Search for the appropriate IGG antibody continues."

"Damn," she said. She felt cut off, abandoned. Jerome Walden was planetside doing who knew what. The others in the research team had turned their back on the Infinity Plague, preferring to work on their own projects. She knew more than any of them, anyway. She had studied the preliminary reports and had proposed new avenues of research. In the twinkling of an eye, a medical doctor aboard a hospital ship had done the work that dozens of highly trained and often brilliant research scientists had failed at.

Anita sagged, resting her head against the bulkhead. Leo had one advantage. Walden had started the computer work, and Walden was nothing short of a genius.

How she could hate and love Walden at the same time was something Anita didn't try to understand. She rushed from Leo Burch's sealed door and found a vidscreen.

"Nakamura, we've got an emergency in the infirmary."

"More cases of the strange fever?" the woman asked. Past Nakamura on the bridge, Anita saw several of the navigation and communications officers wobbling from the disease. How they had become infected mattered less than how to stop the debilitating fever.

"Worse. Leo's got the Infinity Plague. He worked out the structure, did some gengineering on his own, and caught it. The symptoms resemble those in the Frinn."

"He has spread it?" Fear tinged Nakamura's voice for the first time. She glanced over her shoulder at the bridge officers.

"He's sealed in his quarters. I still believe the fever most of us have comes from contact with the Frinn. It *isn't* the Infinity Plague. This is."

Nakamura relaxed a little. ''What do you recommend? Our ability to fight and maneuver is impaired with so many falling ill. Hallucinations are a part of the disease's characterization.''

''Are the robot ships endangering us?''

''Yes, dammit,'' flared Nakamura. She quieted. ''We are unable to remain in orbit if this spreads further. There is no hint of contagion aboard the *Winston*, making me suspicious of the disease's source.''

Although Uvallae might have released it purposefully, she suspected Walden. This had the earmarks of something he might do to retaliate. She swallowed hard. He might even use it for blackmail to get what he wanted out of Nakamura.

Didn't he realize that the Frinn robots still attacked with unabated fury? There might not be a *Hippocrates* left because of his stupidity!

''The Infinity Plague is more important. It's a killer,'' Anita said. ''We were wrong about it not infecting us.''

''Break into Burch's quarters and learn all you can of the virus,'' ordered Nakamura.

''That might spread it throughout the ship,'' protested Anita. ''You know how it spread among the Frinn. It changes its vector. Sometimes it is airborne, other times it seems to enter through the skin. It never repeats itself symptomatically after the first case.''

''What do you recommend?''

''Link me with Jerome. If I can talk with him, I can get his notes out of the ship's computer. I might be able to duplicate Leo's work and help him.''

''Through a sealed door?'' Nakamura's attention focused elsewhere. She struggled at the command chair, using the laser wand constantly. Anita Tarleton wasn't sure she wanted to know what Nakamura faced—what they all faced. Death from the Infinity Plague might be secondary to being blown from space by the Frinn defenders.

''His medbot is inside with him. I can program Albert and maybe save him. It's our only chance.''

''You think Walden has a cure for the plague?''

''He was working on it. Leo didn't think so, but I'm not so sure. He might have kept it to himself.''

''Use your vidscreen. I will attempt to patch you through.

Speak quickly, however. There might not be a second chance.''

Anita clutched the sides of the small vidscreen in the infirmary. The patterns shifted from the bridge to jagged edges caused by a computer trying to establish a link to static fuzz. Over a minute later, Jerome Walden's face came into sharp focus. He was yelling at someone out of Anita's line of sight.

"Jerome, we have an emergency here."

"What else is new? I'm in the middle of one myself. We're surrounded by Frinn armor—and they aren't here to bring us milk and cookies. I don't know how we're going to get away with all our parts intact."

"Leo Burch used your computer work to purify and isolate the Infinity Plague virus. I need your code sequences to see what you were doing. He infected himself with the plague, Jerome. Do you understand?"

Walden's startled expression told her that he did.

"Your codes. I need to retrace what Leo's done. He's locked in his room with Albert trying to perfect a remedy for the plague."

"My notes are under the sequence ANITA ONE. But I didn't—"

"You pointed the way to gengineer the plague to infect humans. You were too sick at the time to realize it."

"Damned *menla* fever," Walden said.

"*Menla* fever? Is that what you have—what everyone on the *Hippocrates* has?"

"I have a cure for the Infinity Plague," Walden said. "I worked it out just before we left. It's not in my computer files." He quickly outlined what he had done and how he had isolated the virus.

"That sounds chancy," Anita said.

"So's dying."

"I'll try it on Leo. He's in a bad way. He . . ." Anita's voice trailed off when she realized that the com-link between the *Hippocrates* and the planet had broken. She didn't waste time trying to reestablish the link. Using her priority numbers, she accessed Walden's computer files and dumped them into her own. Then she put his formula for a vaccine into the computer also, requesting immediate concoction. Only then did she lean back and heave a deep sigh.

"Anita One?" she mused, shaking her head. She wasn't sure how to interpret Walden's use of her name as his security password.

The vidscreen flickered an acknowledgment that the processing equipment in the infirmary had begun work on the vaccine Walden carried with him on the planet. Anita saw that fabrication time was relatively short, less than four hours. Until then, she could do nothing more about the Infinity Plague but sit and fret and hope Leo Burch didn't die.

But on another front, especially the *menla* fever, she could work. Walden knew what it was; she would find out, also.

Anita Tarleton was still trying to isolate the cause of the alien fever when the alarms went off signaling a successful termination on the vaccine processing.

She worked slowly, methodically, not daring to make a mistake. If she had to rerun the vaccine, Leo Burch would be dead.

Injection vial in hand, she went to the secured door leading to Burch's quarters. She stopped and stared. She had forgotten that the doctor had sealed himself in.

"Albert, are you able to accept injectable fluids?"

"That is correct," the medbot responded.

"I'm going to drill through the bulkhead. Accept the fluid and inject it into Leo. Do you understand?"

"Is this a prescribed medicine?"

"I am a medical doctor. I am prescribing it for Dr. Burch's illness," she said, beginning work with the laser torch she'd brought. She worried as the bright light tongued the carbon composite and vaporized it. A small hole appeared, then enlarged as she swung the laser drill around and around. She shoved the vial through and slapped a patch over the hole. Anita spot welded it to the wall, surprised at how she sweat. Before she had finished resealing the room, she was drenched in sweat and shaking.

Such was the power of the Infinity Plague's threat.

"Do you have it, Albert?"

"Prepared to inject."

"Do so. This is a direct order."

"Injection completed," Albert reported.

Anita let out a long sigh and slid down the bulkhead, welcoming its coolness next to her flushed skin. She didn't even realize she slipped into a light sleep until Albert's beeping awoke her hours later.

"What is it, Albert?"

"This is Leo. You . . . your cure didn't work. I'm weaker. Levels of virus in my blood are up."

"It might take a while to work." She looked at her watch and moaned. The drug had been in Burch's system for almost five hours. If it was going to work, it must have begun by now.

"Viral levels up. Weaker than ever. Anita, whatever you gave me didn't work. I'm dying!"

She didn't have any words to soothe Leo Burch. In her way, she felt just as desolate.

CHAPTER
14

"Can she not help us?" asked Uvallae. The Frinn eyed the circle of deadly armament moving toward them.

"Anita is still back on the *Hippocrates*," Walden told his friend. "She's not able to do much except fight the plague. It's started among the crew. Leo Burch has it." Walden hadn't listened carefully to Anita's story about the genesis of the plague. It was enough to know that Leo had contracted it through whatever misadventure. Walden's feelings toward the man were still mixed, but no one deserved to die from it.

"Your cure. It will work for Frinn?" asked Uvallae. "You did not tell me you had solved this problem."

"I'm not sure. I have to find enough victims to test it. It won't matter unless we get out of here alive." He looked from Uvallae to the remaining two Frinn and saw no hope in their catlike eyes. They prepared to die in the sights of their own race's defensive weapons.

"Giving hope, then denying us is worse than having no hope at all," said Uvallae. "We could do so much to save my people, if only . . ."

Walden punched the com-link and sent a laser beam arrowing toward the attacking skirmish tanks. He linked with the one carrying Sgt. Hecht. He thanked every god he had ever encountered for his luck. He knew Sorbatchin would have ignored his plea.

"What can I do for you, Doc? We're on a hot attack pattern right now and can't break off. If we lose formation, they'll find our holes and come at us."

"We're ringed in, Sergeant. Can you break through somewhere? Or try to draw them after you?"

"That's a mighty tall order, Doc. We don't *need* more of them on our asses." The com-link broke apart as another hail of explosive pellets interrupted the laser beam. Walden started to despair until Hecht came back. "Hell, you only live once. We might as well do this up royal. Stand back and put your fingers in your ears. This'll get mighty damned noisy."

Walden saw tiny pinpoints of light spring up from the direction of the distant capital city. He knew that Hecht had launched something—but what?

"Get down and cover up. This might be nastier than he's letting on." Walden dived for sanctuary beside the cargo carrier. He slid along the ground just as the first explosion rocked the area. Wave after wave of detonation rolled down the hillside like marching giants. Then came heat so intense that it blistered the paint off the carrier. Stunned, one Frinn rose to survey the damage.

"Egad, get him. Bring him down!" shouted Walden, finally figuring out what Hecht had sent.

Egad scrambled to his bandy legs and plunged forward, crashing into the back of the Frinn's knees. The alien toppled like a tall tree in a forest. Before Uvallae could protest, heavy laser fire seared the area around them. The lasering went on for several minutes, then died. Only then did Walden poke his head up. A dozen of the attacking Frinn robot tanks had been destroyed. Those remaining spun and raced in the direction of the capital, where the true menace lay.

"What happened?" Uvallae asked in a quaking voice.

The first round had torn apart the hill to slow down the tank attack. The next, the heat, had brought up the thermal profiles of the metal. Hecht had already launched parachute-lasers. They came down slowly, locking on the augmented heat signatures of the robot tanks. By the time the chemical lasers had fired and exhausted their limited energy packs, they had hit the ground and were useless.

Or just about useless. Walden cautioned the Frinn against touching the devices should they see one. Any unused energy might be discharged from capacitors in a few microseconds, turning the device into a small but deadly antipersonnel bomb.

Walden guided the cargo carrier after the skirmish tanks—and the robot tanks—toward the Frinn's capital. The best speed he could squeeze out of the electric motor sent the carrier racing along at barely twenty kilometers an hour. The flatbed truck was made for moving heavy equipment, not for racing.

"Tell me what you can about the city. How did Nakamura pinpoint this one as the capital? I need to know what I can to figure out how best to proceed."

"There are only a half-dozen large cities on the planet," Uvallae said. "This was the largest. Knowing our predilection toward solitary pursuits, it was not difficult for her to guess that the largest became that way because of governmental power."

"Where are your factories?"

"Automated, in space. Many must have been destroyed by the *Winston*. The robot factories might have scavenged themselves to build the fleet of ships we encountered when we entered the system. When I left, we had no such space armament."

"It would take a while to build," agreed Walden. He guided the cargo carrier through the potholes left in the once-smooth grassy plain. The area surrounding the city was like a park. Grass had been neatly trimmed—or grew that way. Walden had often wondered why gengineered grass wasn't used on Earth. That was just another of the quirks a civilization developed as it evolved. Humanity had never trusted robots fully, either, and had kept them in secondary positions.

The Frinn obviously relied heavily on the AI machines. That reliance had saved them from immediate destruction at Nakamura's and Sorbatchin's hands. Even the tanks had the air of being hastily built. Everything Uvallae had said about the lack of strife among the Frinn appeared true. They ordered their robots to defend them—and stood back.

"There!" cried one of the other Frinn. "The city's defense perimeter!"

Walden blinked as a donut of pure energy launched upward, leaving an ionized trail behind. He had seen the compact toroid weapon used before, but it had been fired from a ship in space. The atmosphere attenuated the prodigious torus of energy too rapidly for it to be a true weapon, but Walden saw how it was being used. The ionization channel left behind afforded a laser the perfect path into space. The Frinn had not researched weapons adequately; they used wasteful makeshift devices such as this at every turn.

Only in this way could they hope to reach the orbiting *Hippocrates* with their ground-based lasers.

"What are they used for normally?" Walden asked, indicating the lasers firing steadily into the azure sky.

"Guidance. They track starships as they return. We prefer to detect our vessels from the ground."

"Why not do it from space?" asked Walden, steering around a particularly bad patch of chewed-up ground. The skirmish tanks had turned parts of the ground into glassy slag.

"Religious reasons," Uvallae said. From the terseness of the answer, Walden knew he wasn't likely to get more of an answer. It didn't matter to him. He had heard of Earth-based religions worshiping nature. The planet itself became a deity and the forces of wind and rain occupants of a pagan pantheon.

"Tell me all you can about the city. Where is Sorbatchin most likely to attack? Where can we do the most good? I need to set up a lab and run tests."

"The colonel will plunge through the outskirts and go directly to the government center, thinking he will find the controllers there."

"He won't?"

For the first time in weeks, Uvallae laughed. "The tallest building in Fuonm *is* the government's heart, but it is occupied only by computers and semimobile robots. They conduct day-to-day business. The organic controllers are scattered across the face of the planet. Our communications network is superb." Uvallae's mood darkened again. "It *was* superb when I left. The comsats are likely victims to any space-born attack."

"Nakamura isn't stupid enough to overlook them. Even if

she did, the *Winston*'s commander isn't. He's an old hand at
warfare in a vacuum. And everyone knows you cripple a
country by taking out its space eyes." New York City was
fifty meters underwater because the NAA had failed to detect
the Sov-Lat use of atomics just offshore. The Sov-Lats had
used IR lasers on two key detection satellites, then moved
their nukes in. The skirmish had ended with a tidal wave
more than a hundred meters high washing over Manhattan.

It had also marked the end of nukes as weapons on Earth;
retaliation had come with bioweapons.

"Our controllers serve until they no longer desire to do so,
then another takes their place," said Uvallae. "Anyone can
be a controller, and live anywhere on the planet."

"Are you a controller?"

"I resigned when I volunteered to serve as explorer."

"What if you get a bad controller?" asked Walden. "Aren't
the most venal the most likely to keep the power to themselves?"

"What power?" asked Uvallae, startled. "All a controller does is suggest. If the suggestion is wise, others follow.
If it is not, how can you enforce an ill-advised course of
action?"

Walden laughed. Life among the Frinn was decidedly different from that on earth. He hit the paving at the edge of
Fuonm and shook his head. The skirmish tanks had chewed
up the thin pavement, making the street almost impassable.

He wasn't sure he wanted to proceed deeper into the city—
if city was the word he sought. From space he had seen a
large area he had interpreted as a metropolitan complex. For
the Frinn, this was a major population center. For him, it was
hardly more than a spacious, poorly tenanted village.

"Drive in that direction," said Uvallae. "There is a hospital complex about ten kilometers distant."

"That's why we're here," Walden said. In the distance
he heard the rumble of the EPCT tanks and the firing of
missiles and crackling of heavy laser cannon. He was no
medical doctor, but he found himself torn between setting
up his experimental post and trying to find the cure for the
Infinity Plague and tending those injured by the EPCT attack. He pushed aside the notion of splinting limbs and ban-
daging wounds. He was a scientist, a researcher, and in the

long run could do more good by stopping the spread of the plague.

He guided the cargo carrier through the debris-strewn streets. The buildings were low, some distance away from the road and apparently deserted. Walden sent Egad afield to reconnoiter. The dog came loping back, easily overtaking the slowly moving truck. The gengineered dog's tongue lolled inside his helmet, convincing Walden that the dog was better off out of the environment suit.

Pulling to a stop, he stripped the suit from the dog, then got rid of his own. Having opened the face plate earlier, he knew there wasn't much protection being given by the thin, hot suit.

"Tell me what you saw," he urged Egad.

"Dead. All the pig-faces are dead. Week, maybe more. EPCTs didn't do it."

"The plague?" asked Uvallae.

Egad barked and wagged his tail. Uvallae got even more information from the animal through his acute sense of smell. Walden saw Uvallae's piglike snout working frantically to decipher what Egad told him. Walden didn't need this extra dimension to know that Egad had found desolation. He felt it himself. Everywhere he looked he saw pleasant houses and well-kept buildings—and no Frinn. It was as if they had dropped onto a ghost world.

Walden shuddered at the thought. It *was* a ghost world, a world peopled by ghosts human bioweapons work had created.

"Keep scouting. Look for survivors, Egad." The dog trotted off, happy to be free to roam. Being locked up in the *Hippocrates* had never suited Egad, and Walden was glad to give him this chance. It might not come again soon.

"There," said Uvallae, "there is the hospital."

Walden heaved a sigh of relief. For the first time he saw some evidence of living aliens. Movement against the upper windows of the five-story circular building hinted at more than mere robots rolling along their appointed service routes.

He pulled the cargo carrier up to the front door and got out. Walden felt suddenly out of place. He belonged to the invading race. Somewhere in the middle of Fuonm, Colonel Sorbatchin and the EPCTs killed and destroyed anything opposing them. Vulnerable and aware of it, Walden motioned to Uvallae to go in first. The Frinn nodded, as if knowing what Walden thought.

Walden began unloading the equipment crates, straining by himself. The other Frinn had vanished. He wrestled the last crate to the ground when Egad returned.

"This only place with pig-faces," the dog reported. "We go in?"

"We're going to wait until Uvallae gives us the all-clear sign," he said. His sense of foreboding grew. He tried to push it aside. He was only letting his paranoia take over. To hold the *menla* fever at bay, he used more pentagan.

It didn't do anything to erase his uneasiness.

"Think they will kill us?"

"Me, perhaps. You're safe, Egad. Uvallae can talk to you and you to him."

"Why can't you do like him?" asked the dog. "He can catch little smells as good as I can."

"We're all different. Their eyesight isn't as good as mine. Neither is yours."

"Hearing is better. Run faster."

"But not as long. I can still run you into the ground, if I put my mind to it."

"Do it!" challenged the dog. Egad wheeled and started to dash off. Walden almost tried but his weakness caught up with him. The *menla* fever drained him in ways he still hadn't assessed.

Saving him from humiliation before his dog, Uvallae called from the doorway, "Dr. Walden, this way. I have spoken with several controllers. It is difficult explaining to them what you wish to try. You might be better able to convince them that their cooperation is in everyone's interest."

Walden waved at Egad, then ducked into the building's cool, moist interior. For a few seconds he thought he had entered a large living plant. The walls were soft and yielding. The floor sprang back under his step and the sharp edges where floor met wall and corridors branched were muted and curving.

"We do not live as you do," said Uvallae. "I believe your quarters aboard the *Hippocrates* are similar to those on Earth.

Starlight is considered dangerous duty, not like living here. We are one with our housing. We tend it, it tends us.''

''I can see.'' Walden had the uncomfortable feeling of walking through a giant beast's intestine. He forced away the ramifications of such a stroll and followed Uvallae through the gently undulating passage until they came to a larger room.

The room reminded Walden of a huge stomach. He had to remind himself not to keep ducking to avoid an influx of stomach acid sent to digest him.

''Here, speak to the controllers. Forty are now connected through an emergency network.''

Walden expected to begin by defending Nakamura's invasion. He was again startled. The controllers didn't mention Sorbatchin's lunge into the heart of their capital or anything about what the *Hippocrates* and *Winston* must be doing to orbiting comsats and factories.

''The Infinity Plague, as Uvallae calls it, has raped our world,'' one woman said. It took Walden several seconds to reply. This was the first Frinn female he had seen—and he was certain she was female. Although lacking the obvious secondary sexual features of a mammal, she didn't have the powerful musculature of the males. Paints on her forehead might have been cosmetic; Walden wasn't going to venture a guess about their purpose. It didn't pay to assume his cultural values were shared by the Frinn.

''It was an accidental release,'' Walden said. He detailed all he had surmised about the plague and how he had spent countless hours working toward a cure. ''The splitting of your DNA must be prevented to inhibit the plague. The splitting has to be mended to work a cure,'' he said. ''I think the antiviral agent I've gengineered will stop the spread and even reverse the process, if it hasn't gone too far.''

''Why do you do this? Are you a traitor to your own species?'' asked another controller.

''Releasing the Infinity Plague was an accident, an unfortunate one that has caused too many of my people—and yours—to die. I want to rectify this error.''

''Others from your vessel pound away at the center of our culture with their weapons. Fuonm is being destroyed even as you claim to seek a solution to the plague.''

"Humans are not always of one mind, as are the Frinn," he said. Walden wasn't sure the aliens agreed on anything, yet they seemed to come to unanimous decisions. Perhaps Nakamura could appreciate this more, coming from a society ruled by consensus as she did. Walden wasn't sure if even the Japanese Hegemony enjoyed such unity of mind, though. In spite of what he thought about her, she and the Japanese were human, not alien in thought.

"I seek only to stop the plague. I do not want another Frinn to die from the product of my race's research."

"You lend your expertise to aid us?"

Walden nodded solemnly.

"We would speak with the other human," said still another controller.

Walden started to ask if they could patch through to the *Hippocrates*, preferring that they speak with Anita Tarleton rather than Nakamura. To his surprise, Uvallae brought in Egad. Walden didn't know if he should laugh or cry. The Frinn considered Egad to be human.

And wasn't he? For a dog, he was a genius. For a human, he was out of the ordinary. But Walden wasn't sure what the canine's viewpoint on any of these touchy problems was.

"Egad—"

Uvallae cut him off with a sharp gesture. The communication that went on after that was mostly silent. The surface-acoustic-wave detectors on the Frinn communicators were working overtime, Walden guessed. Egad barked and panted, moved about and rubbed against the SAW-detectors like a cat wanting its back scratched. After ten minutes, a controller broke off the "discussion."

"We are decided. Begin the work. Do what you can to stop the spread of the Infinity Plague."

The vidscreens scattered around the room all went blank at the same time. Uvallae motioned for Walden to follow again. This time they went to a room with more substantial floors and firmer walls. Walden felt more comfortable here—and the equipment he had left outside had been uncrated and set up.

"Do as you will," Uvallae said. "There are no fewer than fifty stricken with the plague willing to test your cures."

"Thank you," said Walden, already beginning to prepare his serum.

He worked twenty hours straight. And Jerome Walden saw his miracle cure for the Infinity Plague fail in forty-eight cases.

CHAPTER
15

"I can't believe my antiviral immune system booster didn't work. Not for a single victim," Jerome Walden moaned. "All my computer projections showed this to have the best chance for success. I don't know what happened."

"Can there have been an error?"

"Dammit, yes!" Walden spun on Uvallae. "Of course there was a mistake. I made it. I just killed fifty of your brothers! Forty-eight died immediately; it took a day longer for the remaining two."

"You did nothing to kill them. Not directly," Uvallae said softly, trying to ease Walden's anguish.

"I did. I said I could save them." Walden stared at the corner of the room where part of the wall grew a large flap and enfolded the last of his experimental subjects. The living membrane absorbed the corpse and assimilated it. Walden had warned Uvallae that this might contaminate the hospital, spreading the Infinity Plague through the walls. The Frinn had not thought this likely. Too many were now dying for regular ceremony in the overcrowded cemeteries.

"You are not a god," Uvallae said. "You tried and failed. The unwrapping of the DNA had gone too far in these subjects. Perhaps the antiviral drug might be used as a vaccine to prevent the plague from taking hold."

"No," Walden said dejectedly. "It wasn't intended to be a vaccine. I really thought it would work."

"Colonel Sorbatchin has demanded the complete surrender of the planet. The controllers are debating the point."

"Let me talk with Sorbatchin. I'll try to convince him that he has to do something to slow the spread of the plague. If he's going to be military governor—"

"We have not yet surrendered," Uvallae pointed out. "We have allowed Sorbatchin to do as he wishes within the confines of Fuonm. This city is *not* the planet. Controllers from across the world suggest destroying the entire capital to rid ourselves permanently of his presence."

"Sorbatchin is no fool. He recognizes the possibility that you'd destroy the city to get him."

"We can do it if it is agreed upon," Uvallae said with assurance. "The widespread use of robots is not our only significant difference from your culture."

"Don't tell me how you'd do it. I don't want to know. All I want to do is stop the plague."

"Your single-minded drive toward this goal is a credit to you, Dr. Walden. However, we have other, more pressing problems. The colonel is but one of the more immediate."

"I know, I know." Walden closed his eyes and shivered. The *menla* fever attacks hadn't worsened—but they hadn't lessened in their severity either. He felt alternately feverish and cold, and the hallucinations sometimes frightened him and kept him from sleeping easily. If only he could separate them from reality.

"Isolation has prevented more of my people from becoming infected," said Uvallae, trying to soothe Walden's guilty conscience. "Try as it might, the Infinity Plague cannot reach them all."

"That's not what I'm seeing. It starts in a form that destroys the autonomic system. It mutates into something else. Organs fail. It's passed along to others by still another vector. It might be an insect vector. If it is infecting a native insect, this means the entire world is rife with the infection. You might consider getting your healthy populace into space and then burning off the world just to rid it of the plague virus. Even this might not be enough."

"There is a protective protein sheath around the virus,"

said Uvallae, nodding. "I know that this might prevent even hard gamma radiation from harming the virus. I witnessed your excellent work tracking down the changes it undergoes."

"It always follows the same evolution. Why? This is tearing me apart, Uvallae. I can't sleep. The *menla* fever is driving me crazy. And I'm failing. I need Anita's help. I need the computer aboard the *Hippocrates*."

"Return," the Frinn said easily.

"Just like that? You want me to leave?"

"Leave, stay, do whatever you feel is best."

"You're being awfully fatalistic about this. It's the fate of your world that's hanging in the balance."

"For the moment, the plague is not spreading as fast as after the exploratory ship returned. Colonel Sorbatchin's threats require more immediate action by our controllers. Why worry about dying from the Infinity Plague if a rocket is likely to blow apart your house in a few seconds?"

"He might not listen to me. I'll try to reach him."

"No, he will not listen to you," said Uvallae. "He speaks only to the *Hippocrates* and to one controller. He refuses to believe more than one person rules my world."

"The Sov-Lat Pact is ruled by a troika. Three out of two billion control everything. I can understand why he thinks your world is run the same way. Cultural myopia." Walden closed his eyes and tried to force away the phantasms edging into his vision. The death he had seen on Delta Cygnus 4 returned to haunt him. Men blown apart. An entire Sov-Lat research facility nuked seconds after he had escaped. And the first contact with the Frinn. How he and the EPCTs with him had botched that meeting.

Walden shivered and wrapped his arms around himself. A soft warmth crept up his back and made him feel good. He relaxed and the crazy hallucination—the vivid memories—went away. He jerked away with a start when he realized the wall was folding a membranous flap over him, swallowing him as it did the dead Frinn.

"It soothes, protects, heals," said Uvallae. "It is as much a philosophical healing as a physical one."

"It took the bodies . . ."

"It serves many purposes, as does your research. You might

find bioweapons, but you also find biocures. The techniques of research are similar.''

"Similar," muttered Walden, still suspicious of the wall's warm, cloying extension even touching him. "You might be right about contacting the *Hippocrates* and getting back to my laboratory. Is there a circuit open I might use?''

"There is only the com-link Dr. Tarleton used to reach you after we landed.''

Walden grumbled to himself. He remembered so little of Anita's call. Something about Leo Burch, and something about the Infinity Plague. He had been trying like hell to avoid the Frinn robot tanks and hadn't paid her much attention. The circuit had been cut too quickly and he hadn't had a chance to speak with her at length. Now he wished he had tried. It had been almost a week—and fifty Frinn under his personal care had died.

Over and over, he returned to his failure. Fifty sentient beings infected with the Infinity Plague had died because of his lack of a decent cure. Never before had he struck such a barrier or been so aware of the result of his failure.

He thought grimly that had he failed before in devising a bioweapon, people *wouldn't* have died. Failure would have been success, in its own way. But now? He forced himself to channel his emotions toward solving the problem, not futilely dwelling on it.

"If you establish contact with the *Hippocrates*, let me know. I need to use the computer and lab equipment up there.''

Uvallae nodded and left the room. Egad trotted in and dropped at Walden's feet. The dog's long tongue lolled out as he panted.

"Been chasing rabbits?'' Walden asked.

"Scouting,'' the dog corrected. "Nice animals to run down. But so lonely here.''

Walden heaved a sigh. He knew what Egad meant. The world had never been bustling in the sense of a human-settled planet. The Frinn did not socialize in the same way that the more extroverted humans did, but even on a world of solitary beings, the profound silence stretched interminably. Knowing the cause did little to help banish the notion of eternal emptiness.

"We might be going back to the ship," Walden said. "Uvallae is trying to reach Nakamura now."

"All dead?"

Walden couldn't answer. He had failed.

"Dr. Walden!" came the call from down the strange, living hospital corridor. "We have a com-link. It might not last long."

Walden jumped to the small vid unit from the cargo carrier. The vidscreen shimmered and focused, giving him a clear two-dimensional picture of Miko Nakamura.

"What success, Doctor?"

"I need to use the ship's equipment." He quickly outlined how he had failed with what he'd hoped was a cure.

"It is good that you desire to return," Nakamura said. "Dr. Burch's condition is critical."

"Did he really infect himself with the Infinity Plague?"

"Dr. Tarleton feels that this is so."

Walden had to guess at many of Nakamura's softly spoken words. The reception quality faded drastically. Shouting, he demanded a shuttle to pick him up.

"Colonel Sorbatchin must be alerted. Shuttle will land within the hour. Home in . . ." Nakamura's picture faded and her words were lost in a hash of static.

"We're going home," Walden told Egad. The gengineered dog shook his big, shaggy head.

"Want to stay. Please."

The request startled Walden. Then he realized that Egad was free to roam and run at will for the first time in almost a year. The *Hippocrates* was no fit place for a dog, much less one as inquisitive and smart as Egad.

"You stay. I'll be back for you. Do what Uvallae tells you, all right?"

"Can't bite the cat-shit colonel?" Egad cocked his head to one side, watching Walden with his mismatched eyes.

"No," Walden said, realizing the dog made a slight joke. "I don't want you poisoning yourself." He patted Egad and then worked to get his notebooks packed for the trip back to the *Hippocrates*.

Nakamura's appraisal of the shuttle's arrival time was precise. Within three hours, he again walked the metal and composite corridors of the hospital ship.

• • •

"He welded himself in?" Walden ran his fingers along the sealed door leading to Leo Burch's quarters. "What's his condition?"

"Still alive," said Anita Tarleton, "but barely. I have some updates from Albert. They don't look promising."

"He actually solved the problem you couldn't—and I failed at?" Walden shook his head. It was easy to claim the alien fever still bringing him occasional hallucinations had dulled his research skills. But the man responsible for the breakthrough wasn't a trained scientist. He was only a medical doctor.

A medical doctor and a traitor.

Anita accurately read the emotions crossing his face. "He wanted to make retribution for what he did," she said. "You solved the problem but didn't know it. The *menla* fever ran wild in you, and Leo took your computer work while you were hallucinating."

"He started the program on another tack?" Walden felt better at learning this—but not much.

"He did some neat gengineering work of his own, using our equipment. The X-ray results are in the computer, but the actual synthesis of the virus isn't."

"Are you sure he's got the Infinity Plague and not some derivative?"

"It might have mutated, but his symptoms are classic from all I've seen with the Frinn victims."

Walden dropped a pair of cerampic computer block circuits into her hand. "Here are photos and field analysis of everything I saw and did on the planet. I hope they help." He turned back to the door and ran his finger along the door.

"You can't go in there. We can get what we need from Albert."

"You said it was acting sporadically. The medbot might be damaged."

"He's working on a vaccine. I don't think he held out any hope for a cure."

"First a vaccine, then a cure," muttered Walden. "That's just the reverse of what we need. Can we reroute the medbot's processing to the ship's computer?"

''No need,'' came a raspy voice over the door annunciator. ''Albert's doing good work. Let him keep on.''

''Leo! What's happening?'' Walden demanded. ''Report on your condition. I can see the med-scan Albert is sending. I want to know how you feel.''

''I'm a dead man, Jerome. But it won't be in vain. Have you left the room sealed?''

Walden looked at Anita, who pointed to the small hole in the wall where she had passed through the antiviral agent Walden had staked so much on.

''Anita gave Albert a drug to counter the virus. It didn't work on the Frinn. Did it on you? The readings are a mishmash.''

''Didn't work on me, either,'' Burch reported. ''But Albert is working on it. He'll come through.''

''He's draining you of blood. You'll die of anemia!''

''Can't breathe anyway. Have to rely on mechanical contraction. So tired, so damned tired all the time. Thank heavens for Albert.''

Walden pounded his fist against the wall, feeling helpless. His mind raced and then came to the only conclusion possible. ''I've got to go in. Get me a complete isolation unit. I'll suit up, but I want the entire infirmary quarantined.''

''All right,'' Anita said quietly. ''I've already gotten authorization for you to use the ship's computer whenever you want. Nakamura isn't having to fend off the constant robot attacks.''

''We've finally worn them down,'' Walden said, feeling worn down himself.

''Why are you doing this?'' Anita asked. ''You don't have to try to save Leo. He may be beyond that—probably is.''

''I've spent my life thinking up ways to kill. Now it's time for me to use some of that knowledge to save a few lives.'' Through force of will he kept the bitterness from his voice. Save? Who was he saving? Not the Frinn, not Leo Burch.

''He's got it!'' came Burch's excited words. ''Albert's isolated the immune stimulus factors needed to fight the plague. Plug in, get the information dump. What a medbot!''

Anita worked at the computer for a few seconds, then nodded. She had the information Leo Burch was dying to obtain. Walden stared at the vidscreen filling with data. Some of it looked familiar; it was the point where Burch had stolen his computer work and taken off with it. Walden had thought it was all a null result. But he had to give Burch his due. The man had pushed back the boundaries of knowledge and had done original work, good work.

It seemed a shame that he had to die for it.

"I'll be inside in a few minutes, Leo," he told the other doctor. "Anita is starting up the automated vat to synthesize enough serum to counter the Infinity Plague in you."

"Too far gone, Jerome. Can't even move. Albert reports massive organ failure, but I noticed some of that years ago with the ladies."

"Leo, stop joking."

"All right." The deadly calm to his voice frightened Walden. He had heard this tone before from men ready to kill themselves. A curious calm descended on them, their decision made. They had come to peace with themselves and the world and nothing mattered.

"Don't, Leo. Don't do it. I'll help. Anita and I can—"

"The entire chamber is being filled with almost pure oxygen. Clear the outer corridors. Seal the airtights as far back from the infirmary as you can. When I blow the place, I want to go through the outer hull and into space. Burial in vacuum. Seems fitting."

"I can't do that, Leo. You've succeeded. You've done what we couldn't, what my entire research team couldn't."

"They weren't interested, Jerome. Don't kid a kidder. Clear the area or there'll be casualties."

"Nakamura isn't going to like this," Walden said, trying to find the proper words to stop him. All he got was a chuckle.

"Good. I'm sorry for all I've done, Jerome. Truly. This doesn't make up for many of the things, but no one ever said you had to cancel the bad with the good before checking out. Good-bye."

"Leo!"

Albert provided the spark that ignited the almost pure oxygen atmosphere. The *Hippocrates* shook and Walden was thrown backward by the explosion. Cracks appeared in the tough carbon composite wall between the infirmary and Burch's quarters. The high-pitched whistle told Walden that they were leaking atmosphere.

He punched the emergency button and got a repair crew to fix the cracks. He had to wait almost twenty minutes before they finished with the more important chore of sealing the hole Burch had blown in the *Hippocrates'* exterior. When they started work in the infirmary, they ended up laminating the entire bulkhead.

"A hell of a way to go," Walden said, staring at the fresh patchwork.

"The computer likes the structure for his antiviral. It's similar to the one you came up with but attaches to a different receptor site. Immune response is extreme and specific to the Infinity Plague."

"To the Infinity Plague in humans," Walden said tiredly. "But does it work in Frinn, also?"

The only way they could find out was to try, and Walden had exhausted the trust Uvallae and the others had in him.

CHAPTER
16

"The repairs are minor to remedy Dr. Burch's unorthodox
. . . departure," said Miko Nakamura. "The damage sustained from the Frinn attacks on the *Hippocrates* before
reaching orbit were worse. The exterior overhaul crews work
well on such damage. The interior destruction is of little concern since we have no immediate plans to use the infirmary."
Nakamura settled back in the command chair, the laser command wand flashing off and on as she scanned the control
boards behind Walden and Anita.

Walden wanted to reach out and block the infrared beam
and see if this would get the woman's attention. She focused
solely on the damage to the ship. Leo Burch, for all his shortcomings, was a human being and had died under emotional
duress. Walden wanted to scream, to reach out and shake
Nakamura to make her understand the importance of the
man's sacrifice and death.

"We think we can save the Frinn," Anita said. "We have
to know if the Burch immune system stimulator will work on
them, though. I've run computer projections and the antiviral
agent looks good for humans. But for the aliens . . ." Anita
Tarleton shrugged and looked at Walden for support.

He saw that Nakamura wasn't listening. She had a small
earphone plugged in giving her a continual flow of informa-

tion. Walden glanced past her at Captain Belford. The man stood gray-faced and unmoving. Like many onboard, he had contracted the *menla* fever released by Uvallae. Walden wondered if the time was right to use this card to gain what he wanted. Nakamura had shown little interest in finding a cure, preferring to let the disease run its course.

Walden knew from personal experience that the alien disease was controllable through drugs and the proper mind-set, but it also didn't go away. The human biosystem didn't produce the right phagocytes to destroy it. He was as possessed of the virus now as he had been when he had accidentally contracted it, probably on Starlight. It might not kill but it hung over his head like a Sword of Damocles.

"Colonel Sorbatchin has lost another skirmish tank and its crew," Nakamura said suddenly. "He has only three tanks and twenty EPCTs remaining from the initial invasion force. But the pacification proceeds well. He speaks of a quick end to the conflict."

"Has he spoken with the Frinn controllers?" asked Walden.

This got Nakamura's attention. The woman's cold eyes focused on him. "It will not be necessary. Their robotic attacks diminish. We have fought a war of attrition and won."

"Attrition? After only ten days of fighting on-planet?"

"The Infinity Plague wore them down before we arrived."

"The plague has been temporarily checked, but it's not contained."

"You state my point for me. The plague has weakened them to the point of surrender."

Walden laughed harshly. "You *haven't* spoken with the controllers. I have. I tried to halt the plague in fifty victims and failed. The controllers might take this as a sign that we didn't do enough for them and that now they should really fight."

"Really fight, Doctor?" Nakamura sneered. "They hit us with robot spacecraft when we dropped into their system. There were space mines. Sorbatchin faced every land-based armament they could throw at him. We prevailed in space. He prevailed on their planet. We have won an unconditional victory. We do not need their formal surrender to acknowledge our supremacy."

"There's more that they can do. This is a strange and alien world. Their hospital isn't what we'd—" Walden stopped talking abruptly when Nakamura turned from him to tend other problems.

"I'm not doing any better with her than I am with the Frinn," he said to Anita. "I've got to get back to the lab. I need more confidence in my results."

"In Leo's results, you mean," she said.

Walden didn't argue the point. Burch had stolen his research and then had botched the experiments establishing parameters for the plague virus. His only real accomplishment lay in gengineering the Infinity Plague to infect humans.

Walden wasn't sure that was any accomplishment at all, not in this company.

He wished Egad had come back to the ship with him, but he understood the gengineered dog's reluctance to return. Being enclosed wasn't natural for the animal, even though he had grown up in labs and had spent much of his time aboard the *Hippocrates*. That didn't make his absence any less painful for Walden. More than any of the humans aboard the ship, Egad was his friend.

Standing in the doorway of his lab brought back all the work he had done—and had failed to do. He went to the large analyzer and started it processing. The computer-driven machine lacked the explicit artificial intelligence shown by most of the Frinn's mobile machines, but Walden had confidence in it. He had grown up on Earth and had a touch of distrust for robots. Even worse than this, he was developing the normal citizen's uneasiness about gengineered products. Few had ever reached the public eye because of the biowar research products.

"Analyzing, processing," the machine told him in its mechanical voice. Walden smiled crookedly; he knew exact human voices could have been programmed into the machine. That one hadn't allowed humans to keep at arm's length from the computer-run world and retain a sense of superiority.

Readouts showed the progress being made. Walden turned from it and went to the computer console and began working. He stared hard at the data parading across the vidscreen, as if this could give him the results he wanted.

"*Menla* fever has reduced the *Hippocrates*' efficiency by

more than fifty percent," he muttered to himself. It seemed too early to reveal what he knew of the fever and force Nakamura into doing—what?

Walden wasn't sure what had to be done to save the Frinn. Sorbatchin roamed through their capital city, thinking he had taken control of the entire world. Walden didn't know what defenses the Frinn held in reserve outside the cities, but he thought they might be significant. They still adjusted to the human way of waging war—of waging *any* kind of war.

If he waited too long to use the knowledge that the alien fever spreading throughout the *Hippocrates* wasn't the Infinity Plague, he might lose all advantage it gave him. Nakamura wasn't the kind to let any epidemic impair her command too long.

Walden sighed. He wished everything had worked out for him on-planet. Frinn still died from the plague. He had sentenced too many to death because he'd thought he had the answer, because Leo Burch had hidden the computer results from him that might have given him a true cure.

He fell asleep with hallucinations caused by the *menla* fever dancing through his brain.

"What do you mean Sorbatchin is jamming transmission? Why should he bother?" Walden stared at Nakamura in wonder.

"He has gone rogue. I am no longer in command of the EPCT unit on-planet," she answered.

Walden looked at Anita, who averted her eyes. He wondered what she knew that she wasn't telling. She and Sorbatchin had worked closely before the Sov-Lat officer had gone down to find glory conquering a peaceful, relatively defenseless world.

"You wanted him to die down there, didn't you?" he accused.

"It would not have been a major calamity to acknowledge his contribution—and his death," Nakamura admitted. "However, this is more than a passing problem. I cannot use the *Winston*'s firepower, diminished though it is, against the city without reducing it to rubble. There is no clear indication Sorbatchin has remained within the confines of the captured city."

"I can find out where he is if you patch me through to Uvallae. You can use the same com-link Anita and I used earlier."

"I have tried it. There is little hope we can reestablish the link."

"Drop a message packet," Walden said irritably. "I need to get in touch with Uvallae."

"You have finished your work?" asked Nakamura, suddenly sly. "You can cure the Frinn of the Infinity Plague?"

"I hope so. Delivering the vaccine is a matter of considerable diplomatic delicacy, though. They aren't inclined to trust any of us too far. I've got to use Egad as a go-between. He can convince them of my sincerity."

"Uvallae is convinced of your candor in these matters," Nakamura said. "He might not believe that you've come up with another remedy for the virus, though."

"He'll believe it. He has to. I've already produced enough of the human blood component for an IGG immuno-factor to inoculate everyone on the *Hippocrates*."

"This is Dr. Burch's legacy," Nakamura said softly. Her eyes focused elsewhere. Walden was sure he was losing her attention as other reports were fed into her earphone. Whatever current crisis built took her full concentration.

"The Frinn *need* this," he said. "Put me in a shuttle and—"

"That would prove too dangerous, Doctor," Nakamura said. "Observe our last attempt to land a probe on the planet near the capital city." The big vidscreen at the front of the bridge flickered and came up in three-dimensional display of a small landing craft from the *Winston*. The small vessel rolled over to equalize the heating on its hull. It exploded with such violence that Walden threw up his hands to shield his face from the vidscreen image.

"A rocket fired from the planet destroyed it," Nakamura said. "We have every reason to believe Sorbatchin is consolidating his position there. He wants to be the commissar of an entire world."

"Let him, if he lets me land and administer the new medicinals to the Frinn."

"He is not inclined to do so. He considers the aliens a bother."

"As do you," Walden said with increasing bitterness. If they would quit their squabbling and power games and let him work, he could cure the world of its viral misery in the span of a month. He knew it. All Walden needed was the chance to deliver the new serum to the Frinn.

"They intrude on my plans," said Nakamura.

"This isn't like the other time," spoke up Anita. "I've checked Jerome's calculations. The computer projections show a ninety-five percent confidence level for success. We can inoculate and prevent the plague and, with Burch's work, even reverse the course of the plague in those already stricken."

"The inoculations for everyone aboard the *Hippocrates* are appreciated," the woman said. Her sallow complexion had turned waxy. Walden wondered if she ever left the command chair. The laser wand that activated the light toggles across the control panel seemed a permanent fixture in Nakamura's hand now.

"Let me finish the job," Walden begged. "No one wanted the Frinn to be infected. We can reverse it and get on with establishing diplomatic relations."

"It has gone past that, Jerome," Anita said. "Vladimir isn't going to agree to any peaceful solution short of completing his genocide. And I doubt Nakamura will, either."

"No wonder the NAA and the Sov-Lats are always wrangling back on Earth. Both sides think alike."

"We contribute to the madness. We're the ones supplying them their weapons."

He looked at her sharply. "What did you give Sorbatchin? You worked on another bioweapon for him. You completed it?"

"I did. There wasn't a chance to test it, though."

"What—never mind," Walden said. He didn't want to know what it did. All he wanted to do was unwind the shroud already wrapped around the Frinn. The Infinity Plague never died, it simply changed. Even in their isolation it would find ways of passing among them and killing them. Its incredible mutability assured that.

Walden glanced over his shoulder and saw many of the bridge officers thrashing about. The *menla* fever worked on them. Captain Belford walked like a zombie through their ranks, dispensing injections of the very drugs that Nakamura used to keep him docile.

"What if we mutinied?" Walden said suddenly. "What if we seized control from Nakamura and turned the ship back over to Captain Belford? We could wash his system of drugs in a few days. We'd be able to deal with Sorbatchin later."

"Do not try it," Nakamura said in a cold voice that brooked no challenge. Walden hadn't even realized the woman had been listening—or could from halfway across the bridge. Her spy devices might be anywhere, everywhere.

"I should imprison you for such talk, Doctor." She went on, "However, I believe you know something about the disease affecting so many of my crew. Cure them, then I will consider allowing you to work on-planet with the Frinn."

Walden saw that the level of the alien fever now annoyed Nakamura. If it increased to where she worried more, he might have a better bargaining lever. Or perhaps not. He might lose any chance if she forced others on his research team to find a cure of Uvallae's *menla* fever.

Walden left, Anita close behind. In a low voice she told him, "Nakamura is lying. She won't let you try. She wants the Frinn dead. An entire uninhabited world is easier to debate than one filled with the original owners."

"Neither the NAA nor the Japanese Hegemony would allow her to remain in charge," Walden said. Even as he spoke, he wondered. If she eradicated the aliens, why wouldn't the NAA look favorably on her? After the destruction of the Delta Cygnus 4 research colony, humanity's leaders might approve of genocide as a means of retaliation.

It turned so many complex problems into simple ones.

"She's caught in a bind right now," said Anita. "Even though she doesn't dare admit it, the *Winston* is too damaged to attack Sorbatchin. If he doesn't do anything stupid, he can control the entire surface of the world. Before long, he will have constructed the means to blow both the *Winston* and the *Hippocrates* out of orbit. When that happens, he's undisputed ruler of a world."

"The Frinn won't let him do that," Walden said firmly. "They fought back with machines, but there's more to their biology than meets the eye. They're solitary beings because they live so closely with certain plants. It's not a symbiosis, but it might be close. The hospital—"

"I've heard about it," Anita said. "The walls wrap the patients and somehow heal them. It explains why the Frinn haven't bothered to develop their biologic sciences more than they have. Everything is done for them."

"I've got to get in touch with Uvallae," Walden said in frustration. "It's the only way I can find out if delivering the serum will help. It might be too late."

"There's a small chance you can make it back down. Nakamura doesn't know everything that goes on aboard the *Hippocrates*. I've been talking with a com officer and he showed me a small laser port we might use. It'd just be a line-of-sight com-link, but you might be able to get through."

"A few minutes is all I need. Information," he grumbled. "It's so important and so hard to get."

"What about the *menla* fever? Nakamura wants that quashed before anything else."

"I've got my analyzer working on it. We and the Frinn aren't too different physiologically. We breathe the same air mixture, can eat the same food—"

"They need more iron than we do. There's also a lack of trace minerals in their blood," said Anita.

"Minor differences," insisted Walden. "The extra chromosomes are the only significant disparity between our species."

Anita Tarleton laughed at this. He knew she had spent more time working on the problem of anti-Frinn bioweapons and probably had uncovered areas unknown to him. He wished they had their old mutual faith back. If Sorbatchin and Nakamura were at odds, so were he and Anita Tarleton. And this hurt him deeply. What hurt even more, Anita didn't seem to miss the trust that had once existed between them.

"Here," she said. "Make it quick. You will only be over the capital for a few minutes, and you can bet Sorbatchin is monitoring everything from the *Hippocrates*."

Walden sat in front of the small com unit. He touched the console and got a two-dimensional picture on the vidscreen. Working methodically, he began sending his message.

"You got it!" called Anita. "The power surged. That means you've got a linkup!"

"Uvallae?" Walden peered at the tiny vidscreen and hoped.

"Walden, we need help," came the immediate answer. "The Infinity Plague spreads through our communications units. It transmits itself on the scent relays. We don't know how this is possible, but everyone on the planet is at risk."

"I've got another serum I need to try. Sorbatchin is blocking delivery. How can I get it to you?"

". . . help us," came the plea. The vidscreen shimmered and Uvallae leaped into focus. Walden's heart almost stopped. The Frinn was wrapped in the gentle folds of the hospital wall, the membrane working slowly to force the air from recalcitrant lungs.

"He has the Infinity Plague," muttered Anita.

"Uvallae!"

Walden's connection broke abruptly, Uvallae's suffering face replaced by Sorbatchin's clean-cut face.

"You deal with our enemy, Dr. Walden," the Sov-Lat officer chided. "Redeem yourself. Kill Nakamura and I will—"

The vidscreen went blank. Walden and Anita stared at each other. Miko Nakamura had intercepted the message.

What would the increasingly paranoid woman think? Had she heard Sorbatchin's request?

Walden pushed back from the vidscreen and got to his feet. The door to the small room burst inward, four armed crewmen blocking the only way out.

"You're under arrest for attempted mutiny," the leading crewman said with contempt.

In the face of their laserifles and the dancing red sighting dot centered on his chest, Jerome Walden could do nothing but surrender. With this surrender came the death of Uvallae and everyone on the alien's home world.

CHAPTER
17

"I can understand Leo Burch's motives for selling us out," said Nakamura, her eyes boring into Walden's. "I do not understand this drive toward treachery for no gain."

Jerome Walden started to tell the woman what he hoped to gain, then stopped. She wouldn't understand that he acted out of altruism. Walden paused before answering. He checked his own motives and shook his head sadly. What drove him was neither altruism nor love for the Frinn. It was guilt for all the deadly research he had done over the years. He had never really thought his bioweapons would be used for anything but defensive purposes, if they were used at all. That they had appalled him.

He, like Burch, wanted to atone for his past deeds. To do so, he had to cure the Frinn. The Infinity Plague wasn't their doing; they had done nothing to deserve such a fate except try to deal with humanity honestly and fairly.

"What you might understand, then, is that your officers are dying." Walden pointed to a bridge officer sitting in the far corner, shaking and clutching his knees tightly to his chest. Walden had no idea what hallucinations tormented the man, but they were obviously extreme. The officer's eyes looked like giant radar dishes, crisscrossed with the thin lacing of burning red blood vessels. The pupils had turned to black holes and sweat poured down his face.

"It'll get worse," Walden said.

"You *do* know of this!" cried Nakamura.

Walden glanced at Anita Tarleton. She had guessed he knew more about the *menla* fever than he'd said. What he said now would come as no real surprise to her.

"I do. I contracted a case on Starlight. You and Sorbatchin were too busy with your invasion plans to notice."

"You spread it throughout the *Hippocrates*?"

"No, Uvallae did that. He saw what had happened on his world and wanted to strike back. This was the only way he knew how. He synthesized the alien virus in his lab and released it through the ship's air system."

"Nonsense," scoffed Nakamura. "The filters would take out any disease-causing particle."

"He introduced it past the main filtration system. The room filters aren't adequate for the task. They only remove dust." Walden pointed to the small electrostatic units spaced around the bridge. "The virus is smaller than ten microns."

Nakamura touched the keypad on the arm of the command chair. The vidscreen blossomed with numbers. The darkness settling on her face told Walden that she had found the answer—and he was right.

"You're responsible. I should have you executed!"

"But you won't," cut in Anita. "You can't."

"You're in this with him—with Sorbatchin! I know you worked on bioweapons for the colonel. Was this one of them?"

"Uvallae released the *menla* fever," insisted Walden, wanting to keep Anita free of the controversy. He wanted to know what weapons she had fashioned for Sorbatchin, but this wasn't the time to muddy the waters with extraneous arguments.

"But Colonel Sorbatchin wanted the weapons before he landed on their world," said Nakamura. "How do I know he didn't use Dr. Tarleton's bioweapon aboard the *Hippocrates* before leaving? He might think we would all die, leaving him in sole control!"

"He didn't," Anita said quietly, forcing Nakamura to calm herself. Walden worried about Nakamura's stability. He had always thought she was the epitome of calm and serenity. She kept her head when everyone around her was panicking. No longer.

Or was it? Did Nakamura play a role to elicit more information? Walden didn't think so. Her responses were too real. He thought it more likely that she had become infected with Uvallae's virus, too, and this was the way she reacted. Others hallucinated, Nakamura lost her emotional control.

"He didn't take *any* of the work I did with him," said Anita. "It's only now reaching the full synthesis—and it is of absolutely no use against humans."

"Like the Infinity Plague," muttered Walden. He remembered how Burch had worked wonders and altered the plague working in seclusion from others on the research staff. It was nothing short of a miracle that he hadn't released the deadly mutating plague inside the ship before he died.

"Execute them both," Nakamura said, using her laser command wand to signal the crewmen acting as guards.

Walden jerked free as one took his arm. "Do that and you're dead, Nakamura. Are you feeling a little feverish yourself? Hallucinating? Or is your iron will keeping the phantasms under control? You're sweating. The bridge isn't that hot. Are you sure you're not dying from the *menla* fever? It isn't a pleasant way to die."

He saw that death held no horror for her. "It's too bad Sorbatchin will end up ruling this entire world. Only you can stop the Sov-Lats from claiming it."

"Will Sorbatchin turn it over to the troika or will he try to reach an agreement with them so he will share jointly in their power? He has an entire world to dicker with," said Anita, seeing Walden's tack and supporting him. The idea that Nakamura would so casually order her executed had shaken the red-haired woman. She, like Walden, fought for her life.

"He'll keep it for himself," said Walden. "Why share? Nobody within a hundred light-years is able to stop him from doing whatever he wants. He's blocking com from both our ships. No one's going to get through to the EPCTs to challenge his authority."

"I am not dying," Nakamura said positively. "I am

medicating myself and devoting several hours a day to meditation.''

"Meditation, medication, it doesn't matter," said Anita. "You have to know how the *menla* fever works to cure it."

"You can cure it?" Nakamura speared Anita with a hot and barren look.

"I can't, not by myself. Jerome and I working together can. We know enough about it."

"Why bother?" asked Walden. "If we do cure her—and the others in the crew—she'll only murder us when we've finished."

Nakamura glanced around, then used the laser wand to summon up a view on the vidscreen that caused Walden to turn cold inside. More of the *Hippocrates* crew had contracted Uvallae's fever than he had thought. He had only seen limited numbers of the bridge crew; Nakamura had replaced many of the stricken officers with those not as far progressed.

He almost blurted out that the *menla* fever wasn't fatal. If he had, Nakamura would have killed him with her iron-edged hand. She would never have forgone the pleasure of his death by allowing him to be executed by any of the crew.

"We can stop the spread. We can cure the ones who are already affected. Only we can do it."

"There are others in your research team. I have sequestered them. Chin, Klugel, Preston, Burnowski—all are separated from the crew. I have even put their research assistants out of . . . harm's way. I can get any of them to aid me. I do not need either of you."

"You do," Anita said with quiet assurance that rocked Nakamura. Walden saw this as another sign that Nakamura fought constantly against the fever with all her will. Never before had he seen her respond to such confidence with anything but complete certainty in her own abilities.

"What?"

"We can save the *Hippocrates*—and your expedition against Sorbatchin. You aren't going to let him remain on-planet and in control. We can cure the fever *and* give you the way to stop the colonel."

"What? How?"

"Execute us or guarantee us our liberty. You can't do both, Nakamura."

"Very well," the woman said quickly. "Cure the disease running rampant on this ship. And remove Sorbatchin as a thorn in my side. Do these things and yours shall be a position of power second only to mine in the new regime."

"We can't ask for any more than this, can we, Jerome?" Anita Tarleton stared at him, her green eyes unblinking. Walden wasn't sure if Anita played the game to save them or thought she could gain the upper hand on Nakamura later. It didn't matter what her motives were. Nakamura had backed down and had given him the chance he needed to save everyone.

Defeat the Infinity Plague, stop the spread of the *menla* fever, those were his priorities.

"Only if we're at your side," he said cautiously. "Nothing inferior to this position will do."

"Agreed," Nakamura said. "Now prepare your medications and get on with it. I cannot operate the *Hippocrates* properly with most of the crew hallucinating."

"We'll start immediately," Walden said, "but there has to be one further promise. No interference with our work. We cannot hope to solve the complex epidemiologic problems with meddling guards jostling our elbows."

"Done. You realize I shall be monitoring your progress, however." Nakamura used the IR wand to shift the vidscreen picture to the research labs where the others on his scientific team were hard at work on their own projects. He almost envied them. They worked oblivious to the troubles outside their small pedantic world.

He had done the same once. Then he had decided to accept responsibility for his actions and the eventual use of his research. It was a heavier burden and had not brought him immediate happiness. But it had brought him more peace of mind about the future.

Walden and Anita left the bridge. Once outside she asked him. "Do you have any ideas about the *menla* fever?"

"I was there when Uvallae released it," he admitted. "I did nothing then because I'd seen firsthand its effects. As terrible as they can be, the fever isn't fatal."

"Not in some of you," said Anita. "Two men shot each

other as they patrolled the halls. Who knows what they saw
stalking them.''

His lips pulled back into a thin, grim line. He had guessed
the infection had caused a few EPCTs aboard *Hippocrates* to
see their comrades as the enemy. Only that explained how
the rigid EPCT mental conditioning could have broken.

''It's not going to be as hard working out a cure for the
fever as it was for the Infinity Plague,'' he said. ''The analyzer can whip up a vaccine in a few hours. Within another
few hours we might be able to counter it in the body by
stimulating the immune system.''

''Don't you think I haven't tried doing that? I'm not stupid,
Jerome. A cure would have given me a strong bargaining
position with Nakamura. It's not going to be as easy as you
make it sound.''

He smiled confidently. He had more than a few hints about
how the fever worked. He had listened to Uvallae describe
its gestation and affect in the Frinn. For them it was hardly
more than a minor childhood disease. This discrepancy gave
him the starting point. Human and Frinn physiology and
biochemistry were similar—a computer check of dissimilar
elements would give him the answer in a few hours, as
promised.

Then he had to deliver the serum countering the Infinity
Plague even now being synthesized in his lab.

''It'll work out, Anita. Trust me.''

''Yeah, sure,'' she said glumly.

Walden closed his eyes and tried to remember when he
hadn't felt tired. Fourteen hours of intense work had been
required to get a handle on the *menla* fever. His idea had
been correct; enumerating the difference between human and
Frinn had helped track down the brain neurotransmitter the
virus altered. It had also taken much longer than he had anticipated.

''Some of the crew are already experiencing relief from
symptoms,'' reported Anita. ''We've done all we can. The
rest is just a matter of time and rest for them.''

''The fever gives me ideas of how to—never mind.'' Walden couldn't shake his training and years of work as a
weapons researcher.

"It *would* make a good infectious agent for an insect vector, wouldn't it?" she asked, smiling crookedly.

"I'm more worried about the Frinn. Uvallae said that the Infinity Plague was being carried by their communications units."

"I doubt that. How could an actual virus be transmitted? The way I understand their com units, the molecules causing odors are electronically reproduced. They couldn't possibly reproduce a living specimen."

"A virus isn't exactly living. Viroids might have RNA but they depend on living cells for reproduction. Perhaps the Frinn's com units create an analog."

"Doubtful. The Infinity Plague's spreading and they're blaming the com-links on it," decided Anita. "It is a fairly unsophisticated response. You said they weren't too sure how communicable diseases spread because of their passion for isolation."

Walden was too tired to care at the moment what caused the new rise in plague cases. All he wanted to do was get down to the planet and administer the vaccine being synthesized in his laboratory. The computer-driven device had produced more than enough for the Frinn's capital city. The rest of the population could be treated after the Frinn automated the process even more.

Their genius for robotics would prove their salvation.

He tapped the vidscreen and got Nakamura. "We're ready to go down to the planet. The *menla* fever is in check aboard the *Hippocrates*," he said. He hinted that the alien disease was not cured, to keep Nakamura honest in her bargaining.

"There is a problem, Dr. Walden. Colonel Sorbatchin has captured an automated factory."

"So?"

"He manufactures surface-to-air and surface-to-space missiles. They lack the sophistication of our genius missiles, but this does not prevent them from being effective."

"I'll chance it. Outfit the shuttle and—"

"The secondary shuttle has been destroyed," Nakamura said somberly.

"I need it to get back! How—"

"The *Hippocrates* needed it for other missions, also, Doc-

tor,'' the woman said. ''Colonel Sorbatchin realized this and
targeted it. Four lives were lost.''

''Contact the *Winston*. They must have a shuttle we can
use.''

''The *Winston* is under constant attack. The Frinn's robotic
factories were *very* efficient and Sorbatchin is making full use
of them.''

Walden held his emotions in check. He had to return to the
planet with his serum soon. The lives of Uvallae and the rest
of his race depended on it.

''Be at peace, Doctor,'' Nakamura said. ''Your first remedy for the Infinity Plague failed. There is some possibility
that this might fail, also.''

''It won't be one-hundred percent effective, but it'll save
millions!''

''I am sorry. There is nothing I can do. Sorbatchin controls
the skies above the planet.''

''There's got to be something. I need to deliver the vaccine. Can you put it in a packet rocket and—''

''What if Sorbatchin blew it up?'' cut in Anita. ''That'd
be worse than negotiating with him. It takes days to formulate.''

''I have spoken with the colonel,'' said Nakamura, ''to no
avail. He requests a total surrender. I have refused.''

''Of course,'' said Walden, his mind racing. No matter
what he did or didn't do, the Frinn would die. Uvallae would
think his promises were hollow. Or worse. The Frinn might
think that Walden worked with Sorbatchin for his race's destruction.

Genocide. That's what Sorbatchin promised the aliens if
Walden couldn't get the vaccine to them soon.

''May I offer a suggestion?''

''What is it, Nakamura?''

''Would aerosol delivery of your antiviral solution be acceptable?''

For a moment, Walden's hope flared. Then he considered
how little of the vaccine he had and how many of the Frinn
there were. To drop an aerosol vapor of the serum in the
upper reaches of the atmosphere would be wasteful. And he
doubted it would work efficiently being inhaled and absorbed

through the mucus membrane rather than injected into the bloodstream.

"It wouldn't work. We don't have enough of it," he said.

"I just ran a half-life estimate on the serum after it's exposed to the air," said Anita, looking up from her computer console. "It would be worthless in less than an hour. Too much contamination from oxygen and other gases."

"Then the Frinn are dead," Walden said, hollow inside. He had come so far to fail.

CHAPTER
18

"There *is* a way of saving the Frinn," Anita Tarleton said.

Walden looked up, startled by the woman's announcement. He started to speak. She motioned him to silence. He sat down, waiting for her to continue. He was willing to do anything to save an entire race from extinction.

"Sorbatchin had me working on other bioweapons," she said. "I came up with one that exploited an ancient evolutionary quirk of the Frinn."

"It has something to do with the extra chromosome pairs?" guessed Walden.

"I found that the chromosomes controlled a hibernation cycle. When the Frinn began socializing, making tools, working their way into a more advanced manipulation of their environment rather than letting it control them, the genes slowed in their functioning. From the look of their bodies, I doubt any Frinn has hibernated in well over a hundred thousand years, and perhaps longer."

"Slowed? The genes are still active?"

"They don't seem to be vestigial like some of our own organs." Anita unconsciously touched the spot where her appendix had been removed. The cosmetic dyes worked as her hormonal and enzyme levels shifted to produce a welter of colors. She was oblivious to the effect, but Walden still found it fascinating.

"You can trigger hibernation at will? What would that do to the ones already stricken with the plague? This must put a strain on their bodies."

"I can't say what it would do. It might kill them outright. But, Jerome, we have nothing to lose—and neither do they. If we don't slow the course of the plague by slowing their metabolic rates, they might all die before we can get onto the planet."

"Is there any evidence that they can go into this hibernation state and get out safely? If it's something from their early evolutionary days, they might have lost the ability to recover."

"That's something Uvallae could tell you."

"There's no chance," said Walden, "of getting through to him. I wish there were." He heaved a deep, heartfelt sigh. Uvallae's help would prove invaluable. As much as he wanted to speak with the Frinn, he wanted to talk with Egad even more. He missed the gengineered dog more than he admitted aloud.

"The chemical trigger for their hibernation would survive an aerosol introduction," Anita said. "It's as much phero-monal as it is actively chemical. I don't pretend to understand the mechanism, but when the Frinn smell this, it begins the process in their bodies, then the chemical itself completes the cycle."

"Just scenting the chemical wouldn't do anything?"

"They'd know it was present, but they wouldn't fall asleep. They have to inhale it in some quantity."

"How much? It'll take millions of liters to cover the planet. And how do we deliver it?"

"Delivery is easy. Manufacturing enough of the organo-acid protein is harder, but we've got to try, Jerome. What else is there to do? Sorbatchin will never let us down onto the planet. He *wants* the Frinn dead. The Infinity Plague is doing it for him, and he'll be content to let it run its course."

"I wonder what he's up to. He must have consolidated his power base on-planet. What would you do in his place?"

"I'm no tactician. Do you want to try this or not?"

Walden said that he did. Anita Tarleton was right. They—and the Frinn—had no choice.

"We don't need as much as you might think," Anita said, working on the computer to get an estimate. She leaned back and stared at him, her cosmetic dyes swirling in crazy patterns across her forehead and around her green eyes. "But we will need several hundred thousand liters to insure hibernation of half the aliens."

"Are there enough of the raw materials aboard the *Hippocrates*?"

"There must be. We've got thousands of kilos of supplies in the cargo bays for use back on Delta Cygnus 4. Since the planet got wasted by the Frinn's cometary sledgehammer, we might as well use it for this project."

Half of the populace in suspended animation meant half dying from the Infinity Plague. Walden wasn't able to cope with "allotted numbers for termination" and "acceptable death rates." He could only think about Uvallae and the other Frinn he had met and liked. They were people, not numbers.

"There's still the problem of delivery. Putting tanks on the *Winston*'s shuttle won't be too hard, if we ever get the use of it. The problems come after that. We need to fly the shuttle low enough into the troposphere to spray the most populated areas."

"Sorbatchin will never allow a fly-over like that, even if Nakamura gets us the shuttle from the *Winston*, which I doubt." Anita grinned broadly. "But you're missing something. Let's *use* Sorbatchin, not fight him."

For a second Walden didn't see what she meant. Then it dawned on him and he, too, smiled. He went to work with a will, knowing that even their best efforts would doom millions of aliens to death.

"These are only unguided rockets," said Nakamura. "Why do you wish to use them? The EPCTs customize them as they see fit, with the proper guidance and armament for specific tasks."

Walden stared at the racks of the large rockets. Equipped with the modular electronics and explosive packages carried by the EPCTs, the rockets turned into genius bombs guided by artificial intelligence circuits. They could dodge and find the enemy, choosing the best trajectory and tactic on the fly.

"We want only the engines and the empty payload containers," Walden said. "And we want a clear communications channel to Sorbatchin when we request it."

On the vidscreen Nakamura shrugged. "There is no chance he will reply positively. He sets up his own empire, issuing ukase after ukase. He envisions himself as a czar rather than a commissar."

"History bored me in school," said Walden. "It still would except we're making it." He watched as Anita expertly directed the robot loaders. Thousands of liters of the complex organic molecule triggering the Frinn hibernation had been generated and put into the rockets under high pressure.

Anita gave him a high sign.

"We want to launch the first flight of fifty rockets," he told Nakamura. "In ten minutes we want the second wave to launch."

"And one hour after that you desire the final one hundred to be expended in this futile plan. What is in the rocket compartments, Dr. Walden?"

"Our first step toward stopping Sorbatchin," he said. He didn't bother adding that it delayed the course of the plague until they could land and administer their antiviral.

"You have honorably discharged your part of our agreement. The alien fever is contained and no new cases have been reported over the past three days."

"They might recur. We need to get in touch with Uvallae to verify our results," Walden said. "Remember how I missed the cure for the Infinity Plague."

"I remember, Doctor," she said. "Your first flight of rockets is being launched, blanketing the planet from equator to northern pole. Please prepare for the launch."

Anita had already left the cargo bag. Triple airlocks opened and the rocket rack moved into position, aimed out into the limitless night of space.

"She knows about the *menla* fever, doesn't she?" asked Anita.

"It sounded that way. She knows there won't be any new cases, and the old victims probably won't suffer a relapse. We've got to be careful with her."

"Not that careful, Jerome. She thinks we've got a way of defeating Sorbatchin. She's got her hands full running the *Hippocrates*. Only if we don't deliver Sorbatchin's severed head to her will she take over again."

"She ought to let Captain Belford return to the bridge. He's still drugged and looking like a zombie."

"Nakamura doesn't like the idea of giving up the power she's seized," Anita said. She looked at him strangely. Walden wondered if her own attempts to take over his job as director of the research team were at an end or if she still desired the insignificant power that gave her.

The *Hippocrates* shuddered as the racks of rockets emptied. One flight after another left the ship's cargo bay until fifty empty slips remained. Anita started the robot cargo handlers on their simple task of getting the next racks into place.

"It'll be ten minutes or more before the first rockets get low enough for Sorbatchin to worry about them."

"He won't want to blow them in the atmosphere. The Frinn's radar surveillance was good. They interdicted us right after we dropped back into normal space," he reminded her.

"They were looking for the residue from a liftspace transition. Inside their atmosphere is another matter."

Walden hoped she was right. They wanted to lay down a barrage across the northern hemisphere that Sorbatchin would have to respond to. If he could knock down a shuttle with its sophisticated avoidance gear, he should be able to intercept noisy, flaring rockets making no attempt to hide their trajectories.

"He might let them through," Walden said uneasily. "He might decide they're packed with bioweapons aimed at him."

"He doesn't have any choice, then, does he? He either tries to intercept or he lets them crash where they're sure to explode on impact and contaminate the area. Either way, he has to respond."

The *Hippocrates* rocked again as the next fifty rockets left in fiery fingers aimed at the planet. The hospital ship rolled slightly and Walden got a quick view of the world spinning below them. It appeared serene and lovely from this height. He had seen the death and destruction on its surface, the death from disease and the destruction from Sorbatchin and the EPCT skirmish tanks ranging through the capital city.

"One more flight to go on the far side of the world," said Anita. She pointed to the vidscreen. "You want to try to reach Sorbatchin?"

Walden keyed the vidscreen to life and began his call for the Sov-Lat officer.

"Doctor, you bombard me from space!" came the colonel's amused response. "What is contained in those tiny bombs? They spray vapors into the air. Surely, you do not think we go about unsuited and vulnerable to such an attack?"

"It's good to see you again, too, Sorbatchin," said Walden. "We want you to let the rockets land. There's nothing in them that will harm you or any of the EPCTs."

"What do you send us? Love letters?"

"The rockets are aimed at the Frinn," Walden said.

"Ah, tell it to your . . . friend." Sorbatchen vanished, replaced by Uvallae's pig-snouted face.

"You bomb us from space," Uvallae said in a choked voice. "All the Sov-Lat colonel has said is true. You try to destroy us for your country."

"Uvallae, it's not like that!"

"Egad still speaks well of you. This is more a reflection on his loyalty than your integrity. You promised to help us. Only Colonel Sorbatchin can do that."

"Uvallae, we're not bombing you. We mean to—" Walden was cut off abruptly by Anita Tarleton.

"Don't give it away. We don't know what Sorbatchin controls on-planet. He might be able to intercept the missiles and render them harmless. If he deflected them into the oceans, they might not break open on impact."

"But Uvallae thinks I've—"

"You're doing this for *him*, dammit," flared Anita. "What does it matter what he thinks, if you're working for him and the rest of the aliens?"

He knew she was right, but it still rankled. He wanted Uvallae's friendship, he wanted his acceptance and cooperation. All he suffered was for the Frinn, and now Sorbatchin had turned Uvallae against him with a simple ploy.

"Get the last racks ready for launching," he said in a dull voice. "I don't want to foul this up, too."

"It'll be all right, Jerome," she said, putting a strong hand on his shoulder. "We're doing the right thing for them. Uvallae will come to see you as his race's savior, you and me and Leo Burch."

Walden stared into the cargo bay until the last of the rockets carrying Anita's chemical blasted toward the Frinn's planet. He cringed at each flare, feeling as if it were a long knife driven into his body. But he knew she was right. They had to do this for the good of the aliens.

"The last of the rockets is away, Doctor," came Nakamura's calm voice. Her composure had returned after he had given her the antiviral for the *menla* fever.

"Good," he said. "We've done all we can for the moment. Anita and I want to prepare to land if it looks as if Sorbatchin has expended all his defensive interceptors."

"There is no indication he has done so, Dr. Walden," said Nakamura. "He has the resources of a world at his disposal now."

Walden doubted that. Uvallae might have thrown in with Sorbatchin, but the others, the Frinn controllers, wouldn't. They had to know where their only hope lay. And it wasn't with a man driving a skirmish tank through the center of their capital.

"Doctor, how many rockets were launched?" asked Nakamura suddenly.

"One hundred in the last wave." He frowned as he looked from the vidscreen to Anita and back. "What's wrong?"

"There is unusual activity on-planet. The rockets we sent were all intercepted easily."

"We intended for them to be," Anita said. "So?"

"There is evidence of hotter rocket flares around the capital. I have analyzed your brief conversation with Uvallae. Is it possible the Frinn have an offensive capability you have not mentioned?"

"They hinted at one, but I think it was mostly a passive resistance. They exist closely with their environment and see us as aberrations since we don't."

"Their space stations and orbiting factories showed no evidence of this." Nakamura frowned, deep in thought.

"They consider their spacemen and explorers as pioneers willing to accept uncivilized conditions. On-planet their houses are more organic than they are inorganic."

"Living houses," mused Nakamura. "All quite interesting but still not explanation of the monatomic hydrogen exhaust picked up after the last of your rockets was intercepted."

"He's attacking," Anita said. "Sorbatchin is returning to take out the *Hippocrates*!"

CHAPTER
19

"That's got to be it. He's launched an attack on us under the cover of our rockets!"

"Absurd," said Walden. "Nakamura has us covered. The *Winston* isn't going to let a shuttle through, even if he repaired the one the Frinn robots destroyed, and what else does Sorbatchin have on-planet to launch an attack?"

"We don't know what the Frinn have lying around," Anita Tarleton said. "Just because the rocket exhaust isn't anything we recognize as dangerous doesn't mean it's not!"

"Nakamura?" called Walden. "Did you hear what Anita just said?"

"I am checking. It is possible Sorbatchin is more daring than I thought. He might launch a counterattack on us."

"Does he have a chance?"

"The *Winston* has ceased to communicate," Nakamura said in a grim tone. "There is some evidence that Sorbatchin spoke with them. They might have defected."

"Nonsense," snapped Walden. "They're NAA. They wouldn't follow a Sov-Lat officer."

"They, like the EPCT unit, have sustained heavy losses. Sorbatchin is a military man and they might see in him a chance for stability and order they can understand."

"Human officers against the Frinn," muttered Walden. He

wanted to rub his forehead in frustration just as Uvallae and the other aliens did. "That's crazy."

"He is persuasive. He did not rise to his rank at such a young age being foolish."

"Are you tracking the missile?" asked Anita.

"Naturally, I am. Its course suggests that it will cross our orbit in less than one hour."

"What do we do? Prepare for boarding like an old pirate ship? Can't you fire on it and blow it up?"

"The *Hippocrates* is in no condition to fight," Nakamura said. "Most of the crew is recovering from *menla* fever. What armament we had has been exhausted or damaged. We relied heavily on the *Winston* for protection."

"Damned traitors!" raged Walden. "We can't let him waltz in here and take us over."

A new thought hit him hard. Sorbatchin might have recruited Uvallae and other Frinn as soldiers. Uvallae thought Walden had betrayed them. What resources could the Sov-Lat officer tap with the Frinn's cooperation? They had a robot-run world that might permit thousands of fighting machines to be sent into the *Hippocrates*.

The lessons of Starlight weren't lost on Walden—and he knew Nakamura thought along similar lines.

"We must prepare," the woman said. "Close the cargo bay doors and return at once to the bridge. We will discuss the matter at length."

"We don't have the time," said Walden. "The ship is maneuvering. He's kicked in more jets. If that's Sorbatchin coming up after us, he'll be here in minutes."

"Vectors intersect in fourteen minutes. That is time enough to leave orbit," Nakamura said briskly. "To the bridge, doctors, immediately!"

Walden and Anita exchanged worried looks. They finished shutting down the equipment in the cargo bay and hurried to the bridge. By the time Walden stepped behind the command chair and Miko Nakamura, he saw the vidscreen detail.

"There's no question," said Nakamura. "Our Sov-Lat friend has found a vessel capable of bringing him back to orbit."

"Can't you blow him out of space?" demanded Anita. "He's a perfect target!"

"He isn't. He approaches from behind us in orbit. We have little that can focus or fire in that direction. I have considered launching some type of space mine and letting it lock onto Sorbatchin's ship. There is nothing left aboard the *Hippocrates* that will suffice."

"The *Winston*?" asked Walden.

"There is still no contact. I can only assume Sorbatchin has subverted them."

"He might be blocking com with them," Walden said. "There's no need to believe he's convinced them to turn against us."

"Yes," said Anita, "if he had, wouldn't they be turning their laser cannon on us?"

Nakamura slumped in the large command chair, her cold eyes fixed on the vidscreen. The shining dot representing Sorbatchin's vessel drew ever closer.

"There is little we can do to prevent him from taking the *Hippocrates*. The crew is still too infirm." Nakamura's fingers stroked the keys on the arm of the command chair. From behind them Captain Belford gasped.

Walden knew what Nakamura contemplated.

"Don't blow us up to stop Sorbatchin," he cautioned. "That's not going to do anyone any good."

"Am I so transparent?" She laughed bitterly. "How do you suggest we fight off the imminent attack?"

The dot reached the area blacked out by the curvature of the *Hippocrates*' hull. The tiny jolt that passed through the huge hospital ship told of a clumsy docking.

"We can do something," said Walden. "How long would it take Sorbatchin to track us down in the ship with the onboard sensors destroyed?"

"A game of cat and mouse?" Nakamura laughed even more harshly. "That only prolongs the matter. Better to meet him squarely and try to reassert control over the EPCTs. Without them he has no power. If they oppose him, he is a corpse."

"He won't let you through to them. They'll be under com blackout for the duration," said Anita. "Finding his command code is almost impossible since it changes thousands of times a second and only the EPCT receivers can unscramble it."

"I am aware of the security aspects," Nakamura said, glaring at Anita.

Walden looked over the array of controls on the bridge. He swung around and demanded of Captain Belford, "Which instruments monitor the ship's interior?"

Belford pointed. Walden went to the bank of instruments and began ripping out the circuits and crushing them under the heel of his boot. The vidscreen winked out.

"You're crippling the ship!" Walden wasn't sure who called this out, but it had to be one of the bridge officers. He ignored the plea to stop until he had smashed every ceramic block circuit he could find under the control panel.

"Let's see how long it takes him to find us now," Walden said, panting from the exertion. In a lower voice so that only Anita and Nakamura could hear, "We lead him on a chase through the ship and see if we can't hijack his shuttle."

"What does this gain us?" asked Nakamura, more interested than she had been in fighting Sorbatchin. Her fatalism vanished as glimmerings of hope replaced it.

"Anita and I can get the antiviral serum down to the planet and the Frinn."

"They no longer trust you," Nakamura said. "Uvallae believes you bombarded his planet."

"Egad can convince them for me. He hasn't changed his mind about me. I've never lied to him before and I won't now."

"Very well." Nakamura looked at the blank vidscreen. She used her laser command wand to power down other equipment. Seeing his interest, she said, "The ship's engines will take much longer to restart than Sorbatchin believes. We have gone entirely to battery power for internal systems."

"Good. He won't notice that for some time," said Anita. "Unless he tries to leave orbit."

Nakamura's answer was an evil chuckle.

Walden's mind raced ahead. The EPCTs would range through the ship to cut off any opposition. The crew was in no condition to fight. This might make the soldiers overconfident when they realized there wouldn't be any resistance. If they became the least bit careless, Walden was sure he could board their craft and get it planetside.

"Get the antiviral, Anita, and I'll see to making Sorbatch-in's chase a merry one."

"I can help in this," said Nakamura. She worked with the laser wand. "They will have to cut through certain bulkheads and airtights to make any headway. Use the time well. You might not find the going as easy as you think."

"I don't think it'll be easy at all," said Walden.

Nakamura smiled and he realized then that he might be facing an impossible task. Sorbatchin wasn't careless like Edouard Zacharias had been. The only chance Walden had for reaching the planet with the vaccine was Sorbatchin's overweening insolence and contempt for the nonmilitary.

"Listen," said Anita. "Hear the hissing?"

"They're cutting through the doors Nakamura locked," said Walden. "And they must be close for us to hear it. Let's get to work." He looked back at Nakamura, who sat calmly waiting for Sorbatchin. Walden wondered what the Sov-Lat colonel would do to her. Shoot her on sight was his first thought, but the woman was a valuable aid in pulling in the reins of power. The EPCTs might not like Nakamura or her position as civilian advisor, but they recognized her as an NAA ally. Sorbatchin would have to tread carefully in dealing with her.

Walden and Anita dashed into the corridor and down toward their laboratories.

"Get the antiviral and meet me in the landing bay as quickly as you can. Wear your full environment suit. They might have blown the air getting into the ship."

"Their shuttle might not be pressurized," Anita said, agreeing. "If it's a Frinn ship, it might be a robot-only vessel."

"I'll decoy them away from the bay. Don't take too long getting everything together." Walden wished he could do this part. He hated to leave such important tasks to anyone else, even Anita Tarleton. In her professional competence he had total faith, but she still remained cool toward him, as if she blamed him for Zacharias' death.

Walden wished they were back on Earth and had never heard of Starlight or the Frinn or Delta Cygnus 4 or any of this. The crackle of a composite deck plate bubbling open under a laserifle beam told him his wish wasn't likely to come true. He had to deal with the EPCTs *now*.

"Halt!"

Walden didn't slow. If anything, he ran faster, expecting the laserifle to cut a hole through his exposed back. The red sighting dot bobbed on the wall beside him, then came back. He knew it centered on his head. He ducked suddenly, rolled, and slammed hard into a wall. Feet kicking frantically, Walden scuttled down a side corridor just as the soldier fired.

"I'm a civilian, dammit!" he yelled. He had been in combat before and hated every instant of it. This almost told him why he preferred the bioweapon to the laser and explosive projectile.

Walden got his feet under him and ducked into a small, out of the way storage compartment to catch his breath. Sweat poured off him in rivers. Outside he heard the steady stride of an approaching EPCT. He longed to open the door a crack and watch to be sure the soldier passed by. To do so would give him away. Walden closed his eyes and forced himself to be calm.

It almost worked.

The door slammed open, and he faced a leveled laserifle. What he did startled him almost as much as it did the EPCT. He kicked the muzzle of the deadly weapon away and spun, his fist swinging. The blow against the EPCT's helmet staggered the soldier. Walden yelped in pain; bones might have broken.

In spite of the pain or because of it, Walden kept moving. He dropped down hard, driving his knee into the soldier's midriff. The man's face was hidden behind the helmet visor, but Walden knew from the way his body had turned boneless that he'd knocked the wind from his lungs. Walden ripped the laserifle from nerveless fingers and stumbled back into the corridor, trying to get his fingers around the trigger guard and onto the laserifle's firing stud. His right hand throbbed unmercifully.

"Get up," he ordered the EPCT.

The soldier rolled to hands and knees and looked up at him.

"I won't kill you," Walden said. "I'm on your side. Ask Sgt. Hecht. But don't ask the *Sov-Lat* colonel."

"Colonel Sorbatchin is our commander."

"He's not an NAA officer."

"He's human. We're fighting the pig-faces."

Walden laughed. Feeling returned slowly to his hand. If the soldier had realized how vulnerable Walden had been, he would have attacked. "Am I a Frinn?"

"You're one of them, a damned traitor!"

"Just like Nakamura and Captain Belford and everyone else aboard this ship? Think, dammit, think! Don't blindly follow. Sorbatchin wants the world for his own. He'll turn it over to the Soviet-Latino Pact. And you're helping him."

Walden took a quick step forward and kicked the EPCT in the chest, sending the man crashing back into the small storage room. Walden didn't stay to see if the man was injured. He turned and ran, skidding around corners and racing as if the legions of hell chased him. He took time after a few minutes of running to catch his breath and melt a control on a door lock. If the EPCT followed, this would slow him down.

But not much. The soldiers were in constant contact with Sorbatchin. He would know what had been said in the corridor and how Walden was armed.

It was time to leave the *Hippocrates*.

Walden made his way back toward his lab, then cut to the infirmary. He found an environment suit near the sealed entrance. Working quickly, he donned the suit and checked the oxygen supply. It was low, but it had to suffice. Walden used the laserifle on the door to the infirmary, blowing a hole that caused a sudden decompression in the corridor. Behind him emergency doors closed and bright red lights flashed warning of pressure loss. Walden levered open the door and hurried into the infirmary. It seemed ghostly to him now, dim lights showing the way through the beds. The earlier explosion caused by Leo Burch had left everything in disorder. But it also left a path to the outside of the ship Sorbatchin might overlook for a few minutes.

He hoped his and Nakamura's sabotage of the internal vidscreen displays hadn't been repaired. Having Sorbatchin watch him was the last thing he wanted.

Walden stared into space at the hard points of stars slowly moving above him. In a few minutes, the planet rose over the horizon made by the *Hippocrates*' hull. Walden made his way slowly and methodically along the ship's exterior until he came to the docking bay. The ship berthed there was of unfamiliar design; he knew it had to be a Frinn craft commandeered by Sorbatchin.

Wedging himself into the space between Frinn craft and *Hippocrates*, Walden wiggled and kicked and dropped toward the docking bay floor. He swung the laserifle around, ready to fight.

There weren't any guards posted. Sorbatchin had decided on an all or nothing tactic. Total offense, no defense. Either he took the *Hippocrates* or he failed, and that made retreat out of the question.

"Jerome?" The helmet speaker in his environment suit cracked and hissed with static. He turned slowly, trying to locate Anita. She waved to him from the open hatch of the Frinn ship.

"All clear?" he asked. He waited until she agreed, both with voice com and with a quick nod of her head. Walden wasn't taking any chances. He had to be sure she wasn't being used as a decoy.

"I've got the serum. We can get planetside and strand Sorbatchin aboard the *Hippocrates*."

"That's not much of a tactic," he said, sliding past her and going to the small vessel's cockpit. The controls appeared simple. Even though he couldn't read the Frinn lettering, he guessed at the function of most of the toggles and rotary switches. "Strap down. We're going down fast."

"Nakamura can stop him, can't she?" asked Anita.

"I doubt it. I ran into an EPCT soldier. He thought I was a traitor. Sorbatchin has him convinced Nakamura is one, too."

"He might have access to the EPCT brain coding," said Anita.

"A wonderful thought. He can use our soldiers against us—and they'd follow him to the end of the universe. Too bad there weren't any officers left."

The rotary switch on his left produced a flare from the simple rockets. Walden cast off from the *Hippocrates*, then used steering jets to swing around.

"Can you fly this thing?" Anita asked.

"What's to know?" he said.

Walden kicked in the rocket and blasted away from the *Hippocrates*. He aimed the prow directly for the planet, praying that the Frinn passion for computer control extended to this ship. If it didn't, they would get very hot—and molten— within a few minutes.

CHAPTER
20

The temperature mounted rapidly. Jerome Walden fought to keep the small craft stable. To begin a tumble now as the buffeting increased meant instant death.

"Are you *sure* you know what you're doing?" Anita Tarleton asked peevishly. "You're scrambling us like eggs in this damned thing!"

"We're getting there." Walden watched the small vidscreen for indication that the *Winston* had fired on them. For whatever reason, the destroyer did not use its laser cannon to turn them into a cinder. Perhaps Sorbatchin felt confident that they couldn't do anything—or they might have misjudged the reason for the *Winston*'s silence and lack of response earlier.

Walden began to worry, in spite of his outward confidence. He had used only four of the ten controls on the board. He had no idea what to do next—or what the other controls did. He simply aimed the vessel at the planet and opened up the jets, counting on safety measures to take over and land them. The mounting heat told him this wasn't going to work.

He began experimenting. Lights flashed on and off in a slow cadence that reminded him of a death march. He began to get frantic when the entire board glowed a dull yellow. The pulsation started slowly in the lights, then increased in frequency until he stared at a stroboscoping control panel.

"You don't know what you're doing, do you?" There was no accusation in Anita's voice. She sounded resigned to death. "It's too bad we couldn't have delivered the medicine. I'm certain my hibernation chemical worked on them. It had to."

"We're not dead yet."

Just as Walden spoke, the controls went dead. Try as he might, nothing changed the rocket thrust, vector, yaw, or attitude. He started to slam his hand against the panel to see if this would free up the frozen controls when he looked at the ship's tiny vidscreen. Robotic controls had cut in and he hadn't noticed. They leveled out and skipped along the upper edge of the atmosphere like a stone. The heat didn't abate—but it didn't increase, either.

"We've made it. Let's hope I can set us down near the capital. I've got to reach Uvallae."

"He's probably soundly sleeping along with the rest of the planet," Anita said, her brittle tone showing that she didn't believe they were safe yet.

Twenty minutes later, the buffeting stopped and the Frinn craft began gliding downward. In an hour, they landed as light as any feather near the capital.

"So," she said, getting out and stretching. Every muscle in her body ached from the pounding they'd endured on the way down. "Do we hoof it or is there some way of catching a ride into town?"

"We walk. If you're right about the hibernation chemical working, the inhabitants are all sound asleep."

The walk to the edge of town took longer than the descent from orbit. Walden began to grow worried as they marched. What could Sorbatchin do to them from orbit? Would he decide to nuke the entire city? Walden was sorry he hadn't checked the *Hippocrates*' arsenal before leaving. The hospital ship had been outfitted to defend itself, but the short, vicious fights since entering the Frinn system had depleted the stock of munitions.

But all it took was one medium-yield nuke to remove the city permanently. If the *Hippocrates* didn't have the requisite megatonnage aboard, he was sure the *Winston* did.

"Are you sure you can't hail a taxi?" complained Anita. She sat down when they reached the perimeter of the city and rubbed her aching feet. Beside her she put the large container holding the antiviral solution that might save as many as half the Frinn from the Infinity Plague. Walden found it impossible for him to take his eyes off the silvered flask. The lives and dreams of a race rested in that single two-liter receptacle.

"The hospital where Uvallae took me before is only a kilometer or two from here." He forced himself to survey the terrain they were going to travel. Sorbatchin's tanks had ripped the city apart and left huge blast craters. At the ten-meter-wide crater to his right Walden saw debris along the sides. He went over and peered down. What had been a Frinn robot lay crushed at the bottom. A single steel tentacle flipped in the air, as if wind whipped it about.

Walden restrained himself from slipping down the side and giving the last rites to the machine.

"It looks alive, doesn't it?" Anita said softly. Walden hadn't heard her join him.

"It does. Let's find some real life. I've been looking and haven't seen anyone anywhere along the route."

"I've been on the lookout, too," she said. "If they've already started to go into hibernation, they might have crawled off into a hole somewhere."

"That might explain their desire for solitude in their normal, everyday lives," Walden said. "Some tiny bit of racial memory tells them to seek the safety of seclusion until they come out of the long sleep."

"I can't imagine them *needing* to hibernate," Anita said, looking past the recent destruction to the world itself. "This is such a lovely planet. It has almost no axial tilt. Perfect climate. And moderate, too."

"It might not have always been this nice," Walden said. "Orbital dynamics might have dictated a more eccentric orbit millions of years ago."

"There," said Anita, grabbing his arm. "That's the hospital you told me about, isn't it?"

Walden approached the large structure cautiously, unsure of his reception. The interior was as he remembered it. The soft membranous walls fluttered slightly as he passed along the corridors. He strained for the remotest hint that Uvallae lay in wait to ambush him.

"Sorbatchin had him to show you on the vidscreen," said Anita. "Who knows where he might be?"

"He wasn't with the EPCT assault force that went back onto the *Hippocrates*."

"We don't know that for sure. We just didn't see him. The fact is, I didn't see any of them. Sorbatchin used his favorite tactic: a lightning strike and no retreat. Uvallae might have been carried along with the EPCT team."

"I doubt it. He would have begun to hibernate before they lifted for orbit," Walden said. "He's here somewhere. I feel it."

"There's an easier way of finding him," said Anita. She let out an ear-piercing whistle.

Walden started to protest, then saw what she was doing. Again she whistled. This time he heard a distant barking. In minutes Egad came loping up. The gengineered dog eyed them suspiciously.

"It's good to see you, old boy," said Walden, dropping to a knee and trying to scratch the dog's ears. Egad backed away and barred his huge teeth. "What's wrong?" Panic seized Walden. His only friend had turned on him.

"You bombed planet. They all hid, then started to die. You said you helped. You killed them!"

"Egad, are you sure they're dead? We have medicine to cure the ones with the Infinity Plague. We brewed it in our lab and brought it down after Sorbatchin left."

"Cat-shit colonel!"

"We know. We need to find Uvallae. We need his help—he needs our help. Take us to him."

"Uvallae dead," the dog declared.

Walden held his gorge down. Burning bile filled his throat and threatened to choke him. He took a deep breath and steadied himself the best he could.

"Are you sure? Show us. Show Anita and me where Uvallae is."

"Over there. In his house. Nice house, all green and growing and made from plants. Machines everywhere to do what I ask."

"I'm happy you've been looked after, Egad. I worried about you, but it was for the best you didn't come with me back to the *Hippocrates*."

"Don't like ship. Like it here with Uvallae."

"Take us to him," Walden repeated. The dog cocked his

massive head to one side, studied them, then spun and trotted off. Walden and Anita had to jog to keep up with him. By the time both humans were gasping for breath, Egad stopped. Like a pointer, he aimed nose and paw toward a shady glen.

"In there? Uvallae has his house in the vale?"

"Go in hole in tree. Follow me." The dog ran off, forcing Walden and Anita to quicken their pace to stay up with him. They slowed to a fast walk when they saw the dark cavity in the large tree bole where Egad disappeared.

"They do live with nature," muttered Anita as she ducked and went inside. A twisting ramp led downward into the ground. Soft green phosphorescent light grew brighter as they spiraled around and around. Walden guessed they were ten meters underground when the stairway stopped and a long straight corridor beckoned. Along it opened a dozen or more doors.

"Here," called Egad. "He's dead here. Haven't eaten him because house gives me food."

"Good for you, Egad," muttered Anita. She stopped just inside the door and stared. Uvallae lay sprawled across the floor, arms pulled in tightly to the sides of his body. His legs bent slightly and came up to his chest. His piglike snout rested firmly between his knees in what would have been an uncomfortable position for a human. For the Frinn, it seemed natural.

"Let me check him," said Walden, pushing past Anita and Egad. He knelt and felt for a pulse. He detected none. Lifting Uvallae's eyelids showed that the cat-slit eyes had rolled up into his head. Something about the appearance of the sclera convinced Walden that the alien hadn't died.

"I can't prove it, but I think he's all right. He must be in hibernation."

"If so, he won't be able to last longer than a few weeks," said Anita. "The Frinn body-fat ratio is too low for them to survive more than a month at the outside."

"Let's see if we can't do something with the serum. Egad, did Uvallae show signs of having contracted the Infinity Plague?"

The dog barked and shook his big, shaggy head.

"This ought to protect him." Walden finished injecting the

one-cc dose. "But we need to get him out of the hibernation to set up manufacture for both a vaccine and the serum."

Walden rocked back on his heels and stared at Uvallae. "How do we get him to come out of the trance?"

"First, the chemical has to be removed from the air. Then we purge his system. I've got a couple ways of doing it. Since he's in good physical condition, we can use the quick way. It puts more of a strain on his system but cleanses the blood-stream fast."

"A gengineered bacteria?" asked Walden. He watched as Anita deftly administered the counter for the artificially in-duced hibernation. In a few seconds Uvallae's eyes rolled down. Several minutes passed before the last effects of the induced suspended animation vanished.

"You have come to kill me with your own hand?" asked Uvallae.

"Dammit, I've come to help!" Walden threw up his hands and turned away. Everyone thought the worst of him when all he wanted to do was stop the deaths.

"I'm responsible for putting you into a hibernation state. It was the only way we could slow the progress of the Infinity Plague." Anita held Uvallae's hand and kept him from flinch-ing away. Their eyes met and locked.

"You know of our past?"

"We've guessed. I got there from studying the function of the extra chromosomal pair. Jerome had more physical ideas about why you once hibernated."

"The plague? You aren't here to destroy us all?" Uvallae rubbed his sloping forehead, then looked to Egad for confir-mation. The dog said nothing, sitting back on his haunches and staring.

"You'll have to take what we do on faith," Walden said. "We've risked our lives to return to help. Sorbatchin has con-trol of the *Hippocrates* now."

"He rules the planet, also."

"Not if he's in space. He saw you falling into hibernation and thought I'd used a faster-acting bioweapon on you in an attempt to stop him and the EPCTs," said Anita.

"Truly, you will help?" Uvallae seemed astounded at his earlier misjudgment.

"Yes," said Walden, hoping they didn't have to make

lengthy explanations to every Frinn. "We need a ton of help, though. We've got an experimental vaccine that will protect those who haven't contracted the Infinity Plague. Anita and I think it will also ease the suffering of those already stricken. It might be a cure, or it might not. We can't say. But the gengineered product works directly on the viral sheath, cracks it open and allows the body's natural defense system to attack."

"This small amount will work across my world?" Uvallae stared at the small flask.

"No. You're going to have to find a way of making more—lots more—and distributing it. How you'd do that, I don't know. We exhausted the raw materials on the *Hippocrates* making even this little amount. There's enough for about two thousand injections."

"If we cannot make more, then we can save only two thousand?"

"I'm afraid that's right," answered Anita. "Jerome said you have a sophisticated hospital." She looked around the chamber with its living walls and undulating ceiling. "Is there any way of getting the, uh, house to manufacture the vaccine?"

"Of course. We live in harmony with our world."

"Do it. Get your tree house working. Or the hospital. Something. Time is of the essence."

"You understand, then, that we cannot remain in hibernation as long as we once did?"

"I know. Weeks," Anita assured him. "No longer. Your bodies have evolved past the need to stop for long winter months."

Uvallae took the flask and went to a wall. He withdrew a milliliter of the vaccine and dropped it into a small cuplike protrusion. The wall tensed and acted as if it were swallowing.

"We will soon know if synthesis is possible."

"The house tells you?"

"Tree talks with smells," volunteered Egad. "Like tree house. Don't even piss on it."

Walden patted the dog's head and wondered at the efficiency of a bioproduction system. The antiviral serum was complicated chemically and biologically and relied on inducing a limited and controllable response in the host's immune system.

"The rocket bombardment sprayed my world with the hibernation fluid?" asked Uvallae. "Was there no other way to dispense it?"

"The shuttles were destroyed. We couldn't take the time to find a better way of introducing the chemical." Walden explained how they had used Sorbatchin's defense network to accomplish their end.

"He lied to me, saying you were a traitor to your kind. He told me he wanted only peace and self-government."

"He's persuasive, but you should have known better. Talk like that from a man driving a skirmish tank through your capital is meaningless. Besides that," Walden said, smiling, "Egad doesn't like him."

"Cat-shit colonel," the gengineered dog grumbled. To emphasize his point, he clacked his teeth shut hard.

"The synthesis of your medicine is now complete," said Uvallae, looking up suddenly. His nose twitched violently. He went to the same spot on the wall and looked into the cup. "It is not exact, but it is close."

Walden and Anita exchanged glances. Was "close" good enough? It had to be. The Frinn's survival depended on it.

"Can you dispense it worldwide? Can you make enough to treat the millions and millions already infected?"

"Let the root system do its work. It might take weeks or even months, but we can reach across the world."

"That's not good enough. The hibernation effect will start killing by then. Slow starvation," Anita said, "is no better than dying from the plague."

"Can the trees inject the serum once they have it?" asked Walden. "Or do you have to go around, find the Frinn already in hibernation, and directly give it to them?"

"The houses can administer a drug by slow infusion."

"This is another reason their medical science is so primitive compared to ours. If we'd grown up surrounded by a patient around-the-clock doctor, we'd never have developed our medical science as rapidly as we did," said Walden.

"Start the drug on its way," Anita urged. "Then you'll have to start production on the gengineered chemical-exuding bacteria needed to counter the hibernation."

''So few will live,'' mourned Uvallae. ''But you have given us a bit of life.'' He began working to allow the tree to send its synthesized vaccine through roots to nearby Frinn households.

Walden watched in wonder and appreciation. The aliens were so different in culture and achievement. For all their reclusiveness, he suspected the Frinn would survive in large enough numbers to repopulate their world.

He closed his eyes and silently prayed that he wasn't saving the Frinn for a Sov-Lat dictatorship led by Vladimir Sorbatchin.

CHAPTER
21

"There's less than a thirty percent survival rate," complained Walden. "We need to see the victims personally, to attend to them ourselves. That's the only way of saving more."

"I'd need to check a computer to agree," said Anita Tarleton. She lounged on a low, firm couch, petting Egad. "The Frinn are more efficient than I'd thought they would be. You have to remember that the Infinity Plague had months to take hold."

"The hibernation technique isn't saving enough, either. There is almost a fifteen percent fatality rate from that alone."

"If it were a bioweapon, you'd say that was pretty good for an aerosol attack modality. Relax, Jerome. There are more deaths than either of us would prefer, but we're saving more than if we'd done nothing."

Walden stewed over this. They were indirectly responsible for introducing the plague in the Frinn. He wanted to do more—and there wasn't anything he could do.

"Dr. Tarleton is correct," said Uvallae. "More of us are alive than if you had abandoned us. The Infinity Plague would have killed everyone on the planet if it had gone on unchecked."

"I want to find out about the virus spreading over your com-link. That seems too incredible for words."

"True," said Egad. "Smelled it. Smelled the disease when Frinn got it over their com." The gengineered dog trotted over to Walden. He idly stroked the animal's head, hardly noticing he did so.

"The vector could have been anything. We know it can pass hand-to-hand or through the air. It's incredibly tough to kill."

"We're engaged in a planet-wide eradication program, Dr. Walden. We feel that within a few months the last traces of the virus will be gone."

Walden shook his head. He didn't think it would be as easily defeated as Uvallae hoped, but they had a good start. In spite of the high fatality rate from the Infinity Plague and adverse reaction to Anita's induced-hibernation chemical, they *had* saved an entire race. Cleaning up would be a long and tedious process, but the Frinn were capable of doing it. Already Uvallae had ordered robots to be designed to ferret out any trace of the rapidly mutating virus and destroy it with a maser.

"The robots are a nice touch," Walden said. "They don't rest and you can put as many of them to work as you want. Now that there is something to save, it's worth the effort."

"What about your houses?" asked Anita. "Are they immune to the plague?"

"I checked them out," Walden said, answering for Uvallae. "Their basic DNA is only eight chromosomal pairs, similar to Earth trees. There's no good way for the virus to cut in to their DNA and begin unraveling it. For all their usefulness, the trees are relatively simple organisms."

"That leaves another problem, then," said Anita.

Walden's gray eyes locked with her hot green ones. He knew what she meant. Sorbatchin had been aboard the *Hippocrates* for over a week. They had had no contact with the hospital ship, nor had any communication from the ship been directed at them.

"We've got to do something about the colonel," he agreed. "Getting there is easier now than it was ten days ago."

"Defense is possible now, also," said Uvallae. "We have examined the automated factories Colonel Sorbatchin ordered built. We can duplicate the missiles he intended to use for defense. The *Winston* and the *Hippocrates* cannot carry enough armament to affect us now that production levels are rising.''

"Don't count on it, Uvallae. There aren't many nukes left up in orbit, but your planet is still recovering from a major catastrophe and will be for years. The two ships might not carry the firepower they once did, but a duck back into lift-space will bring more warships than you can imagine.''

Walden knew that Sorbatchin would return to his Sov-Lat leaders with a proposition that would keep him in power. He'd trade total control of this alien world for supported control. More than a hundred light-years separated Earth and the Frinn's globe. Vladimir Sorbatchin would have considerable latitude in his decisions because of the immense distance and difficulty in communication.

"Nakamura-bitch is not better," said Egad, almost as if the dog read his mind. "No smell. Don't trust her.''

"I don't trust her, either," admitted Walden. "I'm not even sure if supporting her is a better choice than cooperating with Sorbatchin. Both want personal power.''

"We can fight," declared Uvallae.

"Before, you might have had a chance. Not now. What are the estimates on a stabilized, healthy population in five years?'' He looked to Anita for the answer.

"Less than twenty million," she said. "That's not enough to fight off a small NAA battle squadron. Uvallae, we've waged war for centuries. We're *good* at it. Better than you will ever be.''

"Nakamura slipped past our robot fighters easily," the alien conceded. He rubbed the sides of his head in agitation. "What are we to do?''

"We negotiate. We try to get a treaty. We try to call off the dogs of war. No offense, Egad.''

"Like idea. Egad can be fierce.'' The gengineered canine bared his teeth and snarled.

Walden patted the dog. He knew much of the ferocity was put on. The dog had been well treated, even if most of his life had been spent hiding his talents and mental ability. Walden was startled when Egad took a snap at his hand, then backed off and looked chagrined.

"Sorry," Egad said contritely. "Thinking of cat-shit colonel. He mistreated Uvallae and the others.''

Walden looked at the alien. Uvallae said, "It is so. Colonel Sorbatchin did not do well by any of us he took prisoner. Only after you began dispensing the aerosol canisters of the hibernation chemical did he see in us an ally."

"Some ally," scoffed Anita. "This isn't getting us into a better position to decide what to do next." She looked up as if she could see the orbiting *Hippocrates* through the ceiling of Uvallae's underground house. "How do we find out what's *really* happening there?"

"Ask?" Walden went to the small vidscreen and found the keypad under it. He spent a few minutes punching in different combinations. Nothing worked. The *Hippocrates* remained a silent threat hanging above their heads.

"If the doorbell doesn't work, why not walk on in?" asked Anita. "We've got a shuttle that will get us back into orbit. It's the only way we're going to finish this, Jerome."

"There's a great deal to do here," he muttered.

"We can do much for ourselves, now that you have shown the way," said Uvallae. "Dr. Tarleton is correct in saying the *Hippocrates* and *Winston* constitute the bigger menace to us now. And they are threats only you can address."

"Let's go. You want to come along, Egad?" He looked at the dog. The huge head turned to one side and the mismatched eyes closed for a moment. Then Egad barked sharply.

"Yes! Can I rip out cat-shit colonel's throat?"

"You wouldn't like the taste in your mouth," Anita assured him as she ruffled his hairy ears.

"Will come anyway," Egad decided. "Want to return, though. Like it here. Fun to chase rabbits."

Uvallae smiled as he regarded the dog. "They're not rabbits, not the way he explained them to me. They're more like your wild field rodents."

"We'll be back. Look after yourself—and all the rest," Walden said. He motioned to Anita and Egad, who followed him out of the subterranean chambers and into the balmy, warm sun. Walden knew Uvallae would have the robots working on the shuttle. It would be ready long before they arrived. For the moment, he wanted nothing more than to enjoy the sun's warmth and the soft breeze blowing in his face. He had forgotten how wonderful all this could be working in sealed, buried laboratories and on starships. It was stimulating enough to make him want to join Egad chasing the rodents or rabbits or whatever the creatures were.

All this vanished when they arrived at the shuttle and launched for space. Again he entered a hostile environment— and was heading for one even more deadly.

Three hours after lifting from the planet, Walden saw the small, bright dot of the *Hippocrates* above him in orbit. The shuttle slowed and the orbit widened. Two more revolutions were required to dock with the hospital ship and leave its womblike confines.

Then he found hell.

"No approach guards," observed Anita Tarleton as she edged along the wall in the docking bay following Walden and Egad. "They have to know we're here. Nakamura only killed the interior sensors, not the external radar."

"They still might not know we're here," Walden said. He held down his gorge when he saw the decomposing body a few meters down the deserted corridor. Even though his environment suit prevented him from smelling the obvious decay, he turned up the oxygen level, as if this would wash away the taint.

"What happened to him?"

"Her," Walden said. "I think it was a woman. It looks as if the flesh started rotting from the inside and worked outward."

"Something got loose from Willie Klugel's lab," Anita said. "His T-odd bacteriophages . . ."

"Starvation from killing the flora in the gut isn't going to cause this. The body started working against itself. This is total body rejection."

"The Infinity Plague?"

"Possibly, but I doubt it. Leo Burch gave us the way to prevent it in humans. Nakamura knew about it. She wouldn't turn it loose, not on the crew." Walden walked gingerly, as if the decking might turn to vacuum under him. Occasional glances down branching corridors hinted at even worse carnage than what he'd already seen. Dozens of crew members lay dead, no one caring that they decomposed where they lay.

"Did Sorbatchin do this? Or Nakamura?" asked Anita. "She would kill everyone to get him. You know how she planned to kill herself when Sorbatchin and the EPCTs came up on us.''

The attempts to contact the *Hippocrates* had failed because there was no one to answer the com. Walden steeled himself to find everyone aboard the ship dead.

"Egad, can you scout for us? Don't you dare open your helmet. Whatever killed them might work on dogs.''

"Can't sniff around,'' Egad said.

"Just look—and report straight back if you find anyone alive. Anyone.''

The gengineered dog raced off, his head swiveling back and forth as he ran.

Walden said to Anita, "Let's check the labs. The cause might be in Klugel's lab, or Chin's, or any of the others. Who knows what they were working on.'' If he had remained on the ship, the biological destroyer of so many people might have originated in his own synthesis machines.

Walden sidled into the corridor. Doors on each side opened into his research team's laboratories. Walden opened the first door; the lab was empty. Anita checked two more. Nothing. The fourth door they opened produced an unexpected result.

Walden dived forward, carrying Anita out of the line of fire. A laserifle hissed and left a trail of ionized air behind it. Almost instantly came the shouted apology. "I'm sorry! I thought you were with them!''

"Who's them?'' asked Anita, getting to her hands and knees. She peered up at Willie Klugel. The short, balding man had a wild expression and his hands shook. It was nothing short of a miracle that he hadn't cut them in half with the laserifle. It had been set on fan-pattern blast intended for fighting crowds rather than individuals.

"Sorbatchin and the damned EPCTs. They're roaming the ship, killing anyone they find.''

"We saw a half-dozen crew, and they'd all died from a bioweapon. Anita thought it might be one of your T-odd phages.''

"Not mine. Paul Preston whipped it up and released it. Nakamura told him to. Three days after Sorbatchin got here. Most of the crew died, but only a few of the EPCTs, damn them! They were supposed to be NAA soldiers, not Sov-Lat flunkies!''

"Sorbatchin and the EPCTs are still in control?"

"What's control? Nakamura wanted the *Hippocrates* turned into a death ship. Sorbatchin can't work freely from inside his combat gear. The engines are shut down and getting out of their suits to relight them is sure death. Jerome, I've lived in my e-suit for a full week. I reek!"

"Who else is still alive?"

Willie Klugel shook his head. Walden saw tears forming in the small man's eyes. "Claudette is dead. I think Marni Donelli is, too. I know Paul died. He made a mistake with the bug and started decaying within minutes. The flesh melted right off his skeleton."

"A week of this," muttered Walden, feeling almost guilty about the relatively pleasant time he'd spent on-planet. The fresh air and honeyed sunlight and hope for combating the Infinity Plague had buoyed him. Klugel had spent the time amid panic and death.

His headphones whistled. Walden turned slightly until he got a stronger signal. Egad barked twice. He told the gengineered dog to report.

"Got Nakamura," Egad said. "Holed up like rabbit in her quarters."

"Any sign of Sorbatchin?"

Egad growled. Walden took that for a negative response. "Bring her to Willie Klugel's lab right away. It's time we started consolidating our forces."

"We're still blind inside the ship," said Anita. She toggled the vidscreen off in disgust. "Nobody's bothered to repair the internal sensors."

"How many of the EPCTs are left?" Walden asked.

Klugel shrugged. "Haven't seen any of them in the past couple days. Their combat suits aren't going to leak, not to whatever Paul released. I tried to analyze it, but working in my e-suit is too hard. It's been easier to just sit and wait to laser anyone coming into my lab.'

"It's a good thing you're a lousy shot," Anita said sarcastically.

Before she could say anything more, Egad came in, leading Miko Nakamura. The sallow woman had lost weight. Her environment suit hung on her in thick folds of plastic. She smiled slightly when she saw Walden and Anita Tarleton.

"So you have succeeded on-planet. Amazing."

"The Frinn will survive. Enough of them," said Walden. "But what about here? What did you do?"

"Dr. Preston had a new bioweapon. I suggested immediate release to hold the colonel at bay. With the engines cut down and the internal sensors sabotaged, I knew it would be difficult for Sorbatchin to make any progress. Adding the element of the Preston Plague, as he called it, to the equation would keep Sorbatchin too busy to concentrate on my assassination attempt."

"Did you murder him?" Anita asked pointedly.

"His Sov-Lat training stood him in good stead. I tried and failed. The Preston Plague affected the crew but not the EPCTs and Sorbatchin."

"Weren't there enough e-suits?"

"No," Nakamura said in a tiny voice. "Not after Sorbatchin destroyed most of them."

Walden was speechless. Between Nakamura and Sorbatchin, they had killed most of the crew aboard the *Hippocrates*. The entire might of the Frinn had been unable to cause the casualties these two had among their own species in one short week.

"How many are left?" Walden asked in a choked voice.

"A dozen, perhaps more," said Nakamura. "Of Sorbatchin's soldiers, only a handful remain. I have been effective in stopping them. EPCT training leaves curious blind spots."

"Is Sgt. Hecht still alive?"

"I do not know," said Nakamura. She settled down on the deck, sitting cross-legged and staring into a distance only she perceived.

"How about it, Egad? Can you find the EPCTs?"

"Find them faster without helmet," the dog said.

"No! Keep the helmet on. We might have to destroy the *Hippocrates* after this. There's too much released inside for the few of us to clean."

"We can borrow some of the Frinn robots, when they're finished on-planet," said Anita. "It might take a long time to free them up, but we're in no hurry to get back to Earth." She looked squarely at Walden. "At least, I'm not."

"Come on, Egad, let's find Hecht and the others."

Walden stopped for a moment and touched Anita's cheek.

He was pleased when she didn't flinch away as she had done before. But in her eyes was no real warmth. He hurried on, hard-pressed to keep up with the dog. He wished he had brought the laserifle Klugel had used against them. He couldn't outfight even a wounded EPCT, but it would make him feel better having something to hang on to.

He turned up the gain on his headphones and listened intently. Noises from ahead alerted him. Wary, he advanced.

"Hello, Doc," came Hecht's familiar voice. "I wondered when you'd stumble across us."

"You overheard us talking back in Willie's lab?"

"Been monitoring whatever I could. About all I'm good for now." He pointed to a leg that had been ground to a bloody pulp. "Got caught in one of Nakamura's traps. She's a devil, that one."

"Sergeant," Walden said slowly, unable to take his eyes off the man's ruined leg, "that's dangerous. You need it taken care of immediately."

"Aboard this ship? No way. I'd sooner die of septicemic shock then the creepy-crawlies that were released. Never did care for biologic weaponry. A nuke is cleaner by far."

"We can get you down to the planet to work on your leg. Their medical facilities are . . . different," Walden said, words failing him. He didn't know how else to describe the hospital trees used by the Frinn. Even their gentle healing might be lost on Hecht's leg. He needed a major operation to restore any use of the leg.

"Is it all over?" Hecht asked.

"You mean between us and the Frinn or just among us?"

"Both, either, I don't know. I'm so drugged out right now, it's hard to tell what I do mean."

"Egad, where's Sorbatchin?"

"Don't bother with the colonel," Hecht said, slipping to the deck and putting his mutilated leg out to one side at an unnatural angle. "He's got something. One of the bugs. He's dying."

"Nakamura isn't in good shape, either. Can we call a truce? Will the EPCTs follow you, if you do?"

"All three of them?"

"Three?" Walden's stomach tied in knots. Humans had

almost destroyed the Frinn. What they had done to themselves aboard the *Hippocrates* was no less brutal.

"We've been hunting survivors. Everyone's holed up somewhere. Your radio broadcast was the first hint I'd had in two days of anyone else on the ship."

"It's over," Walden said firmly. "We'll get you to the planet and take care of the others."

"I'd like that."

"Egad," called Walden, "fetch Anita. Tell her—" He looked around but the gengineered dog had vanished. Walden knelt by Hecht and said, "You'll be all right for a few more minutes. Egad's gone off. I'd better find him."

"Take your time. I've been living like this for days, Doc." Hecht slipped to the deck, looking more dead than alive. The telltales on his combat suit showed a strong heartbeat and shallow, ragged breathing. He had been kept alive by the drugs, but his strength had to flag soon unless he received medical attention.

Walden broke into a run when he found the dog's helmet on the deck. He spun around a corner and saw Egad advancing on the Sov-Lat officer. Egad's tongue lolled and he barked once, then fell silent.

"Sorbatchin!" Walden cried.

"Doctor, so good to see you." The Sov-Lat officer propped himself up on one elbow. He lay on a crude bed made from discarded material. He had skinned out of his ill-fitting combat gear and lay half naked on the bed. "I am an invalid from Nakamura's gengineered disease. But I am happy to see you, the architect of all my woe."

A heavy laser pistol came out of the folds in Sorbatchin's rude bunk. He never fired. Egad ripped his throat out in a single crimson gush.

"Wanted to do that," the dog said. "Sorry."

"Don't be." Walden held the dog close. "You saved my life. Even in his condition, he wanted to kill me."

'You were right," said Egad. The dog forced himself away from Walden. "Cat-shit colonel tastes *bad*."

CHAPTER
22

"Contact has been reestablished," Miko Nakamura said solemnly.

"What happened aboard the *Winston*?" Walden asked, distracted. He worried over the tests he ran on Egad. The dog had been without a helmet in the disease-laden air in the *Hippocrates* for several minutes. Even worse, he had both Sorbatchin's diseased flesh and blood in his mouth. Walden wanted to be absolutely sure that nothing happened to the dog. Egad bore up under the scrutiny with increasing restlessness.

"Want to go back to Uvallae," he had said repeatedly.

"Soon," was all Walden could tell him. For the most part, the gengineered dog looked none the worse for his deadly excursion and mouthful of Sorbatchin's throat.

"The ship experienced a major breakdown." Nakamura cleared her throat. "There was also a mutiny inspired by a faction supporting Sorbatchin's leadership. Much important equipment was destroyed during the uprising."

"The *Winston* can't lift for Earth, either?"

"Doubtful. We rely on the Frinn for cleaning the *Hippocrates* and important parts for the *Winston*."

"Forget refitting the *Winston*," Walden said. "Concentrate

on the *Hippocrates*. There's hardly enough crew from both ships to make a skeleton crew on this one.''

"Agreed," Nakamura said. "Our temporary evacuation to the planet is almost completed. Will you come, on this trip?''

"It's the last one down for some time," said Walden. Anita Tarleton had preceded him hours ago. He had stayed to get more equipment the Frinn could use in stanching the spread of the Infinity Plague. And he had needed to run the tests on Egad.

"Go now?" demanded Egad.

"Sure, pal, let's go. You'll be chasing rabbits before sundown.''

"Good time to chase them," agreed Egad. "More are out then.''

Over Egad's protests, he picked up the heavy dog and made his way to the docking bay. They had cleaned up a bit, but bodies still littered the *Hippocrates*. Walden paused when he saw Hecht being strapped onto the shuttle floor, flat to prevent further damage to his leg.

"Will I walk again, Doc?''

"Hobble, maybe. We might have to get you back to Earth before we can replace that leg.''

"I've been talking to Egad," the EPCT said. "I'm in no hurry to get home. This sounds like a nice place to do some R and R.''

"It might be, it just might be," Walden said. He didn't mention how the Frinn had been devastated by the plague. For the most part, the world looked untouched. Only when the numbers who had died were revealed did the true magnitude of the disaster emerge.

"Uvallae is well?" asked Nakamura as she got into the shuttle and seated herself beside him.

"Hale and hearty, the last I saw.''

"Good. He will make a good go-between. The NAA must establish formal diplomatic relations with the Frinn.''

"With you as the Earth's first ambassador?" Walden rebelled at the notion. Nakamura had been instrumental in the deaths caused by the Infinity Plague.

"The position is open," she said. He saw the calculating begin behind those cold, dark eyes. Already she maneuvered for what benefitted her most.

Walden took one last look at the *Hippocrates*. It had been home for almost a year, but he wasn't sorry to leave it behind. In a few weeks or months, the Frinn robots would begin scouring its interior. One day its interstellar engines would be relit and a crew would return to Earth with the history of mankind's first meeting with an alien intelligence.

Walden let the shuttle's acceleration crush him back into the hard cushions. This first meeting with an alien civilization had been a nightmare. And he had been pivotal in making it that way. Without the bioweapons research team aboard the *Hippocrates*, much of what had happened would have been impossible.

As the shuttle touched the fringes of atmosphere, another thought occurred to him. Without him and Anita Tarleton and even Leo Bruch, the Infinity Plague would never have been brought under control. The Frinn would have died totally.

By the time the shuttle landed outside the destroyed Frinn capital, he was feeling almost sanguine about the future.

Walden waited for Hecht and the others to be taken from the ship. Miko Nakamura had rushed off as soon as the hatch popped open. She sought Uvallae or a controller willing to sponsor her as Earth's first ambassador. Let her, Walden decided. Let her change her ways from war to diplomacy. There wasn't much difference in the two, except for the techniques used.

Wind blew in his face and the yellow-orange sun warmed him. He started walking, Egad at his side.

"You like it here, Egad?" he asked.

"Better than in ship," the dog told him.

"It might not be so bad to stay here for a while," he decided.

"Going to, anyway. Uvallae said he'd give me place to sleep."

Walden was startled and hurt by this revelation. His dog had already made plans to leave him for the alien. Then he smiled. In a way, it was like losing a child to maturity. Egad was finding what he wanted and needed from life. Uvallae was a good choice now for Egad's development. The alien communicated better with the gengineered dog than any human ever had—or could. Egad would make a better ambassador between humans and the Frinn than Nakamura ever considered being.

Egad let out a yelp of joy and frolicked off, chasing down one of the furred creatures he called a rabbit. The big front teeth and floppy ears reminded Walden of a rabbit, but the stubby legs and pale green and brown stripes were unlike any earthly lagomorph. Walden wondered if the Frinn used the animals for research.

He shook his head. He didn't want to return to bioweapons work. There were other chores to be done for the Frinn. The Infinity Plague had ruined their world. He wanted to help rebuild it.

Walden smiled broadly when he saw Anita Tarleton atop a distant hill. He started walking faster, then slowed when he saw what she was doing. A small metal plaque had been placed on the hill. He scanned the simple words and felt a desert grow within him.

The red-haired woman turned and looked at him. She had never looked lovelier—or more distant.

"I had to, Jerome. It's not just a monument to Edouard Zacharias but to all the EPCTs and to everyone who died. *Everyone*, Frinn and human."

"You loved him," Walden said.

"In some ways, no. But in the way you mean, yes."

Walden stared at the metal plaque and then lifted his gaze to the woman. Tears shone like jewels in her eyes. They had loved each other once. They could again. They *would* again if they got away from the deadly research and the killing.

He put his arm around her shoulder and held her close. She didn't move away.

CLASSIC SCIENCE FICTION AND FANTASY

___ **DUNE Frank Herbert** 0-441-17266-0/$4.95
The bestselling novel of an awesome world where gods and adventurers clash, mile-long sandworms rule the desert, and the ancient dream of immortality comes true.

___ **STRANGER IN A STRANGE LAND Robert A. Heinlein**
0-441-79034-8/$4.95
From the *New York Times* bestselling author—the science fiction masterpiece of a man from Mars who teaches humankind the art of grokking, watersharing and love.

___ **THE ONCE AND FUTURE KING T.H. White**
0-441-62740-4/$5.50
The world's greatest fantasy classic! A magical epic of King Arthur in Camelot, romance, wizardry and war. By the author of *The Book of Merlyn*.

___ **THE LEFT HAND OF DARKNESS Ursula K. LeGuin**
0-441-47812-3/$3.95
Winner of the Hugo and Nebula awards for best science fiction novel of the year. "SF masterpiece!"—*Newsweek* "A Jewel of a story."—Frank Herbert

___ **MAN IN A HIGH CASTLE Philip K. Dick** 0-441-51809-5/$3.95
"Philip K. Dick's best novel, a masterfully detailed alternate world peopled by superbly realized characters."
—Harry Harrison